P9-BYU-843

10TH ANNIVERSARY

Special thanks to our well-wishers, who have contributed their congratulations and support.

"The best historicals, the best romances. Simply the best!"
—Dallas Schulze

"Bronwyn Williams was born and raised at Harlequin Historicals. We couldn't have asked for a better home or a more supportive family."
—Dixie Browning and Mary Williams, w/a Bronwyn Williams

"I can't believe it's been ten years since *Private Treaty*, my first historical novel, helped launch the Harlequin Historicals line. What a thrill that was! And the beat goes on...with timeless stories about men and women in love."
—Kathleen Eagle

"Nothing satisfies me as much as writing or reading a Harlequin Historical novel. For me, Harlequin Historicals are the ultimate escape from the problems of everyday life."
—Ruth Ryan Langan

"As a writer and reader, I've always felt that Harlequin Historicals celebrate a perfect blend of history and romance, adventure and passion, humor and sheer magic."
—Theresa Michaels

"Thank you, Harlequin Historicals, for opening up a 'window into the past' for so many happy readers."
—Suzanne Barclay

"As a one-time 'slush pile' foundling at Harlequin Historicals, I'll be forever grateful for having been rescued and published as one of the first 'March Madness' authors. Harlequin Historicals has always been *the* place for special stories, ones that blend the magic of the past with the rare miracle of love for books that readers never forget."
—Miranda Jarrett

"A rainy evening. A cup of hot chocolate. A stack of Harlequin Historicals. Absolute bliss! Happy 10th Anniversary and continued success."
—Cheryl Reavis

"Happy birthday, Harlequin Historicals! I'm proud to have been a part of your ten years of exciting historical romance."
—Elaine Barbieri

"Harlequin Historical novels are charming or disarming with dashes and clashes. These past times are fast times, the gems of romances!"
—Karen Harper

Ana Seymour

A Family For Carter Jones

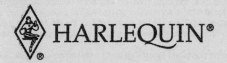

HARLEQUIN®

TORONTO • NEW YORK • LONDON
AMSTERDAM • PARIS • SYDNEY • HAMBURG
STOCKHOLM • ATHENS • TOKYO • MILAN • MADRID
PRAGUE • WARSAW • BUDAPEST • AUCKLAND

If you purchased this book without a cover you should be aware that this book is stolen property. It was reported as "unsold and destroyed" to the publisher, and neither the author nor the publisher has received any payment for this "stripped book."

For my daughters
Kathryn and Cristina
with admiration, pride and love

ISBN 0-373-29033-0

A FAMILY FOR CARTER JONES

Copyright © 1998 by Mary Bracho

All rights reserved. Except for use in any review, the reproduction or utilization of this work in whole or in part in any form by any electronic, mechanical or other means, now known or hereafter invented, including xerography, photocopying and recording, or in any information storage or retrieval system, is forbidden without the written permission of the publisher, Harlequin Enterprises Limited, 225 Duncan Mill Road, Don Mills, Ontario, Canada M3B 3K9.

All characters in this book have no existence outside the imagination of the author and have no relation whatsoever to anyone bearing the same name or names. They are not even distantly inspired by any individual known or unknown to the author, and all incidents are pure invention.

This edition published by arrangement with Harlequin Books S.A.

® and TM are trademarks of the publisher. Trademarks indicated with ® are registered in the United States Patent and Trademark Office, the Canadian Trade Marks Office and in other countries.

Printed in U.S.A.

"Perhaps it's just the brandy," Jennie said aloud.

Carter looked down at her in surprise. "Perhaps what is just the brandy?"

She made a little twist with her mouth. "Nothing."

"Oh."

In a minute they would be at their rooms. He would open her door and say good-night like the gentleman he promised to be. Suddenly she blurted out, "I was wondering if it was the brandy that was making me remember the night you kissed me."

She could feel him stiffen beside her. It was a relief to have let it out. Now he'd probably laugh and tell her that she was perhaps a little tipsy, and then they could part and get some sleep.

Instead he said in a voice that had grown slightly hoarse, "I haven't needed brandy to remember it, Jennie...."

Prologue

Vermillion, Nevada
May 1881

Unlike most girls who blossomed into womanhood at the same sedate pace they used to walk across the room at their first adult social, Jennie Sheridan reckoned that she'd pretty well completed the process at a gallop within the space of six weeks.

Sitting on the porch swing with a lump in her throat the size of a rolled-up pair of socks, she looked away from her sister and counted backward. Six weeks. The first snowdrops had already started appearing on the hills outside of town the week they'd lost first their mother, then their father two days later. Her entire world had turned itself inside out within six short weeks. And now this.

"When?" she asked Kate, forcing the word out and avoiding her sister's eyes.

Kate's voice was almost inaudible. "Well, it's nine months, right? That would make it sometime around Christmas."

"Some Christmas present, huh?" Jennie tried a smile, but her lips threatened to quiver, so she tightened her mouth again.

"Oh, Jen, I'm so very sorry," her sister murmured.

Jennie's unshed tears drained back down her throat as she looked up to see Kate's eyes filling. Jennie reached to take her younger sister's hand, then changed her mind and slid across the wooden slats of the swing to enfold her in her arms.

Kate put her head down on Jennie's shoulder and began to sob. "I never thought I could be so wicked, Jennie," she said, taking big gulps of air. "It almost makes me glad that Mama and Papa are gone."

Jennie straightened up at that and took a firm grasp of her sister's shoulders. "That's nonsense. You're not wicked and you're certainly not glad that our parents are dead."

Kate gave a little jerk at the harsh sound of the last word. "Can you imagine what they would have felt, Jen? What would they have said to discover that their unmarried daughter was about to have a child? I was always supposed to be the perfect one, you know."

Jennie gave a sympathetic nod. Her sister's bright blue eyes were full of anguish. And she was right. Their parents would have been devastated by this news. Jennie had always been headstrong, allowed her stubborn ways and occasional childish tantrums. But Kate had been the perfect one.

Well, *nothing* was perfect anymore.

"Isn't there some way you can contact him?" she asked.

Kate looked up in horror. "To tell him about the baby? I wouldn't even think of trying. He *left* me, Jennie. Without so much as a goodbye. You can't know what that means after you've...you know... *given* yourself to a man...."

Her voice trailed off and the tears started flowing again. Jennie gave a deep sigh. She would not be afraid to confront the blarney-talking Irishman who had swept in and out of town like a cyclone, scattering her sister's reputation and pieces of her heart in its wake. But perhaps this wasn't the moment to pursue the subject. "I suppose this is a silly question, but...are you sure, Katie? You haven't been to see Dr. Millard."

Kate moved away from her sister and set the swing in motion with a push of her heel. "I'm pretty sure, Jen. I haven't had...you know. And it was always every fourth Sunday...like clockwork. Now I've missed twice. And I'm...ah...tender up here, like the womenfolk say."

Jennie nodded, miserable but not embarrassed by her sister's frank description. She and Kate, just sixteen months apart in age, shared even the most intimate details of their lives with each other. At least, they used to share, Jennie amended, until Kate met up with that scoundrel. "Well, the first thing is...you have to see the doctor."

Kate took a deep, jagged breath. "I'd die first. It would be almost as bad as telling Papa."

Gentle Dr. Millard had taken care of their childhood hurts and illnesses since they were born. The week her parents had died, he'd stayed at the Sheridan house day and night, even though there were other influenza cases in town. "Sweetie, you have to tell him," Jennie said. "You'll need him to take care of you and...and the baby."

Kate looked down at her lap and shook her head

firmly. "I'm going to take care of myself. Mama had us without any doctor helping."

"But only because they were living up in the mountains then. And besides, she had Papa."

"Well, I have *you*."

"Kate Sheridan, I don't know the first thing about babies." Jennie tried to keep her tone free from the desperation that was creeping over her.

Kate set the swing rocking at a more frantic pace. "Well, I don't, either. But I'm afraid we're both about to find out."

The tears had ended, and suddenly there was determination in Kate's tone. Jennie let out a long stream of air. Together they could do this. No matter how bad it got. They had always supported each other, and since the deaths of their parents, it had become something like a sacred pact between them.

When Kate had broken down at their dead mother's bedside and refused to leave, it had been an equally heartbroken Jennie who had pulled her away and tucked her into the bed Kate hadn't slept in for the previous five nights.

When Harmon Wentworth, the banker, had told them that their parents had left them virtually without funds, it had been calm, logical Kate who had kept Jennie from total despondency. They were capable, able-bodied women, she'd insisted. Not girls any longer. They would find a way.

Now it was Jennie's turn to be strong again. And this time it appeared she'd have to be strong enough for the both of them.

Chapter One

August 1881

"**I**'m sorry, ladies, but I don't see how that particular task falls under my jurisdiction," Carter Jones said crisply. "It's a job for the sheriff."

Mrs. Henrietta Billingsley, Miss Margaret Potter and Mrs. Lucinda Wentworth stood before him in a row, shirtwaists billowing. Carter looked down at the papers on his desk and shifted uncomfortably, creaking the leather of his chair.

"Sheriff Hammond won't be back from visiting his sister in California for another three weeks, and by then that…that person's shameful condition will be apparent to God and every man wearing trousers in this town," Mrs. Billingsley insisted.

Carter looked up at the florid face of the town's leading matron. "I reckon God's aware of the problem already, Mrs. Billingsley. After all, isn't he the one responsible for creating a new life?"

"Not this life, Mr. Jones. This was the devil's work, pure and simple."

Carter sighed. "Sheriff Hammond left your son, Lyle, as deputy, Mrs. Wentworth. You could get him to serve the papers."

Margaret Potter stared down her long nose with a look that had been known to freeze truant students twice her size dead in their tracks. "He refuses to do it, Mr. Jones. He says we have to wait for the sheriff. Lyle has always been a difficult boy. And everyone knows he's always been sweet on Kate Sheridan."

Lyle Wentworth may be difficult, but he wasn't a boy. He had to be at least twenty-three, Carter reckoned. But in the few weeks since he'd arrived in Vermillion, he'd realized that Miss Potter continued to treat her former pupils as recalcitrant adolescents even though some of them had begun sprouting gray hair.

"Lyle's not difficult." Lucinda Wentworth defended her son in a voice so small it sounded as if she hoped Margaret Potter wouldn't actually hear her.

"Sounds to me like Lyle has the right idea," Carter said. "Let's just wait until Del gets back to handle this."

"Delbert Hammond will be no more eager to serve these papers than Lyle," Miss Potter said with one of her chronic sniffs. "It's your responsibility representing the interests of the territory to see that the decisions of the court are upheld."

Mrs. Billingsley leaned over Carter's desk, her formidable breasts perilously close to his face, and slapped down the sheaf of papers she'd been holding. "Those two Sheridan hussies have no business opening their home as a so-called boardinghouse in a respectable part of town. If they want to run something like that, they'll just have to go down to Tinkersville and hang a red lantern in front like the others."

Carter grimaced. He'd not met either of the Sheridan sisters since he'd taken over the post of district attorney, but he'd caught glimpses of both young ladies, and they had not struck him as likely candidates for the tawdry streets of the notorious Tinkersville district.

Miss Potter continued, "It's taken us a month to get the order to shut them down. And now that we've got the papers, we're not willing to have that situation continue one more night."

"Have they been disturbing the peace in some way, ladies?" he asked mildly.

"They've been disturbing the harmony of this community," Mrs. Billingsley huffed.

"And twisting the minds of the innocent schoolchildren," Margaret Potter added, her words punctuated by vehement nods from her friend.

Carter stretched his long legs under the desk, then picked up the bunch of papers and looked at them with distaste. "I'll see what I can do," he said.

As he walked toward the neat white clapboard house at the end of Elm Street, Carter went through a mental rehearsal of the speech he was about to give, with little enthusiasm for the task. He knew that the Sheridan sisters had lost their parents and fallen on financial hard times recently. And if it was true that the younger sister was bearing an out-of-wedlock child, as the town rumor mill had it, then Carter would have preferred to stay ten leagues away from the entire situation.

The house was well kept up with a flourishing vegetable garden to one side and neat rows of geraniums along the front. No one could say that the Sheridan boardinghouse represented an eyesore. But, of course, that had nothing to do with the court's ruling. Nor did the unwedded state of Kate Sheridan.

The ruling was based strictly on the town ordinances that had been passed not a year ago carefully separating the business part of town from its prosperous homes. It was the latest idea in city planning. Carter had never seen much sense to it, himself, but he was an ambitious man, and if zoning regulations were popular with the people, he would not be the one to argue against them.

As he mounted the front steps, he tried to get a picture in his mind of the sisters as he remembered seeing them about town. One had been striking, blond and tall, willowy. He wasn't as sure about the other. She'd been shorter, he thought, with mousy brown hair. Rather nondescript, if memory served.

It was neither young lady who opened the door to his knock, but a young lad of about twelve. "Who are you?" the boy asked without a smile.

"The name is Carter Jones. I'd like to talk with Miss Kate or Miss Jennie Sheridan."

"What about?" The boy had intense brown eyes that looked old in the middle of his youthful face.

Carter hesitated. It was absurd, but he almost felt as if he owed the boy an explanation. "I'll state my business to the Misses Sheridan, if you don't mind, lad,'' he said finally.

"Come back later. Miss Jennie said I wasn't to let anyone 'sturb Miss Kate.''

To Carter's amazement, the boy began to swing the door shut in his face. He put a hand out to hold it open. "Well then, I'll talk with Miss Jennie.''

"Can't. She's gone to the store.'' He paused and held up a hand to shade his eyes from the sun. "Oh. There she comes now.''

Carter turned to look down the street. Walking toward them with an almost childlike skip to her step was the Sheridan sister he'd dismissed as "nondescript.'' Carter's mouth dropped open.

He knew he'd been working too hard since he'd come to Vermillion, but up to now he hadn't thought that the overwork had struck him blind. Had he actually seen this girl in town and not paid her any attention? He ought to make an appointment with Dr. Millard that very afternoon to have his eyes examined.

Granted, her sister with her statuesque blond good looks had drawn his eye, but this girl was exquisite. She was not as tall as her sister, but her figure was perfection, with curves that were tantalizingly outlined by the worn spots in her faded green dress. Her hair was not the least bit mousy, but a rich mahogany brown that glinted in the morning sunlight. And her face would stand out in the portraits of *Godey's Lady's Book.*

He closed his mouth and swallowed away the dryness. Busy with his fledgling career, he'd been without a woman for too long. And under normal circumstances, the delectable Miss Sheridan would have seemed to be a perfect victim for his well-developed skills in the art of seduction. Suddenly his present duty seemed more than unpleasant—it seemed downright inconvenient.

"This gentleman's looking for you, Jennie," the boy yelled to her. "And I wouldn't let him 'sturb Kate, just like you told me."

The young woman's pace became more sedate as she approached them. She smiled first at the boy, and said, "Thank you, Barnaby." Then she turned the smile toward Carter, causing his heart to skip a beat. But her smile died as she glanced at the papers in his hand. "What can I do for you, sir?" she asked. Her huge brown eyes had grown wary.

"Ah…" Carter fished about for an opening gambit. It was an uncharacteristic hesitancy for his normally glib tongue. He prided himself on always knowing what to say in every situation. The consummate politician. Someday he hoped the skill would take him to the heights he had secretly dreamed of since he was a boy not much older than the lad who stood in the doorway staring at him.

The sudden childhood memory restored some of his power. The Sheridan girl was beautiful, but that didn't mean he had to lose his wits talking to her. "Perhaps we should go inside and discuss it," he said smoothly.

Jennie looked from Carter to the boy. "Barnaby, you go on in and see if Kate needs anything." Then she mounted the four steps to the stoop to stand directly in front of Carter. She was several inches shorter than he, but somehow it seemed as if her eyes were level with his as she said gravely, "My sister is...indisposed. I'd rather talk right here, if you don't mind, Mr. Jones."

The sound of his own name surprised him. "Ah, you know who I am, Miss Sheridan. I apologize for not introducing myself immediately."

"This town does not keep secrets, Mr. Jones. Everyone knows about the new young prosecutor from the fancy law school back East."

"Harvard," Carter put in with a smile.

"Harvard," Jennie agreed with no softening of her own expression.

Carter blinked, trying to concentrate on the business at hand instead of the way the morning light brushed Jennie Sheridan's high cheekbones with the faintest blush. Irrationally his heart was beating a tattoo inside his chest. Yes, it had been too long since he'd been close to a woman. At least a woman the likes of the older Sheridan sister.

He tried another of his politician smiles and willed his voice to sound smooth. "Nevertheless, it was remiss of me. We've never been formally introduced and perhaps you—"

"Mr. Jones," Jennie interrupted. "It's been some weeks now since anyone in this town has bothered to observe good manners with me or my sister. And this is heavy." With her free hand she gestured to the basket of groceries hanging over her arm. "If you would be so kind as to state your business, I'll let you be on your way."

Carter tried to take a step back to distance himself from the intensity of those brown eyes, but his heel hit the edge of the stoop. He stopped himself just in time to keep from tumbling backward onto the ground. Jennie Sheridan watched him without blinking.

"I could come back if this is an inconvenient time." His smile was not quite so self-assured.

"I guess that would depend on the nature of your business. Recently, my sister and I have had to deal with a lot of things that aren't much convenient at any time. Is this that kind of business, Mr. Jones?"

Carter hid his chagrin at the coldness of her tone. With his tall good looks and practiced charm, Carter had been able to soften the hearts of the haughtiest of debutantes in Boston society. But he had a feeling that Jennie Sheridan was regarding him with no more interest than she had in the black ant that was crossing the wooden stoop at their feet.

"I guess you'd put this in the category of inconvenient," he admitted, giving the papers in his hand a shake.

"It's the court ruling, isn't it?"

Carter met her eyes and nodded. She held her head stiffly, her delicate chin up, as if she were waiting for a blow. "They've turned down your petition. You're not allowed to have a business in this part of town," Carter said gently.

Jennie closed her eyes for just a moment, but when she opened them, they held anger, not resignation. "Three renters. That's all it is. Three people to fill out the bedrooms in this big place." She gestured to the house behind her. "Why, it should be a crime *not* to let the rooms out, with the silver boom in town. People need places to stay."

Carter ruffled through the papers in his hand. "You have an employee, it says..." he began.

"Barnaby?" Jennie gasped in disbelief. "He's twelve years old. And he had nowhere else to go—"

"That boy is the employee?" Carter interrupted.

Instead of answering the question, Jennie backed down the stairs to the wooden walkway and pointed up the street. "You see all those fancy houses, Mr. Jones? There's not a one of them that doesn't have a servant of some kind. Gardener, maid, livery man. We have Barnaby. One boy and two women. We run this place. We muck the horses and grow the food. When the pump broke out back, I was the one who fixed it. When the roof leaked this June, I was the one on a ladder patching it up."

She seemed to gather steam as she continued to talk, her features becoming more animated. Carter was so entranced that he found himself losing track of what she was saying. When she paused, evidently expecting a reply, he could only manage to say, "It does seem a bit unreasonable to classify that boy as a business employee."

"Well then, tell that to your precious courts, Mr. Jones." She marched up the stairs past him, her basket nearly knocking the papers out of his hand. "And tell them that if they want to force two orphan sisters, one of whom is ill, to leave their home, they'll have to come in here with the sheriff and a passel of deputies and carry us out."

As Carter tried to formulate an answer, she wrenched open the door, stalked inside and slammed it in his face.

"Well, what was he like?" Kate asked.

"Who?" Jennie was kneading bread dough. Lord, it seemed as if she spent half her time kneading bread these days. She couldn't understand how just three men and a boy could go through so many loaves each week. Goodness knows, she and Kate hardly touched the stuff. Jennie was always too busy or too tired to eat, and Kate had had no appetite since she'd started getting sick early in her pregnancy. Her face had grown gaunt and, except for her now obviously protruding stomach, she was alarmingly thin. Jennie had pleaded, alternating tears and threats, but Kate still refused to be seen by Dr. Millard, which was not only dangerous to her health, but pointless, since by now everyone in town knew that she was with child.

"The new district attorney," Kate said with slight exasperation. "What's he like?"

"I don't know…he's…he's just a man. Who cares?"

Kate sighed. "Just because he's a man doesn't eliminate him from consideration as a human being, Jen dear. There *are* good men in the world. Not all of them disappear leaving…problems in their wake."

"Not all of them are like Sean Flaherty, you mean."

As usual, her sister's eyes chilled at the mention of her erstwhile lover's name. Jennie hated that look.

"Think of Papa," Kate said after a moment. "He was a good man."

"He left us, too," Jennie said under her breath, slapping the bread as if it were Carter Jones's handsome face. The new district attorney *had* been handsome, she would admit that much to herself, if not to Kate. But then, Sean Flaherty had been handsome, too, and look where that had led her poor sister.

"Jennie! How can you say such a thing? Papa didn't leave us—he *died*."

Jennie stopped pummeling. Her shoulders sagged, and she gave the ball of mixed dough an apologetic pat. "Yes, he died. It wasn't his fault, but he's gone, nevertheless."

"Well, maybe it's not Mr. Jones's fault either that they gave him those papers to bring here. If you'd been a bit nicer to him, we might even have gotten him on our side."

Jennie used the edge of her hand to chop the mass of dough into loaf-size chunks. "Oh, I'm sure the fancy *Haah-vard* man would take the side of a couple of unimportant, disgraced, utterly poor women against the whole rest of the town."

Kate looked gloomy. "I'm the one who's disgraced, not you. It's not fair that you should pay for my sins."

Jennie smiled at her. "My sister, the sinner."

"I am. I *did*."

"You were in love, Kate, and falling in love's not a sin." She dropped the last loaf into its pan with a satisfying plop, then added, "It's just stupidity."

Kate shook her head. "I'm afraid I've soured you on men for good."

"'Twas Sean Flaherty soured me on men, not you. Not that I ever had much time for them in the first place."

"Because you never met the right one."

Carter Jones's smile flashed through Jennie's mind. She'd been thoroughly irritated by his smile, but beyond the irritation, she'd felt another sensation. Equally disagreeable, she decided, kind of like the prickling of a heat rash. "There is no right one for me, Katie dear," she said breezily. "I intend to grow old as a happy and peaceful old maid."

Jennie finished wiping her hands on the dish towel and hung it on the rack, then turned to look around at their tidy kitchen. "And what's more, I don't care how many Mr. Joneses they send after us—I intend to do it right here in my very own house."

"So what are we going to do about the papers?"

"They can go to the devil with their papers. I'm not leaving here. And since we can't afford to stay here without the money from our boarders, *they're* not leaving here, either."

Kate slid awkwardly off the stool where she'd perched to watch her sister's labors. Jennie refused to let her help much with the cooking anymore. The heaviest job Jennie would allow her was wiping the dishes after dinner. And even then, Jennie herself took over when it came time to put away the heavy pans. For weeks Kate had been too sick to argue with her sister's proclamations and now, though she was feeling better, she seemed to have adapted to the unusual circumstance of allowing her sister to take care of her. "Are we going to tell them about it?" she asked.

"Tell the silverheels?" The silverheels was Jennie's nickname for the three miners who had taken rooms at Sheridan House while they hired on at the Longley mine up the canyon. She'd called them that from the first day the three young men had arrived, joking that they hoped they wouldn't track too much silver dust onto her mother's prized Persian rug in the parlor. Jennie had laughed and welcomed their business and had never let on to them that a bit of silver dust would be a godsend in the Sheridan sisters' lives at the moment.

"Well, they'll probably find out about it. Especially if Mr. Jones takes you up on your invitation and comes trooping back here with the sheriff to shut us down."

Jennie felt the pulsing behind her right eye that always preceded one of her headaches. "The sheriff's away in California. They told me so in town today."

"Well, they're not just going to forget about it. Didn't Sheriff Hammond leave a deputy?"

Jennie fixed Kate with a look. "Lyle Wentworth's the deputy."

Kate colored. Lyle had tried to court Kate since they were children, much to the wealthy Wentworths' dismay. Before Sean Flaherty showed up in town, some people thought Lyle would go against his parents' wishes and ask Kate to marry him. Kate had refused to see him since she had found out about the baby. "I suppose you could go talk to Lyle," she said, her voice subdued.

"Me?" Jennie said, her hands on her hips. "I suppose *you* could go talk to him."

"Jen, you know I can't do that."

"Criminy, sis. Someday you're going to have to talk to people again. It doesn't make much sense for us to go through all this effort to hold on to this place if you're going to shut yourself away in here the rest of your life as if you'd been buried right along with Mama and Papa."

Kate clasped her hands over her big stomach and looked down. "I can't see Lyle, Jennie. Please don't ask me."

Jennie gave a little huff but didn't pursue the matter. "I think I will tell the silverheels that those old biddies are trying to shut us down. Maybe they'll have some ideas."

"And maybe you should talk to that Mr. Jones again. He's a lawyer, right? At least he should be able to tell us what our options are."

Jennie stared straight ahead as another quick memory of Carter Jones's striking face flashed in front of her like the image from a stereopticon. How odd, she reflected. Perhaps it was somehow connected to her impending headache.

"I'll go see him in the morning," she agreed finally. "Tonight I'm going to let Barnaby help you with the dishes while I nurse one of my megrims."

Carter Jones sat in his small office and stared at the bookshelf on the opposite wall as if willing one of the leather tomes to magically open up with the answer he sought. He'd been at it much of the afternoon, more time than he could afford to spend on a matter that, after all, was not even his concern.

Zoning ordinances were so new that it didn't appear that there was much body of law on them. And, though he'd read the court's decision half a dozen times, he'd been unable to come up with any ideas as to how to render it null. He had no doubt that the self-appointed moral guardians of the town, Mrs. Billingsley, Miss Potter, Lucinda Wentworth and their cronies, would be back tomorrow in full force when they learned that nothing had been done to change the situation at Sheridan House.

Carter threw his pencil down on the desk and pushed back his chair. His stomach was rumbling its disapproval of his decision earlier in the day to skip lunch. He hadn't felt much like eating after his encounter with Jennie Sheridan. The prospect of one of the Continental Hotel's shoe-leather steaks was not thrilling, but it would at least fill the hole in his middle.

He leaned back toward his desk to straighten the piles of work. No matter how hungry he was, he wouldn't leave an untidy office. A cluttered desk meant a cluttered mind, he'd always believed. The pencil he'd thrown in disgust was carefully retrieved and put in its tray—on the used side of the tray, not to be confused with the freshly sharpened ones that he put there every morning.

He ran his hand over the neatly arranged writing instruments with a certain satisfaction. At least it was possible to inject order into a certain portion of his world. He didn't want to admit how unsettled he'd been by his trip to Sheridan House. He still wasn't entirely sure why. The girl was pretty. The young boy was engaging. But none of it was his problem.

There was a soft knock at the door. He jerked his hand away from the pencils and said, "Come in."

It was the temporary sheriff's deputy, Lyle Wentworth. Carter wasn't particularly pleased to see him. Though they were both eligible young men in town, the two had not become friends. Carter found him overbearing and petulant. He'd seen Lyle kick back a chair and stomp out of the bar over a two-bit poker game. Of course, as the only son of the town banker and the pretentious Lucinda, Lyle had probably been raised to believe he was a cut above the rest of the world. Carter, on the other hand, had known at a young age that he'd better start climbing, because he was starting life at the bottom rung.

"Evening, Lyle," he greeted his visitor.

"What in blazes are they trying to do to the Sheridan sisters?" Lyle asked without preamble.

Carter raised his eyebrows. The demanding tone was characteristic, but for the life of him he couldn't think what interest Lyle Wentworth would have in the plight of the Sheridans. He leaned over his desk and put his hand down flat on the court order that he'd not served that morning. "The court says they can't take in boarders in that location. They have to stop it or move to another house."

"They don't have any money to move. Or to survive if they can't get that extra rent money. What are they supposed to live on with both their parents fresh in their graves?"

Carter let a stream of air out threw his nose, still mystified as to the motivation behind Lyle's inquiry. "This order doesn't concern itself with what they're going to live on. It just states that the way things are, they're in violation of the law."

"It's damned nonsense, fostered by a bunch of the town's old biddies. The Sheridan sisters aren't hurting a thing in that house."

Carter slid his hand off the papers and grinned. "Well, according to the oldest Sheridan sister, the only way we're going to get them out of there is to carry them out."

Lyle's scowl softened. "That sounds like Jennie, all right. So you talked to them already?" At Carter's nod, Lyle stiffened and asked, "Did you see Kate, too?"

"The younger one? No. Her sister said she was ill."

Lyle's head jerked up. "Ill? What's wrong with her?"

The motive behind Lyle's interest was becoming more apparent. It appeared he was smitten with one of the girls. Which one? he wondered. Carter was surprised to realize that he was very much hoping that it was not Jennie who held the rich young man's interest, though she would be the most likely candidate. It would be tough for any man to be in love with Kate Sheridan under the current circumstances.

"What's wrong with Kate?" Lyle insisted. The slight tremor in his voice gave Carter the answer to his question.

"I'm sorry, Lyle. Her sister didn't elaborate. I assumed it had something to do with…" Carter hesitated. Surely Lyle *knew* about Kate Sheridan's condition.

"With her having a baby," Lyle finished for him, his voice tight.

"Yes."

Lyle kicked the heel of his boot backward into the door frame, gouging the soft pinewood. "I don't want them bothered, Jones," he said. "Not by you nor by those old gossips who are trying to run them out of town."

Carter pushed back his chair and looked up at the young man. After a moment he said, "I intend to see what I can do to straighten this out."

Lyle nodded and spun on his heel to leave. Carter could hear the clatter of his fancy, high-heeled boots all the way down the stairs. This was an interesting development, he thought, since the way he understood it, one of the "old gossips" Wentworth had referred to was Lyle's own mother. Carter wrinkled up his nose. Small-town politics. He had little patience for it. But if he had to put up with the foibles of the local denizens in order to proceed up that ladder he was determined to climb, he'd put aside his distaste.

And in the meantime, straightening things out meant that he'd have to pay another visit to Jennie Sheridan. Which was not such an unpleasant prospect.

Chapter Two

By the time he'd washed down the last piece of the Continental's totally flavorless meat with a third mug of beer, Carter was ready to admit that the prospect of a return engagement with Jennie Sheridan had him interested. Hell, it had him downright bothered. He'd planned on postponing the encounter until tomorrow, but with the pleasantly warm hum of beer singing inside him, he stood on the steps of the hotel wondering if he should change his mind and go immediately.

"Evening, Carter." The gruff voice of Dr. Millard was unmistakable. It could be intimidating to someone who didn't know the disposition of the town's only doctor.

"Dr. Millard," Carter acknowledged. "You out seeing a patient this time of night?"

"I came looking for you. I'm concerned about this campaign against Jennie and Kate Sheridan."

Yet another champion for the beleaguered sisters. Carter smiled. It was beginning to look as if the two lovely orphans might cause a regular civil war in town.

"I was just about to head over there," he told the doctor.

"To the Sheridan house?"

Carter nodded.

Dr. Millard looked up and down the street. Only a few evening stragglers were still out. "Now?"

Carter gave one of his self-assured nods. "I imagine those poor girls are quaking in their shoes wondering when the sheriff is going to show up to move them out of there."

Dr. Millard looked doubtful. "Have you met Jennie?"

"Yup. This morning. She was…"

"She's not exactly the quaking type," the doctor interrupted.

"No. Perhaps not. But I imagine she'll be pleased to learn that I've decided to help her and her sister out of this muddle."

Dr. Millard looked amused. "I'm relieved to here it, Carter. Ah…just how do you plan to do that?"

Carter peered into darkening street and blinked to find it empty. "I don't know. I'll…file an appeal or something. Get the court order blocked. I can talk to Mrs. Billingsley and get her to forget the whole thing."

"That's about as likely as a blizzard in July."

Carter gestured grandly. "Would you like to come with me?"

The doctor grinned. "My boy, I'd love to see Jennie's face when you give her the good news that you've gallantly decided to ride to her rescue.''

"Well, come along then."

Millard's smile died. "I can't. Kate's been avoiding me since the beginning of her...problem. She refuses to see me, and I can't go over there without her welcome. She'll let me know when she's ready for my help."

"Hey, Doc. Haven't you learned by your age that women don't always *know* what they want. Sometimes a man just has to step in and take over to keep them from making a mess of things."

"Is that what you learned at that fancy Eastern school?"

"I learned it long before then. Give a woman a chance to argue and you're sunk. If you want to help out Kate Sheridan, you should just march on over there and tell her so. Don't let her get a word in edgewise."

"And that's the approach you intend to take with Jennie tonight?" he asked.

"Actually, it's what they like," Carter answered with a firm nod.

Dr. Millard made a click with his mouth. "Yup, I surely would like to see that."

"Do you want to change your mind and come along?"

The doctor shook his head with a slow grin. "Nope. But you give Jennie my regards, you hear?" He turned to leave, and Carter could hear him chuckling all the way down the street.

* * *

"I thought I told you that you would need reinforcements when you came back here, Mr. Jones."

Jennie Sheridan's voice was even frostier than it had been that morning, but Carter was concentrating more on the way the neck of her maroon silk evening dress scooped out a circle of creamy white skin. The sight made the air stick in his throat. He'd tried to hold on to the idea that his interest in the Sheridan case was all in the name of justice and fair play. But standing here in the doorway looking at her, he had to admit that his motives were at a baser level.

Simply put, the diminutive, curvaceous Miss Sheridan made the blood race through his veins.

"I didn't come to put you out of your home," he said when he could trust himself to speak. "I came to offer my help."

Jennie looked skeptical. "Your help?"

Carter looked up and down the darkened street. The new street lanterns had not yet been placed in this part of town. "Is it too late to invite me in?"

She bit her lower lip, drawing Carter's eyes to her full mouth. "I guess not."

She looked down at his hands as if expecting to see the papers he'd brought earlier. He held them out, palms up. "No concealed weapons," he said lightly.

The smile she returned was slight, but it was enough to restore the confidence that had slipped a notch when he'd felt the visceral effect of seeing her in that dress. She was, after all, a woman. And if there was one thing Carter had always been able to handle, at least since the time he'd graduated to long pants, it was women.

"I suppose you can come into the parlor for a few minutes," she said, holding the door open for him to enter. "Our board...our *guests* are there playing cards."

He followed her inside and placed his hat on the hall table. "And your sister...?" he asked as she started toward the curtained archway that evidently led to the parlor.

She whirled to face him. "What about my sister?"

He held up a peacemaking hand again. "I just wondered if I would meet her, too. I was talking earlier tonight with a friend of hers who seemed concerned about her welfare."

"What friend?"

"Lyle Wentworth."

Jennie made a face. "He used to be sweet on Kate."

"Still is, if you ask me."

Jennie ignored his comment as she led the way under the drapes into the cozy room where three men sat around a small round table covered with playing cards. A fire burned cheerily behind the grate of the painted brick fireplace. "Mr. Jones, I'd like you to meet Dennis Kelly, Brad Connors and Humphrey Smith."

The men looked up from their game in acknowledgment of the introduction, but did not stand and offered no words of greeting. The one she'd called Mr. Kelly was a heavyset blonde with muttonchop whiskers. He said to Jennie, "Is he bothering you with those papers again, Miss Jennie?"

"Mr. Jones says he's come here to help, Dennis," she told him with a smile.

"Why can't the town just leave these girls alone?" Kelly asked, turning his gaze on Carter. "Ain't they got enough problems?" The other two men at the table nodded their agreement.

Still more defenders for the Sheridans, Carter noted. "That's what I came to talk over with Miss Sheridan. I'd like to help her and her sister out of this dilemma."

The three men didn't reply, but sat staring at Jennie and Carter, making no move to resume their game. After a couple minutes of awkward silence, Jennie said, "Why don't we go in the kitchen, Mr. Jones? I'll pour you a glass of cider."

Carter nodded and after a distracted "Nice to meet you" to the boarders, he followed her to the back of the house, relieved that he didn't have to talk with her in front of such a partisan audience.

"So it's the presence of those three men that's causing all this ruckus?" he asked her as he sat on the stool she indicated.

She stood with her back to him, filling two glasses from a clay pitcher. "Yes. But, of course, they're not the real reason."

"They're not?" She turned back and offered him one of the glasses. He took it, trying to keep his eyes off the way her slender white arm disappeared into a ruffle of maroon silk.

She perched on a stool on the opposite side of the table. "It's Kate who's the problem," she said. "She's going to have a baby."

Carter was a little taken aback at her bluntness, but he recovered quickly, saying, "It's not illegal to have a baby."

"Well, you wouldn't know it to talk to the people in this town. They'd just as soon lock her up and throw away the key."

Carter knew a lot about bitterness, but it was hard to hear it coming from Jennie Sheridan's beautiful lips. "I've met a passel of nice people in this town in the few months I've been here. I find it hard to believe they're as vindictive as you say. In fact, besides Lyle Wentworth, I had another person offer support for you two today—Dr. Millard."

Jennie's expression softened. "Dr. Millard's a good man. A lot of the people in town are. But then there are the ones like Henrietta Billingsley. I'd thought she was my mother's friend. Now she comes around here and tries to blame Kate for my parents' deaths."

Jennie took a big swallow of cider and Carter could see that her hands were shaking. Unlike his own bitterness, which had been long-standing and coldly calculated, Jennie's was raw, sharply edged with hurt. "I had heard that your parents died of the influenza last spring," he said gently.

"They did. Kate's condition had absolutely nothing to do with it—the very idea is absurd. They didn't...know about it before they died. *Kate* didn't even know then."

"People say cruel things sometimes without thinking."

"Oh, Henrietta thinks about them, all right. Then

she goes ahead and says them, taking joy in the process.''

She held herself stiffly erect on the stool, and Carter had an almost uncontrollable impulse to walk around the table and pull her off the stool into his arms. He'd met the woman only today, but he was already feeling as if some invisible thread had wrapped itself around the two of them, tangling up her feelings with his own.

''You'll have to learn to ignore her, then,'' he said instead. ''Just deal with the people who are worth your attention—people like Dr. Millard.''

His comment was rewarded with another half smile. ''Yes, we do have some friends left.''

Carter started to extend his hand toward where hers rested on the table across from him but changed his mind. He had the feeling that Jennie Sheridan would have to be gentled more cautiously than a wild young mare. He withdrew his hand. ''I'd like to be counted as one of those friends,'' he said simply.

She smiled again, this time with a rueful twist to her mouth. ''Aren't you the one who's supposed to be shutting us down?''

''I'm an officer of the court, and there's a court order shutting you down.''

The smile disappeared. ''So there you have it,'' she said softly.

''Which is why I spent a great portion of my afternoon going through law books trying to find a way out for you.''

He could see the sweep of her long lashes all the

way across the table as she blinked in astonishment. "You did?"

He nodded. "I told you, I'd like to help."

She cocked her head to one side. "Why?"

It was a logical question, he supposed, but he hadn't expected it. And he had no idea what to answer. It didn't seem that it would advance his case with her any to say, "Because you made my entire body come alive this morning when I saw you walking down the street toward me." It was a woefully inadequate answer, even to himself.

"I don't like injustices," he said finally.

Jennie regarded him with genuine surprise. "I've misjudged you, Mr. Jones," she said softly. "I think I owe you an apology for yelling at you this morning."

Carter grinned. "I'll forgive you on one condition."

"What's that?"

"That you call me Carter."

The glow in her brown eyes dimmed. "I don't think I could do that."

"It's not so much to ask. You call Lyle by his first name."

"We've known Lyle since we were children."

Carter slid off the stool and walked around to stand in front of her. After a moment's hesitation, he plucked her right hand from where it rested on her knee and wrapped it in both of his. "You have lots of old friends in town. I'd like to be a new one."

Jennie's breathing deepened. She looked up into his eyes and nodded slowly without words.

"So you'll call me Carter?" he asked softly, his voice persuasive, a little husky.

She gave another slow nod.

"Let me hear you say it," he insisted. "Say, 'good night, Carter.'"

"Good night, Carter," she repeated, her eyes never leaving his.

He dropped her hand in her lap. "I'll come by tomorrow after I've had a chance to wire the district judge in Virginia City about this case."

Her only response was another nod and the wide gaze of her brown eyes.

He gave a satisfied smile and said, "I'll see myself out." Then he turned, crossed the kitchen and went out through the front hall. By the time he got to the stoop, he was whistling and thinking to himself that perhaps the gentling of Miss Jennie would not be quite as slow a process as he had feared.

Flapjacks had been their father's specialty. Or rather, they had been the only item that he ever cooked in his entire life, so it had been customary to make a big fuss whenever he, with great ceremony, donned their mother's apron and took over the stove. Jennie and Kate had avoided the food for the first few weeks after the deaths, but when the silverheels had asked about flapjacks for breakfast, Jennie had decided she would take over her father's duties.

She stood over the pan ladling and flipping until there was a platter of the fluffy cakes big enough to feed, as Kate pointed out each time, the entire Seventh Cavalry...or three hungry miners.

"He said he wants to help, but he didn't say how?" Kate asked her sister as Jennie watched carefully for the first bubbles to rise on the last batch.

"He said he'd get back to us today with more ideas," Jennie answered carefully. She'd had no choice but to tell her sister about last night's visit from Carter Jones. The silverheels would have revealed it if she hadn't mentioned it first. But she wasn't sure she was ready to discuss the encounter with Kate. It had left her too confused.

"So what did you talk about?"

"I don't know…just…well, Lyle, for one thing." That ought to shut her sister up, Jennie thought smugly.

But she was wrong. Kate continued the interrogation. "What about Lyle?"

"Mr. Jones says he's still smitten with you."

Kate shrugged. "That's his problem, I guess. Any man who would be fool enough to carry a torch for a fallen woman deserves to suffer."

Jennie knew it was unhappiness, not cruelty, behind her sister's brittle words. "Fallen woman, indeed," she snorted.

But Kate would not be led away from the subject. "Well, what did you think of the man? You never answered my question about him yesterday."

What did she think of him? "Think" wasn't precisely the word she would have chosen. It had not been rational thought that had made her turn into a speechless goose last night when Carter Jones had taken her hand and looked at her with those riveting gray eyes. "I think he was sincere about wanting to help. And, Lord knows, we can use all the friends we can get these days."

"And he's a lawyer, which is good. But why does he want to help us?"

What had he said? Something about injustice. Jennie didn't completely buy it. Carter Jones didn't strike her as the idealistic type. But she was afraid to offer the only other explanation that seemed logical, because it was a possibility that she didn't even want to consider. He *couldn't* be attracted to her. For one thing, they'd barely met. For another, the last thing either Jennie or her sister needed in their lives was another fast-talking, charming scalawag of a male.

She piled the last three flapjacks on the platter, then put down the turner and wiped her hands on her mother's apron. "I don't know. It's probably a lawyer thing. They're always trying to see if they can find an angle that no one else has thought of."

Kate started to pick up the platter, but Jennie pushed her sister's hands out of the way and lifted it herself. By now Kate had stopped protesting when Jennie took over her share of the work. "Well, it doesn't sound as if he left a very good impression on you."

Jennie headed toward the door of the dining room. "Good enough," she said, keeping her voice light. "At least I didn't yell at him and slam the door in his face like the first time."

Kate giggled. "Dorie Millard says when you treat men badly it makes them want you more."

Dr. Millard's daughter, Dorothy, was notorious for giving advice on romance to anyone who would listen. Jennie would have liked to discount her words as giddy nonsense, but the truth was that Dorie had always had more suitors than any other girl in town.

She hesitated a minute before she said, ''Mr. Jones doesn't *want* me, Kate. The idea's absurd.'' Then she pushed her way through to where the miners were impatiently awaiting their breakfast.

Kate had perked up her head at Jennie's last words. She'd only been teasing by bringing up Dorie's proclamation. But the break in her sister's voice had been unmistakable. And unprecedented. Could it be possible that Jennie was finally feeling what it was to be attracted to a man? Kate smiled, then clasped her hands over her stomach and addressed her unborn child. ''What do you think, sugarplum? It sounds to me like we'd better have ourselves a look at this Mr. Carter Jones.''

Jennie tried to tell herself that she was acting no differently than she would on any other day. She and Barnaby cleaned up the breakfast dishes while Kate lay down for her morning rest. Then she deliberately made herself put on her gardening dress, the least attractive thing she owned, and went out to weed and pick the vegetables. She refused to admit that she was hurrying through the task so that she could clean up and change her attire. And she picked her *second*-best day dress, the yellow one with five pink primroses tucked along the bodice. Of course, it *was* the one she'd been wearing when Jack Foster had told her that the yellow dress and her glossy dark brown hair made her look as pretty as a black-eyed Susan.

If she was jumpier than normal during the day, it was because she hadn't slept well last night, still nursing her headache and thinking about that blasted court order. It had nothing to do with the fact that every time that broken shutter in front blew open she'd thought it had been footsteps coming up the walk.

In the end it was nearly five before he came. And by then she was more or less convinced that she truly *didn't* care if she saw him again. But when she opened the door to see him standing there holding a nosegay of delicate purple flowers complete with a trailing ribbon, she knew that she was in trouble.

"How are you, Mr. Jones?" she managed to say calmly enough. "Come in."

Carter frowned. "We'd progressed farther than that last night," he said, handing her the flowers with a slight bow. "You called me Carter, remember?"

Jennie remembered every second of last night's encounter. But she said, "It was done under duress, I believe."

Carter laughed. "Turning legal on me, are you?"

"It's *your* profession, Counselor." The banter was making Jennie feel giddy. Growing up, she'd avoided the casual flirtations with the boys in town, preferring the solitude of home with her books or her music. Kate had always been the one who'd drawn the boys' eyes, and that had been fine with Jennie. After Kate's disaster with Sean Flaherty, Jennie was even more strongly convinced that men were not a necessary ingredient for happiness. Indeed, they could sometimes be the major obstacle to it.

Which didn't explain why she was standing in her

front doorway, grinning up at Carter Jones as if he were the candy man at the circus. She forced her face into a more sedate expression, took the flowers from him and gestured for him to come in.

"You can finally meet my sister," she told him over her shoulder. "She's back in the kitchen shelling some peas for supper."

Carter touched her arm. His fingers were warm through the soft yellow muslin of her dress. "Would you mind if I spoke to you alone first?" he asked.

His suddenly serious tone made her stop at once. She turned back toward him. "Of course. We'll go into the parlor."

Once again they entered under the draped archway, but this time the room was empty. The table the miners had used for their card game was pushed back against the wall and held a vase of freshly cut flowers. Carter pointed across the room to the piano. "Do you play?"

Jennie nodded. "Yes. And Kate sings. We're kind of a team," she added with a smile. She sat down in one of the tufted chairs and motioned for Carter to take the settee.

"You and your sister watch out for each other," he observed.

"Yes. We always have. But now more than ever since our parents are gone. Kate's all I have."

Carter's face was still grave. "This has been difficult for you, then."

"Losing one's parents is one of the most difficult things…"

"No, I mean about your sister. Her...ah... problem."

Jennie was silent for a moment. Finally she said simply, "Yes."

"Then I hope you won't think I'm presumptuous when I tell you I've been doing some work today on your dilemma."

"Of course not." She smiled at him. "I told you yesterday that I was sorry our first meeting was so...abrasive. I appreciate your help. Truly. Both Kate and I do."

Carter gave a brisk nod. "First I should tell you that it appears that the court's order on your zoning infraction is perfectly legal."

Jennie's smile faltered. "You mean, they have the right to make us stop renting to the silverheels...to the miners."

Carter nodded. "So I decided we needed another approach."

Jennie leaned against the back of the chair. Something about Carter's businesslike manner was beginning to make her feel uncomfortable. He seemed different than he had in the dim kitchen light last night when he'd taken hold of her hand. Now he seemed more lawyerlike, more like the overbearing males who'd dealt with her case when she'd gone to the district court to give her side on the zoning issue. "Another approach?" she asked warily.

"I talked to the members of the town council."

Jennie's shoulders sagged against the back of the chair. "You mean you talked with Henrietta Billingsley. Because Henry Billingsley runs the council and Henrietta runs him.''

''Yes, Mrs. Billingsley was involved in our discussions.''

''I'll *bet* she was.''

''But I think we were able to come to an agreement that will satisfy everyone.''

''Now *that* would surprise me very much.''

Carter smiled at her, but his smile didn't make her insides do the same flip-flops that it had the previous evening. ''They're willing to give you an exemption to the zoning ordinance to rent rooms here to a maximum of four boarders.''

Jennie's eyes widened. ''They are?''

''Yes.''

''I can hardly believe it.''

''I think you'd be surprised to find that many people in town have a lot of sympathy for you and your sister. They know that it's not your fault that you lost your parents and were left in less than desirable financial circumstances.''

Jennie gave another disbelieving nod. ''So we can keep on just as is?''

''Well, not exactly. It seems that the objection is not so much to the boarders as to the presence of…the…ah…''

''My sister,'' Jennie supplied, her voice suddenly hard.

Carter nodded kindly. ''There's an asylum in Carson City where she can stay until such time as she is sufficiently recovered and the adoption of the child is arranged—''

Jennie was on her feet before he could finish. "An asylum!"

Carter rose from the settee more slowly. "It's a home, really. A home for girls in trouble like your sister."

Jennie literally sputtered with fury. When she could shape the words into speech she leaned close to Carter and said, "The only *trouble* my sister has is meddling busybodies like you who can't leave decent people alone to live out their lives."

"I'm trying to work out a settlement that will—"

Jennie reached to grab Carter's hat from where he had laid it beside him on the settee and she went up on tiptoe to jam it onto his head, taking care to crush the brim in the process. Then she picked up the delicate nosegay from the table and stabbed it into his chest. "You can just take your settlement *and* your damn flowers and get out of here. My sister is waiting for me to help her fix dinner in *our* kitchen in *our* house, the house where she's going to have her baby and raise him or her to be a more caring, tolerant person who will be worth more than every hypocritical member of the town council put together."

Carter made a halfhearted attempt to straighten his hat with one hand while he held on to the mangled flowers with the other. Jennie finished her speech and, without giving him a chance to reply, whirled on her heel and stalked out of the room. As she disappeared under the doorway drapery, she fired back over her shoulder, "You may see yourself out, *Mr.* Jones."

Chapter Three

If Carter had any intention of soothing his feelings by forgetting the existence of Jennie Sheridan, he was doomed to be disappointed. For the next three days, as he awaited the ruling he'd sent for, a constant stream of visitors paraded through his office arguing the pros and cons of the sisters' case. Even the three shaggy miners who were boarding at Sheridan House put in an appearance, shuffling and looking ill at ease among books and papers instead of their accustomed tools and rocks.

Just about the only person who didn't show up was the one person he secretly kept hoping to see each time the creaky office door announced a new arrival. The person who'd unceremoniously thrown him out of her house at their last encounter.

This morning the advocate for the Sheridans was once again Dr. Millard, who had finally been called in to consult on Kate's condition.

"Something's got to be settled in this matter. And I mean, immediately," the doctor said, his expression unusually serious.

"Unfortunately, courts don't seem to be too good at getting things done anywhere near immediately." Carter frowned at the number of pencils scattered around his desk and began to replace them in their appropriate trough.

"They'd better make an exception this time. The health of a young woman might depend on it."

"Kate Sheridan's not doing well?"

"I'm not at liberty to discuss the condition of my patients, Carter. You're a lawyer—you know that. But I'll tell you that I'm making a professional recommendation that the Sheridans not be subjected to any more anxiety."

Spending half his time on a dispute over a minor zoning infraction was not what Carter had envisioned when he'd taken the district attorney position. He'd been hoping for some kind of high-profile trial of the century that would have put him in the political spotlight for the entire state. Part of him wished the whole thing would go away. Another part of him wished he could yet come up with a solution that would make him a hero to the stubborn but lovely Jennie.

"I'll send another wire to the court," he told the doctor. "And in the meantime I could see the Sheridans and tell them that no one will be closing them down until we've heard on the appeal. Do you think that would help?"

Dr. Millard nodded. "It's just not healthy for Kate to be sitting over there waiting for the sheriff to appear any moment. She needs total peace and rest."

"A house full of men doesn't seem too peaceful to me," Carter observed.

"Jennie's handling things. She won't even let Kate make the beds anymore. Jennie does the cleaning, cooking, fetching water and cares for Kate, as well."

Carter made no comment. He'd seen Jennie handling things. Himself, for one. But he'd also seen her turn shy and tongue-tied as a schoolgirl that night he'd taken her hand and asked her to call him Carter. Which was the real Jennie? he wondered. He wasn't likely to find out if his last-ditch appeal on her case came back rejected, as he was almost certain it would.

Dr. Millard stood, pushing heavily on the arms of the chair. "Old bones don't want to work some days," he muttered. Then he looked across the desk at Carter, his eyes as piercing and sharp as any man half his age. "Go talk to them, my boy. Make up a story, if you have to. I'd wager it wouldn't be the first time you've stretched the truth to tell a pretty girl what she wants to hear."

Dr. Millard softened his accusation with a wink, and Carter grinned as he answered, "You'd win that bet, Doctor."

He waited until the doctor had slowly made his way down the office stairs, then reached for his hat. He wasn't sure he was ready to face Jennie Sheridan yet, but he would send that wire. At the very least, it would get him out from behind this desk.

Throughout his childhood Carter had watched the comings and goings of Philadelphia mainline society from hidden corners in laundry rooms and butler's pantries. He'd not merely watched, he'd *studied* them until he could imitate the haughtiest Pennington or the most tiresome Witherspoon.

He'd learned early to keep out of their way, to allow no opportunities for the rich young offspring of the people his mother worked for to taunt him for his lack of a name. But it had been a lesson learned in heartache. His mother, Maude, had usually been too tired from her days of scrubbing floors and polishing mahogany staircases to lend comfort to the small boy who had, after all, been the result of an entirely improper upstairs-downstairs liaison that had been the one mistake in her circumspect life.

So Carter was left on his own to watch and plan. His blood was every bit as blue as these elegant men and women who passed him by each day as if he were no more than one of the marble statues currently in vogue. His father had given him the heritage, but not the name. Nor would he ever have the chance to do so. According to Maude Jones, Carter's father had been sent off in disgrace on a grand tour of Europe after impregnating the family servant and had died in a carriage accident in Italy.

Sometimes Carter used to spin fantasies about what would have happened if his father had returned from that trip. He would have visited Maude in the tiny apartment she'd been forced to take to await the birth. There he'd have seen his son and would have been so full of fatherly pride that he would have resisted his entire family and taken Maude to wife. And Carter would be living in one of the fine stone mansions instead of lurking there in shadows, waiting for his mother to finish her endless toil.

Walking slowly down the main street of Vermillion toward the telegraph office, he wondered what had triggered his sudden reverie into the past. It had been months since he'd indulged in those memories. Months, too, since he'd written to his benefactor, a Mr. Arthur Trenton, one of his mother's employers who had finally noticed the boy in the shadows and had seen fit to send the abnormally bright child first to prep school and then to Harvard.

Before his mother's death, Carter had spun fantasies of Mr. Trenton falling in love with Maude and marrying her, which would finally give Carter the name he craved. But, of course, by then Maude was no longer the pretty English immigrant fresh off the boat. Years of labor had roughened her skin and dulled her bright eyes. Arthur Trenton never so much as glanced her way.

He'd send Mr. Trenton a wire instead of a letter. That would show him how prosperous Carter was becoming, how important. No time for pen and paper. Just a wire, businesslike and expensive. He'd tell him what an important position he'd obtained—district attorney. It sounded impressive. In a wire there would be no space to provide the exact details of his jurisdiction. He wouldn't be able to tell the old man that his days consisted mostly of farm disputes and dealing with small-town politics.

His thoughts came to an abrupt halt as he nearly collided head-on with a solid wall of them. Henrietta Billingsley, Margaret Potter and Lucinda Wentworth, coming directly toward him with all sheets to the wind.

"Good morning, ladies," he acknowledged with a forced smile and a tip of his hat.

"We need to talk with you, Mr. Jones. We were just going to your office," Mrs. Billingsley said. She planted her substantial form directly in front of him, causing him to abandon any hope of slipping easily around the group to continue on his course.

"Let me guess the topic."

Like a helpful sergeant at arms, Miss Potter continued, "It's been four days, Mr. Jones. What's the delay in dealing with those girls?"

"They still have that house open as if there's not a thing wrong," Henrietta added.

Carter waited, looking at Lucinda Wentworth. He was curious to see if she would add her voice, or if her son had convinced her to stay out of the fray. She darted nervous glances at her two friends, her pinched face looking strained, but remained silent.

"There's been an appeal of the ruling," Carter said finally. He wasn't about to add that he himself had engineered the appeal. Not in front of this crew.

Henrietta huffed loudly, her face beginning to color. "We've already *gone* through an appeal. What are they going to do, appeal from now until the day that bastard child pops out for the entire town to see?"

Mrs. Wentworth gasped, then blanched and swayed toward Margaret Potter, who in turn was pushed toward Henrietta. As Carter watched with growing horror, the matrons began to topple like a row of buxom dominoes. In quick succession he threw his upper body to block Mrs. Billingsley's fall, then reached his long arms around her to ward off the further descent of Miss Potter, who by now was entirely supporting the weight of an apparently unconscious Lucinda.

When Carter was assured that Mrs. Billingsley's significant bulk would maintain her upright, he stepped around her, lifted Mrs. Wentworth from Margaret Potter's shoulder and leaned her up against the post that sustained the wooden awning over the Billingsleys' dry goods store. Her head hit the column with a thud and her eyes fluttered open.

Henrietta had recovered her balance and her voice. "Not another of your swoons, Lucinda. Honestly, you're such a goose."

Mrs. Wentworth's pale cheeks grew pink with indignation. "Any decent person would be liable to swoon at that kind of language. I'm shocked at you, Henrietta."

"It's not the language that's shocking. It's the situation. To think of that hussy shamelessly flaunting her condition as if she had all the right in the world..."

Mrs. Wentworth appeared to be recovering rapidly, so Carter stepped back. Mrs. Billingsley's eyes widened and her voice trailed off as she focused over his shoulder. Whether it was Lucinda Wentworth's suddenly shamefaced expression or the slight hint of fresh lemon scent, he knew without seeing her that the new arrival was Jennie Sheridan.

He whirled around but could find no words of greeting. Her lips were tight, nearly bloodless. Carter watched, fascinated, as her eyes drilled into each of the three older women, then settled on Mrs. Billingsley. Her small chin went up and she said stiffly, ''Far from flaunting anything, the hussy you refer to has not left her house for three months, thanks to people like you. Though I don't recall you thinking she was so shameless when she spent a whole summer taking care of your twins when your mother was dying from consumption.''

She took a step to the side and fixed her gaze on Margaret Potter. ''And I can't remember that you thought Kate was a hussy, Miss Potter, when she stayed after school every day to help you set up the school library.''

She moved over one more step to the edge of the sidewalk. ''And, Mrs. Wentworth, Kate was evidently good enough for your precious Lyle to set his cap for her.''

''He never...'' Mrs. Wentworth began, but faltered as her two friends sent her withering looks, as though this lapse of discretion in her only son was entirely her fault.

Carter's neck had grown sticky with sweat, causing his starched collar to prickle. ''Ladies, I don't think we're going to solve anything....''

The women found common ground in ignoring him. All four seemed to be talking at once and mysteriously understanding what each of the other three was saying.

''And now that the entire town has begun this crusade against us, you all have her so upset that Dr. Millard says her health is in danger,'' Jennie continued.

This statement brought a moment of silence into

which Carter ventured once again. "Dr. Millard informed me this morning that Miss Kate Sheridan is not well," he said, supporting Jennie's assertion.

"Will she lose the child?" Mrs. Billingsley asked with a touch of eagerness that even she immediately realized was unseemly. "I mean…she's not terribly sick, is she?"

Carter could see the rise and fall of Jennie's breasts as she fought to keep her emotions under control. He himself wouldn't be averse to giving Henrietta Billingsley a shove right over the edge of the sidewalk.

"I'm on my way to fetch the doctor now," she said. The quaver in her voice told Carter that she was a lot more scared than she had let on in her feisty confrontation with the town matrons.

"I'll go with you," he offered.

Mrs. Billingsley looked stricken. "We were having a discussion, Mr. Jones."

"I'm sorry, ma'am. If you'll stop by my office tomorrow morning, I'll be happy to consider any matter you'd like to bring up."

He took Jennie's arm and stepped off the sidewalk into the street so the two of them could outflank the three older women before they could make any further protest. She let him pull her along without speaking until they were safely out of earshot, then she slowed her pace. "Thank you for the rescue," she said in a stilted voice. "I wasn't in much of a mood to deal with those women today. But you don't have to come with me."

He looked down at her and said simply, "I want to."

She wrinkled her nose. "Why?"

"Let's say I feel involved. Dr. Millard came to see me this morning and warned me that this situation was becoming unhealthy for your sister."

Jennie nodded. "She worries too much. And she cares too much about what everyone else thinks."

"But you don't."

"I care what *Kate* thinks. Or worthwhile people like Dr. Millard. But I certainly don't care about the views of a bunch of old biddies with time on their hands and nonsense in their heads."

"Good for you, Miss Sheridan. I've been known to ignore the court of public opinion a time or two myself."

Jennie had continued walking along at Carter's side in the direction of the doctor's office, but now she stopped and looked up at him with a curious expression. "I thought you were a politician, Mr. Jones. Your kind lives and dies by public opinion."

Carter grinned. "It's a matter of picking your battles. That and knowing when it might be worth it to fight on the other side awhile."

"Well, I don't know why you've decided that this is one of those times, but I'm grateful, Mr. Jones."

"Grateful enough to call me Carter, like you did the first day we met?"

The tense look in her eyes was gradually being replaced by a warmth that was kindling another kind of warmth in Carter's midsection. "Those guardians of the town's morality you were just talking to will think it scandalous if they hear me."

Carter grimaced. "It will give them something to think about besides your sister, then."

Jennie smiled. "Yes. That's a strategy I haven't used yet. If I become a greater scandal, they'll turn their attention away from Kate." She moved closer to him and linked her arm through his. "I shall call you Carter. And you must call me Jennie. Loudly enough for them to hear it all the way back to Mr. Billingsley's store."

Carter chuckled. He had his doubts about the wisdom of her so-called strategy. As far as he could tell, the town matrons had plenty of ammunition to lob at Kate Sheridan and her sister both, if given cause. But he was enjoying her good humor. "Jennie it is," he said with a grin.

"Thank you...Carter," she replied, raising her voice as she said his name.

They turned their heads in unison and, sure enough, the three matrons were staring after them with appalled expressions.

Jennie and Carter smiled at each other, then started toward Dr. Millard's once again. As they walked down the street, Jennie began to giggle. Carter had heard her raging and had heard her determined. He'd heard her with worry cracking her voice. But nothing he'd heard from her up to now affected him like that giggle. He found it more enchanting than a choir of angels.

Dr. Millard had been with Kate for over an hour. By the time he emerged from her bedroom at the far end of the hall, Jennie was pacing the parlor, taut with worry. Carter had left her at the doctor's office after telling Jennie that he'd be interested in hearing a report on her sister's condition.

She'd spent the first few minutes after arriving home going over the conversation she'd had with the handsome prosecutor. Carter Jones wasn't *so* bad, she reckoned. Perhaps Kate was right that not all men were like Sean Flaherty.

But as the minutes ticked by and Dr. Millard still had not emerged from Kate's bedroom, she began to get more and more nervous. She snapped unreasonably at Barnaby when he pushed aside the parlor door drapes, just because she'd hoped it was the doctor.

When Dr. Millard finally did come through the arched doorway, he looked tired and suddenly old. Her father and Dr. Millard had been the same age and the greatest of friends. But Papa's cheeks had never had that pallid, puffy look. His lips had not grown crinkled with lines. And now, of course, they never would. Jennie felt a sob rise in her throat. She'd lost so much. Dear Lord, not Kate, too.

"You look like a child who's had its toys snatched away, Jennie," the doctor said gently. "Come on. Kate needs you to be strong right now, not weepy."

"What's the matter with her?" Dr. Millard's words had hurt her pride and stiffened her back, which was most likely exactly the effect he had intended.

"Honey, some girls are blessed to have babies by the baker's dozen without batting an eye, but your sister's turning out to be a more delicate sort."

Jennie bit her lip. "Is she going to be all right? I mean…is the baby…?"

Dr. Millard pulled on Jennie's arm and led her to the settee, where he lowered himself into the down cushion with a heavy whoosh. "She's bleeding, Jennie. That's not supposed to happen. Could be she'll lose the little tyke. Now, maybe that's what's meant to happen. Poor little thing without a father. You know sometimes the Lord…"

Jennie had let him pull her to a seat, but she sat erect, and when he began the last statement she jumped to her feet again. "Dr. Millard, this baby may not have a father, but it *will* have a family. A loving, caring family. So don't tell me that it's not meant to be. Just tell me what we have to do to be sure my sister has a healthy child."

The doctor leaned back and closed his eyes with a sigh. "The only thing I can tell you is that she's got to rest. Keep her off her feet as much as possible. I know that puts a lot of burden on you."

"I don't care about that."

"You should have some help."

Jennie gave a little snort. "Shall I post a notice in the town square and see how many people come rushing to help the two wicked Sheridan sisters?"

"That's not fair, Jennie. You know you have friends here. Lyle Wentworth came to see me about your sister. He'd help out around this place."

"Kate doesn't want to see him, Dr. Millard. And I don't imagine you'd want me upsetting her."

The doctor shook his head. "Definitely not. But there are others. That young Carter Jones seemed a bit taken with you when he escorted you to my place today. I bet he'd lend a hand."

To Jennie's amazement, she felt her cheeks begin to grow hot. Could she be blushing? Only silly girls blushed. Silly, lovesick girls. "I'm sure Mr. Jones has more important things to do than worry about us," she said. "We'll get along fine. I've got Barnaby to help out. And the miners will lend a hand, if I ask them. We'll make sure Kate doesn't so much as fluff the pillow from her bed."

Dr. Millard pushed heavily on the arm of the settee and stood. He leaned over to put a soft hand on Jennie's still-blushing cheek, which seem to burn under his touch. "You've got your parents' spirit, girl. The same spirit that took them through all those winters in the mountains. Strong, independent people they were. Some of the finest I've known."

Jennie nodded, her throat too full to answer.

"So you and I will do our best to take care of our Kate and of that grandchild of theirs," he added.

As the doctor quietly left the parlor, Jennie stood staring blindly at the bombazine curtains. She'd been thinking of all the problems this coming child was causing, but what about the child itself? Her parents' grandchild. Her sister was going to have a baby—a new life to carry on the proud tradition that her parents had done such a good job of passing on to her and Kate. Yes, she'd take care of Kate and of the baby, too. She wouldn't let them down. And Dr. Millard was wrong. She didn't need help from anyone to do it.

Chapter Four

Like the eye of a hurricane, Kate sat on a stool in one corner of the kitchen, viewing the scene with one of her serene smiles. Around her the room was in chaos.

Jennie stood next to the stove, sleeves rolled up, her hair fallen in damp ringlets around her neck. Dark patches had begun to show across her back where her dress clung to her sweaty body.

Barnaby had climbed up into the tin sink and was balancing precariously while he picked the good china plates one by one out of the high cupboard and handed them to Dennis Kelly, who took each fragile dish in his meaty hands and set it down on the table as if it were a piece of spun sugar.

Brad Connors and Humphrey Smith were standing together at the cutting counter, jostling each other and grumbling as they chopped vegetables.

"Smitty ain't doing it right, Miss Jennie," Brad complained. "He's not cutting off enough at the tops."

"You're throwing away half the carrot, Connors,"

Smitty replied. "I didn't break my back picking those out of the garden for you to waste 'em like that."

Jennie set aside the big spoon she'd been using to stir the stew and reached to put the cover on the big pot. "It doesn't matter, boys. However you chop them will be fine. We have plenty of carrots."

"Well, someone else is going to have to go grub in the dirt and find them," Smitty said under his breath, but he moved a step back from where Brad continued to chop furiously, throwing the top two inches off each vegetable into the garbage bin on the floor beneath them.

"I'm just grateful you've all agreed to pitch in and help," Jennie said, her voice sounding a little weary. "Mr. Jones and the Millards have been quite a help to us and I don't think I would have dared ask them to supper if Barnaby and I had to do it all by ourselves."

"If you'd let me help…" Kate began from her corner seat, but she fell silent as Jennie fixed her with a stern look.

"We've told you to count on us, Miss Jennie," Dennis Kelly said. He had finished stacking the plates Barnaby had handed him and was now warily transferring crystal goblets.

Jennie leaned back against the warm stove, heedless of her damp dress, and regarded the three men fondly. "I don't know how we were so lucky to have you three come along just when Kate and I needed friends so badly."

The skin around Dennis's muttonchop whiskers turned bright red. "It's a downright shame how the people in this town turned their backs on you two girls," he said, his voice hoarse with indignation. "Why, you're two of the sweetest little gals we've ever known. Right, boys?"

Smitty continued chopping, but Brad turned and said, "Sure as shootin'. Two of the prettiest, too."

Dennis shot him a look of reproof. "We'll help you through this. And I'd just like to see that old battle-ax try to stop us."

Jennie's smile broadened. She wouldn't like to predict the outcome of a showdown between Mrs. Billingsley and her silverheels. Blood might be drawn. "Smitty, I think we have enough—honestly. You can put the rest of those down in the cellar."

Barnaby handed down the last glass, then jumped to the floor. "When will Mr. Jones be here?" he asked.

Jennie pulled her mother's silver watch from around her neck. "Goodness! It's past six already."

Kate slid off the stool. "Jen, I want you to go upstairs and get washed up. I'll supervise the rest of this." She held up a hand as Jennie began to protest. "I won't make a move. I won't lift a dish. I'll just give orders to this handsome crew here." She indicated the three miners and Barnaby with a smile and a wave of her hand.

Jennie looked doubtful. "Someone needs to drop in the dumplings."

"I'll do it," Dennis offered. "Kate can show me how."

"And the apple crisp should be done any minute

now. You need to keep watch because that stove burns.''

Kate came up behind her sister and gave her a little shove toward the door. ''We'll handle it. If you don't hurry on upstairs, you'll be greeting your guests looking like the scullery maid.''

Jennie took a look down at her bedraggled frock and gave a wail. ''I wanted everything to go so well.''

Kate laughed. ''I wonder why. Dr. Millard and Dorie have eaten in this house dozens of times. Which means it must be Mr. Jones you want to impress.''

Jennie frowned. ''I don't want to impress anyone. I just feel that we should thank the people who have stood up against the rest of those close-minded—''

Kate gave her a hug and a more forceful push. ''Don't get started, sis. We're here to have a pleasant evening. So go upstairs and get yourself beautiful.''

Jennie sagged a little against her sister's arm, which tightened against her. It felt comforting. She took a deep breath and a last look around the kitchen. Most of the meal was ready. Barnaby had disappeared into the dining room with the first of the good plates, which he evidently intended to transport one by one. Kate was right. Everything was in good shape except herself. She leaned over to give her sister a peck on the cheek, then darted out of the kitchen toward the front hall.

Barnaby stood by the front door looking up at her with wide eyes. Behind him was Carter Jones. She gave a little shriek.

''Am I early?'' he asked.

Bits of dumpling dough clung to her hands. She

put them behind her back. "No. I'm...ah...late. I mean, I'm not quite ready yet."

"Shall I come back later?" he asked uncertainly.

"No, of course not." She wished there was some way to keep his eyes from roving up and down her stained old dress that way. She pushed at the hair that had fallen down her neck, but stopped as she felt it stick to her doughy fingers. "Barnaby, take Mr. Jones into the parlor, please. Then ask Miss Kate to come out and sit with him until I...until I come downstairs."

His gaze had followed the movement of her hands and seemed to fix on where the tendrils of hair just under her left ear were now stuck to her neck with dough. Jennie could feel the beginning of one of those blushes whose existence she had so recently discovered.

He smiled at her, his gray eyes warming. "I'll be fine, Jennie," he said softly. "Take your time."

She let out a long breath, irritated that her heart refused to slow to anything near normal. With a lift of her chin, she returned his gaze directly and said, "I'll be down in five minutes."

Dorie Millard had worn her hair styled in the same blond ringlets framing her face ever since Jennie could remember. She was two years older than Jennie, approaching old-maid status by Vermillion standards, but her single state wasn't for lack of offers. Jennie reckoned she'd be hard-pressed to find an eligible male in town under the age of fifty who *hadn't* asked for Dorie's hand. But the doctor's breezy daughter seemed perfectly happy to continue being the unmarried belle of the church ice-cream socials and the harvest dances at the back of the feed mill.

Jennie watched with unusual interest as Dorie turned her sunshiny smile on Carter, waiting for the inevitable male response. But to her surprise, Carter seemed to divide his attention equally among the ladies present. In fact, he addressed just as many comments to Dr. Millard and the silverheels, or at least Dennis. Brad and Smitty weren't much for conversation.

She wouldn't admit to herself that she was gratified by Carter's apparent failure to be charmed by Dorie. After all, it was possible that he was just being polite. He was a politician, used to having to stay on good terms with everyone. With three women at the table, he probably knew enough not to play favorites.

Nevertheless, she couldn't help noticing that Carter's eyes followed Jennie herself when she began to help Barnaby clear away the dishes. And while Dorie was in the middle of one of her most vivacious stories, Carter was smiling at Jennie and seemed not to be paying the least attention.

She hummed a little ditty to herself as she went swinging through the door to the kitchen, her arms full of plates.

"The dinner went well, didn't it?" Barnaby whispered when they were both on the kitchen side of the door. He seemed to sense her good mood.

Jennie smiled. "It certainly did, young man. Thanks to your help."

Barnaby looked pleased but embarrassed. "I only put out the dishes," he mumbled into his chest.

"You did a fabulous job." Jennie reached over to give his small shoulders a squeeze. "You served the meal like a real waiter from the most elegant restaurant in Virginia City."

He looked up at her with a grin. "Maybe we should open our own eatery. That would give old Pruneface Potter something to really complain about."

Margaret Potter *did* have something of a prune face. Jennie struggled not to smile, but felt obliged to say, "You shouldn't talk that way about your teacher, Barnaby."

The lad shrugged, unchastened. "Shall I spoon out the apple crisp?"

Jennie nodded. "A ladle of cream on each one. I'll bring the rest of the plates."

She turned back toward the dining room, still smiling. She could hear Dorie's merry laugh before the door swung fully open. Her friend was standing directly behind Carter, her hands on either side of his neck, pulling up on his starched collar. "I don't know how you men stand these things," she said in a teasing voice. "Why, look…you're as chafed as a newly saddled bronc. Now would you care to repeat those words about women suffering for vanity?"

Carter looked uncharacteristically embarrassed and had his hands up trying to hold the collar in place as Dorie tried to tug it off. The three miners were grinning, Kate looked mildly shocked and Dr. Millard sat shaking his head at his daughter with a look of long-suffering resignation.

"Miss Millard, I think I'll keep my ensemble as is, if you don't mind," Carter protested.

Dorie laughed again and pushed the four inches of collar back down into the neck of the shirt. "You see, you men suffer for vanity, as well."

Jennie felt an uneasiness in the pit of her stomach as Dorie's slender fingers rubbed up and down Carter's neck. It *was* a bit chafed, she could now see. But it would be hard to imagine him without the snowy-white collar. It seemed almost part of him.

Dorie gave one last stroke to her victim's neck, then let him go. "We're not so different—men and women," she said. "Old and young. Town and country. Everyone likes to think they're so different, but we're all human. Deep inside we're all the same."

As usual, Dorie's seemingly frivolous words sank in with surprising weight. Jennie looked over at Kate, who was endorsing Dorie's observation with a serious nod.

Carter had relaxed his stiffened position and was regarding Dorie with an odd expression. The heightened color was fading from his face. "You may be right about that, Miss Millard," he said with a glint of admiration in his voice. Jennie's heart plummeted. Another conquest. How did Dorie manage?

The happiness she'd felt in the kitchen with Barnaby had disappeared. With a strained smile she took the plates from in front of Dennis and Brad and turned toward the kitchen.

Dorie was still on her feet. "Shall I help you with those, Jennie?" she asked. It was impossible to be resentful of Dorie, in spite of her ability to turn the head of any male she wished. She was simply too much fun and too nice to dislike.

"Sit back down and entertain the folks, Dorie," Jennie said with a little laugh. "Barnaby and I will bring in the sweets directly." She looked back at the group over her shoulder. "How many want coffee?"

When every male voice answered in the affirmative, Carter pushed back his chair and said, "She's right. You must continue to provide the entertainment, Miss Millard. I'll help Miss Sheridan with the coffee."

The three miners looked over at Carter with surprise. It appeared that the stiff public prosecutor had had more than his collar loosened.

Jennie hesitated, then finally said, "All right. I'd appreciate a hand." She continued on into the kitchen, her arms just a little shaky from the heavy plates.

Carter was right behind her. "Miss Millard is quite a debater," he said softly, for her ears only. "She should consider a career in politics."

"Some folks in this town might say she already practices her own special brand of politics," Jennie said dryly.

"Politicking with the men in town?"

"With the eligible ones, at least. Dorie wouldn't make time with someone else's husband, but every other male out of short pants is pretty much fair game."

Carter grinned as he stacked the dirty dishes he carried on top of the pile. "Do I detect a note of jealousy, Miss Sheridan? I thought you two were friends."

"We are friends. And I'm certainly not jealous of her. In order to be jealous, I would have to care about making time with the men in town myself."

"Which you don't," Carter clarified with an amused smile.

"No, sir."

"Is this enough cream, Jennie?" Barnaby interrupted their exchange by stepping between them holding out a bowl of apple crisp.

Jennie gave the boy a grateful smile. What was it about talking with Carter Jones that made the breath stick in her throat? "That's just perfect, Barnaby. You can begin taking them out to the dining room. Remember to serve the ladies first."

Barnaby drew himself up proudly and marched toward the door, holding the bowl of crisp like a tournament trophy. Jennie's smile turned tender. Their little foundling was always so eager to please.

Carter appeared to read her thoughts. "He glows like a lightning bug when you pay him a compliment."

Jennie nodded. "You should have seen him when he first came here. He was so shy that he could hardly utter a sentence. He used to hang back in the shadows hoping no one would notice him."

An odd expression flickered across Carter's face, but after a moment, he smiled and said, "He's learning fast. He had no problem with shyness the other day when he was barricading the door against me."

Jennie nodded. "He's grown very protective of Kate and me. It's quite touching."

Carter tipped his head in the direction of the dining room. "You seem to have a room full of protectors out there."

Jennie laughed. "I guess we do. The miners are great. They even helped with the dinner tonight."

Carter leaned back against the kitchen counter and surveyed her. She presented quite a different picture than the harried young woman with dough sticking to her neck he'd encountered before dinner. Her hair was back up in a proper chignon and she was wearing some kind of bustled blue silk thing that sculpted her slender silhouette as if she'd spent the entire afternoon being pinned and stitched by a seamstress.

Carter reckoned that nine men out of ten would pick either of the two blondes in the next room over Jennie Sheridan. Kate was a sleek beauty and Dorie a vivacious charmer. But there was something about Jennie. Half the time she was acting stubborn and prickly, daring the rest of the world to say something bad about her baby sister. But then she had those moments of looking like a child who had lost every anchor she'd ever had in life. And somewhere in between both those Jennies was a glimmer of the woman she refused to admit to being, a woman whose passions might fit the sensual promise of that sculpted, low-necked dress.

Suddenly he realized he'd been staring for too long. And that Jennie was staring right back. Barnaby had whisked past them three times now, carrying the bowls of dessert one at a time into the dining room.

He cleared his throat. "So he was lucky to find you," he said.

Jennie looked confused and blinked her unfocused eyes. "Who?"

Carter smiled gently. There was definitely a woman inside there waiting to find her way out. He wouldn't mind being the one to help make it happen. "Barnaby. He was lucky to find this place to live with you and your sister."

Jennie swallowed hard and said, "Well, we were lucky to have him. He's been a tremendous help." She reached out and gave Barnaby's shoulder a pat as he passed by with another bowl. Then she and Carter lapsed into silence as they watched the boy swing through the door. Neither one was thinking about Barnaby.

"Goodness," Jennie said suddenly. "The coffee!"

She was slightly flushed, and just at the side of her slender neck in the precise spot where the dough had stuck earlier, Carter could see her pulse beating. "Relax," he said, in a voice that was lower and more intimate than any he had yet used with her. "There's no hurry. Everyone's having a good time. Including me."

He leaned over and brushed a kiss on her mouth, then backed away almost before Jennie could realize what he had done. He waited for a protest, but she simply stood and looked up at him, her eyes grown wide. Finally he flashed a smile and turned to cross the room to the sink. "All right," he said briskly. "Put me to work."

* * *

All the parlor lamps were lit, the wicks turned up full, but it seemed to Jennie as if a kind of haze hung over the room. She was feeling much the same kind of fog she'd felt after her parents' deaths, though without the pain. She'd worked hard all day and knew that she was nearly giddy with exhaustion as they'd sat down to eat. But this was something else. It had started when Carter had followed her into the kitchen. As soon as the door had swung shut, closing them off from the other guests, her heart had begun to accelerate. When he'd touched her with his lips, it had settled into a fast staccato that was still drumming away inside her chest.

It was silly, of course. Carter was a handsome, eligible man, used to flirting, used to teasing. The little peck he'd given her had meant nothing. He'd have done the same to Dorie. In fact, it might have been more than a peck with Dorie. She bit her lip.

Her animated friend was addressing him this minute. "So someday you might be *governor* of the state, Carter?" Dorie asked breathily. "I can't imagine knowing anyone so important. Will you still come back and talk to us little folk in Vermillion when you're such a famous man?"

Carter did not look the least embarrassed by the question. In fact, he appeared to consider it before he answered. "A good politician is able to relate to people at all levels, Miss Millard. I would hope that I'll keep my friends wherever my career might take me."

Dorie made a show of sliding nearer to him on the settee and took his elbow in both hands. "Just in case you don't ever come back here, I want to be able to say that I touched the future governor," she said with a flirtatious giggle.

Carter looked over Dorie's shoulder and gave Jennie a conspiratorial smile. Jennie wasn't entirely sure, but it looked to her as if his expression said, "Your friend's a bit of a goose." At least that was the way she chose to interpret it.

Her attention turned abruptly from Dorie and Carter when Dr. Millard said suddenly, "Are you feeling all right, Kate?"

With a pang, Jennie realized that Kate's wan face was even whiter than normal. Jennie'd been so busy working that she hadn't thought to ask about her sister's condition today. Though she hadn't let Kate do anything in preparation for the dinner, she had allowed her to sit with her in the kitchen all afternoon instead of taking her usual nap.

She jumped up and went to Kate's side, laying a hand on her shoulder. "You should be in bed, sis. You've been on your feet for hours now."

Kate put her hand on top of Jennie's and gave it a little pat. "I'm fine, my little nurse. You worry too much about me. You too, Dr. Millard," she added, giving the old man a smile.

The doctor's expression was grave. "Perhaps I should have you stay over with me and Dorie for a couple nights so I can keep an eye on how you're doing."

Jennie felt a panicky sensation in her middle. She and Kate belonged together. She could face anything as long as the two of them were facing it side by side.

But she waited for Kate's reply, which was as she expected.

"Nonsense, Doctor. It's not that I don't appreciate the offer—"

Across the room Carter stood and interrupted. "What Miss Sheridan undoubtedly needs is some rest, which she's not going to get if her visitors sit around all night talking."

Dorie jumped up next to him. "Carter's right. It's been a lovely party, Jennie dear," she said. She smiled at her friend, then let the smile dance its way around to each of the gentlemen in the room.

Jennie was not going to argue. There was a definite pallor around Kate's mouth. She wanted to get her to bed. Besides, she'd had just about as much as she could take for one evening of struggling to keep her eyes and her mind off Carter Jones. And if Dorie didn't stop grabbing his arm that way, there was a likelihood that Jennie would end up giving one of her very dearest friends a smack.

Dr. Millard stood slowly, his eyes still on Kate. "I'm coming over tomorrow morning. If your color's not any better, we need to think about having you see an obstetrician in Virginia City."

"What's an obste...?" Jennie stumbled over the word.

"A special doctor who looks after ladies," Dr. Millard told her. "It's a person who specializes in birthing babies. They have one at Mercy Hospital in Virginia City."

Carter frowned. "Perhaps she should see one anyway."

"Sounds like a good idea to me," Dennis Kelly added. "You've been looking mighty peaked, Miss Kate."

Kate took her hand off Jennie's and straightened up in her chair. "You're all very kind, but I wish you wouldn't make such a fuss. I'll be perfectly fine."

Jennie could tell that having a room full of men discussing her personal health was making her sister decidedly self-conscious. She gave Kate's shoulder a squeeze as she shifted uncomfortably in the hard-backed chair. "I don't mean to be rude, but I think what my sister needs most right now is some rest. We should say good-night."

The three miners had shuffled to their feet and begun mumbling apologies for keeping their pretty landlords up so late when Barnaby appeared, ducking under the parlor entrance curtain. "There's a visitor at the door," he told Jennie.

Jennie's surprise came from more than the late hour. The only visitors she and her sister had had for weeks were already in the room. "Who is it?"

"Mr. Wentworth."

"Lyle?" Kate asked, her hand fluttering to her throat.

When Barnaby nodded, Jennie looked at her sister, then said, "I'll go speak with him."

Kate nodded and whispered. "I can't see him." The hand moved from her throat to her rounded stomach.

"He says he wants to see both of you," Barnaby said. "He says it's important."

Jennie hesitated and the others in the room remained silent. Finally Carter stepped over next to Jennie and took her arm. "I'll speak to him with you. There's no need for Kate to see him if she doesn't want to."

Kate's look of gratitude was not lost on Jennie. She herself was feeling grateful for the solid support of Carter's hand at her elbow. In spite of her brave words to Kate, Jennie had also felt herself affected by the ostracism of the town. It wasn't easy to be shunned by people you'd known for years. In addition, Carter's warm hand brought back the moment in the kitchen earlier when he'd kissed her. The sudden memory gave a lift to spirits that had been dampened by the sight of Kate looking so drawn and exhausted.

"Thank you," she said to him, starting toward the door.

"Yes, thank you, Mr. Jones," Kate said. "But I guess if Lyle's braved his mother's wrath to come to this house, the least I can do is hear what he has to say." She stood, swaying a little, the exertion flushing her cheeks.

Carter reached out with his free hand to steady her, guided her toward Jennie, who slipped an arm around her waist. "Are you sure, Katie?"

At Kate's nod the two sisters went into the front hall, followed by Carter, the Millards and the three miners. There was scarcely room for Lyle Wentworth to enter the narrow vestibule when Barnaby opened to door to admit him.

His eyes went immediately to Kate's, then to where her shawl discreetly covered the now noticeable pregnancy. There was a flicker of pain in his eyes, but his voice was businesslike. "Evening, Kate. Evening, Jennie."

"It's a late hour for a social call, Lyle," Jennie said. She noticed that Lyle was bigger than Carter and softer. Carter's hand on her arm was strong with long, lean fingers. Lyle's hands, rubbing across the top of his thirty-dollar felt hat, were short and puffy.

He nodded. "It's not a social call. I came to tell you that Sheriff Hammond's back in town and old lady Billingsley's after him with the rest of her pack, my mother included." He turned to Kate with a shrug of apology. "I'm sorry, Kate. She usually listens to me, but Mrs. Billingsley's so all fired up about you girls…"

Jennie felt Kate stiffen. "We don't need to talk about this tonight," she began, then stopped to stare behind Lyle and out the open door. Sheriff Delbert Hammond, a shotgun cradled in his arms, was marching up their front walk, followed by a veritable army of women.

Jennie tightened her hold around Kate's waist. "Don't let them bother you, sis," she said quickly in an undertone. "They're just busybodies with too much time on their hands."

"We'll protect you, Miss Kate." Brad Connors pushed past Lyle toward the front door, pulling a derringer from his boot en route.

After a minute's hesitation, Dennis and Smitty moved to each side of him, forming a flank, pushing Dr. Millard heavily against the hall whatnot.

Dorie shouted, "Papa, are you all right?" then

scooted around Jennie to grab Brad by the shoulder and spin him around. "Don't be an idiot!" she barked.

The delegation had reached the front stoop. Sheriff Hammond looked shamefaced and, in spite of the weapon in his arms, not the least bit fearsome. But the two women directly behind him, Mrs. Billingsley and Miss Potter, were skewering Kate with frightening stares.

"Do your duty, Sheriff," Mrs. Billingsley said coldly.

"What's this all about, Hammond?" Carter asked.

The sheriff stammered for several seconds, but finally managed, "I'm serving these here papers, Counselor. Closing the place down. I've got an order from Judge Hickory. Says here 'for immediate execution.'"

Carter stepped around Jennie and reached out to take the crumpled paper the sheriff had pulled from his pocket. No one spoke as he began to read it silently, his expression hardening. Jennie's breath stopped in her throat. Surely they couldn't close them down just like that? They wouldn't turn her silverheels out on the streets of the town in the middle of the night with nowhere else to go? It was a lucky thing that Carter was here tonight. He'd take care of it.

She studied his face as he bent over the paper. The hard line of his jaw was dark with evening whiskers. She'd felt the barest touch of them when he'd kissed her. In spite of the circumstances, a smile played about her lips. She wondered what Mrs. Billingsley would say if she knew that only an hour ago the town prosecutor had been kissing the older of those sinful Sheridan sisters. It almost made her want to giggle. Henrietta would explode when Carter told her that he was on the Sheridans' side now.

Carter looked over at her, his gray eyes stormy. Then he said, "The sheriff's right. You men are going to have to get your gear together and head on out of here or the sheriff will have the right to seize this place and turn everyone out."

Jennie looked up at Carter in shock. Had she heard him correctly? What had happened to his promises to help them?

"It just don't seem fair," Dennis Kelly was protesting. "Miss Jennie and Miss Kate need the money and we need the place to live."

Mrs. Billingsley poked her head around the sheriff and said, "I'm sure you'd all like to continue with whatever...*arrangements* you gentlemen have made with these...*girls*...but this is a decent part of town. And we decent folks aren't going to put up with it."

"No, we're not," Miss Potter echoed.

Behind her Lucinda Wentworth had the grace to look embarrassed under the withering glance of her son.

Jennie heard Dorie's gasp of indignation through the sound of blood rushing behind her own ears. She let go of Kate and took a step toward the women. She addressed them, totally ignoring Sheriff Hammond and his shotgun. "I don't know how you can call yourself decent when you come here in the middle of the night to a house of bereavement and say vile things—''

She broke off and whirled around as, out of the corner of her eye, she saw Dr. Millard straighten himself up from the whatnot, shove Dennis Kelly aside and take two surprisingly spry steps across the hall, just in time to catch a collapsing Kate.

''Kate!'' Lyle Wentworth yelled, helping the doctor as he bent with the weight of Kate's unconscious form. Together the two men lowered her to the floor.

''Lordy!'' Brad Connors breathed, still holding his derringer pointed toward the sheriff.

Jennie wailed and sank down next to Kate, her eyes on the doctor. ''What's happened?'' she asked in a choked voice.

Dr. Millard shook his head gently. ''I'm not sure, child. Perhaps she's just fainted. We need to get her to a bed.'' With a minimum of words, he instructed the three miners and Lyle on how to lift Kate gently and bear her upstairs toward her room. ''I may need your help, Dorie,'' he told his daughter, and she turned to follow him up the stairs.

Jennie stood immobile as an icy fear spread through her. When the procession had disappeared around the curve of the stairs, she turned to face the group who stood waiting around the doorway. ''Get out of my house,'' she said to them.

Sheriff Hammond turned around to scan the faces of the women. Even Henrietta looked a bit taken aback at the turn of events. Turning back to Jennie, he said, ''I'm not sure this will change the order, but I guess we can wait to deal with it until tomorrow.''

Jennie looked first at him, then one by one at the women behind him. Most wouldn't meet her gaze. "If my sister dies," she said, "it will be on your heads. You will be responsible for the death of a sweet, gentle angel who's never harmed a soul in this town. Her crime was to love too much and give too much. But *your* crime will be murder."

At the very end she let her stare rest on Carter. "All of you," she ended.

Then she turned, put a shaky hand out to the banister and started up the stairs.

Chapter Five

Jennie had never much liked Lyle Wentworth. As son of the town banker, he'd always seemed to consider himself a cut above the rest of the students at Vermillion School. When it was time for lunch out on the enclosed dirt play yard, most of the children brought out tin pails full of cold biscuits or dried bacon slabs. Lyle had had a cloth-lined wicker basket that every year seemed to overflow with more delicacies—tins of salmon paste, marchpane candies— foods that Jennie and Kate had never even heard of.

Jennie remembered the first time that Lyle had offered to share some of his bounty with Kate. They'd giggled about it on the way home that day, but it had become less funny to Jennie as the days passed and it became increasingly obvious that stuck-up Lyle Wentworth was sweet on her baby sister.

Fortunately, Kate never seemed to find much appeal in the idea, either, though she was too sweet to ever tell Lyle to his face. She couldn't even bear to turn him down when he'd asked her to the harvest dance the year she turned sixteen. He'd tried to kiss her, she'd confided to Jennie later. Jennie had been shocked.

But tonight she was happy that Lyle had stayed. It was comforting somehow. He was one of Kate's oldest friends, a man with money and power. He'd help see that nothing happened to her.

"How is she?" he asked as she started down the stairs. He was still standing in the front hall where she'd left everyone over half an hour ago. The others had left, including Carter.

"She's awake. The doctor sent me down for some tea." Lyle looked almost as worried as Jennie felt. She forced a small smile. "Kate's strong."

Lyle shook his head. "No, she's not. You're the strong one, Jennie. Kate's always depended on you to take the lead."

Jennie's smile died and tears filled her eyes. "I wish there was something I could do for her now."

Lyle took her arm as she reached the bottom step and said with surprising gentleness, "There is. You can bring her some tea, like the doctor said. All Kate needs is to know that her family is there by her side. That's all she's ever needed."

There was a touch of wistfulness in his voice. Another surprise. Perhaps she'd misjudged Lyle. Suddenly she felt almost sorry for him. She was sure the Wentworth family had never had the kind of closeness shared by the Sheridans.

"Jennie, I want to talk with you." Dr. Millard had appeared at the top of the stairs.

Jennie clutched Lyle's arm. "Has something happened? Is she all right?"

The doctor gave a wave of assurance as he descended the stairs. "She's fallen asleep. Just a natural sleep, I think. She's exhausted."

"We've been careful, I promise. I haven't let her do a thing."

The doctor reached to pat her cheek. "You've been doing a fine job of taking care of her, little one. But your sister's condition requires professional care."

"Then she'll get it," Lyle said firmly.

"You mean we need to make an appointment with that special doctor you were taking about?" Jennie asked.

Dr. Millard leaned against the banister and looked from Jennie to Lyle, then back to Jennie. "Do you want to talk about this with Lyle here?" he asked.

The question took Jennie aback. She hadn't been thinking about the propriety of discussing her sister's condition with an unrelated male present. But looking at Lyle's determined face, she had the feeling that he wouldn't leave without protest. And, anyway, she and Kate could use a friend. She'd thought Carter would prove to be one, but that illusion had been thoroughly smashed tonight. "Lyle's concerned about Kate," she answered finally. "You can speak in front of him."

Dr. Millard nodded. "Kate admitted to me that she's had the bleeding again."

"She didn't tell me." Jennie threw an agonized glance up the stairs.

"I know." The doctor's eyes were warm. "She said you had enough to worry about, keeping the house running for everyone and trying to work out the finances. But she's in serious danger of losing her baby, which at this stage could put her own life at risk. She's going to need constant care.''

''I can do it,'' Jennie said. ''Barnaby and I will take turns with her. And I'll get the miners to do more of the cooking…why, they all helped out tonight…and…''

Dr. Millard gently grasped her shoulder. ''No, Jennie, you can't do it this time. You have all the will in the world…and all the love. But right now Kate needs medical skill.''

Jennie looked down at the hall carpet. It was threadbare in spots. Mother had been talking about ordering a new one from back East. ''What do we have to do?'' she whispered without raising her head.

''There's a hospital in Virginia City with a maternity ward. She needs to be there.''

''For how long?'' Jennie asked, scuffing her good patent leather shoe against the side of the stair.

''Until the birth most likely.''

Jennie swallowed. ''Two more months?''

Dr. Millard nodded. ''If it goes full term.''

She let out a long breath. ''Can I stay with her?''

Dr. Millard pursed his lips. ''Well, now. I don't know. I don't think they'd let you stay right there in the hospital for two months, but I suppose you could find a boardinghouse nearby. I hate to think of you in a strange city by yourself.…''

His words drifted off and there was silence as all three considered the ramifications of the move.

Finally Jennie said, ''And what about my own boardinghouse in the meantime? Who takes care of that? How do I pay my bills?'' A sudden thought hit her. ''Will this hospital be expensive?''

''I'm afraid so, Jennie. But you have no other choice. I could help you out with some of the bill—''

Lyle interrupted, ''The money is unimportant. If Kate needs the care, she'll get it. I'll pay for it.''

Dr. Millard raised an eyebrow but didn't say anything. As far as Jennie knew, Lyle had no funds of his own. He'd just begun to work for his father at the bank.

''Kate and I pay our own way,'' Jennie said, finally lifting her head and looking at first Lyle, then the doctor with a strong gaze. ''I'll find the money. We can always sell this house.''

''And live where?'' Dr. Millard asked. ''That baby's going to need a place to come home to once it's born.''

Jennie's head had begun to pound. ''Kate's sleeping now, right? We won't be doing anything until morning?''

Dr. Millard nodded.

''Then if you don't mind, gentlemen, I still have a kitchen full of dishes to clean. Tomorrow we'll work this out. Whatever it is that Kate needs, I'll see that it's done.''

Jennie thought she'd cried every tear in her head when her parents died, but by the time she was halfway back to Vermillion after leaving Kate in that sterile room in Virginia City, she realized that she must have an endless supply. She was sunk in the cushions of Dr. Millard's comfortable carriage, oblivious to the scenery they were passing.

"I'm sorry," she said between hiccups. "I can't seem to stop. She looked so alone there in that stiff bed."

Dr. Millard kept his eyes on his horse. "Just cry it out, child. You're almost as worn-out as your sister. I should have made you stay at the hospital for a rest, too."

"You know I couldn't do that. I have to go back. We need the rent money." Kate had been scared and reluctant when Jennie had sat down this morning to tell her about the hospital stay, but both sisters had realized that without the rent money, they'd lose their house. Jennie would have to stay in Vermillion. Kate would have to be alone.

"I wish you'd let me help."

Jennie shook her head. "I'll manage. I intend to get another boarder to take Kate's room."

"But what about the court order?"

"At one time, Mr. Jones said that the group moving against us would be willing to allow me to have four boarders if my sister was not living there. I intend to talk to him about that offer." In spite of the fact that she'd rather pet a rattlesnake than talk with Carter Jones about anything, she would swallow her pride and ask for his help.

"Good. He seems like a nice young man, Jennie. He could prove to be of help to you."

A nice young man who could kiss her one minute then turn his back on her an hour later. "All I want is the compromise on the court order. I don't intend to have any other business with Mr. Jones.''

Dr. Millard turned his head to give her a sharp look. ''You sound angry.''

''No. In order to be angry with Mr. Jones, I would have to care what he does or says or thinks. Which I don't.''

''Ah.'' The doctor reached an arm around Jennie and pulled her against his side in a fatherly hug. ''You've taken on a big burden, Jennie. Just remember that it's not a crime to ask for help from your friends.''

Jennie sagged a little bit against his wool serge coat. ''I know. I don't want to sound ungrateful. But, Carter Jones is not one of those friends. In fact, Doctor, sometimes I think that you and Dorie are the only friends we have left.''

The doctor gave her another quick squeeze, then she straightened up and they continued along the rutted road in silence. Jennie's eyes stung and she could feel the trace of dry tears on her cheek, but their flow had ceased. The thought of once again confronting Carter Jones had stopped them cold.

Jennie had never been in the district attorney's office on the second floor of the tiny Vermillion courthouse. It wasn't anywhere near as impressive as the law offices she'd visited in Virginia City when she and Kate had gone for the reading of their parents' will and then later for help with the boardinghouse fight. In fact, it was small and bare, with a cheap desk that made it look as if it might be a tiny cubbyhole for the janitor rather than the man entrusted with justice in Vermillion and six surrounding communities. Carter may be a fancy Harvard man with clothes to match, but his workplace was more than modest. Jennie found it comforting.

"How's your sister?" was the first question he asked.

"Fine, thank you." She wanted to leave no doubt that they were no longer on the social terms that had been implied by the invitation to dinner three nights ago.

"I heard that you got her situated in a hospital in Virginia City."

"Mr. Jones, I didn't come here to discuss my sister. I came to find out the status of the order closing down my boardinghouse."

Carter shifted, making his chair creak. Jennie's eyes went to his long fingers, which were playing with a row of pencils. "I just thought we'd wait a few days until you could take care of things with your sister…"

"My sister is no longer living at Sheridan House. You once told me that under those circumstances, the town council was willing to give me a permit to take in boarders."

Carter nodded. "That was the original vote of the council."

"Good." Jennie was determined to get through this interview without the nerves that had seemed to afflict her every previous time she'd been in the presence of Carter Jones. "Then I'd like to request that you inform the council that we have agreed to these terms and would like for them to issue the permit or proceed with whatever bureaucratic nonsense they require as soon as possible.''

Carter leaned back, creaking. ''You're angry with me.''

Jennie managed a small laugh. ''I have no emotion toward you whatsoever, Mr. Jones. I merely need to get these formalities out of the way so that I can return to my duties. I'm a busy woman.''

''No, you're angry with me,'' he insisted. ''Is it because I backed up the sheriff the other night?'' His gray eyes roved over her, taking in the plain blue cotton dress and bonnet. Her *plainest* dress, which she had donned purposefully that morning. His voice grew softer. ''Or is it because I kissed you?''

The tiny upstairs office was sweltering in the late autumn heat, and the heavy cotton was suddenly entirely too warm. Jennie stood, holding the edge of the desk with her fingertips for support. ''I'm going to assume that this matter is now settled,'' she said, her voice cool. ''I'll continue to operate my establishment just as I have been doing. And I won't expect to be bothered by this discussion again.''

Carter rose to his feet more slowly. The teasing smile was gone and his expression grew serious. ''Are you going to be all right over there alone with those miners, Jennie? Is there anything I can do to help you?''

Jennie picked her reticule off his desk and adjusted her gloves. ''As I was saying, Mr. Jones. I consider the matter settled. I won't expect to be bothered by you again, either." She met his eyes for a full ten seconds, then turned to leave.

Jennie threw two more green beans into the pail, then straightened up, rubbing her back. She'd started her day before dawn fixing flapjacks for the miners. It was clean sheet day. The morning had been taken up boiling the linens, and now she'd spent three hours this afternoon working on the garden. She missed Kate. She missed her so that it had become a kind of ache, like a bad tooth. And like a tooth, every now and then the ache would turn into a painful twinge when she'd remember how sick her sister had looked when she'd left her in Virginia City. Lord, don't let anything happen to my sister, she mumbled under her breath in a prayer that had become as natural as breathing.

Criminy, the silverheels were coming down the street and she hadn't even started on supper. They were always ravenous the minute they arrived home. She looked up at the trio with an apologetic smile as they came up the front walk. "I've gotten behind today, boys. You'll have to wait a bit to eat."

Dennis Kelly stepped over a small hedge to stand next to her and reached for the pail. "Poor lassie, you look as if you've been wrestling a den of grizzlies today."

Jennie swiped back the hair that had fallen around her face. "Nope. Just a kettle full of sheets and a garden full of weeds. I made some apple crisp, though." It was the silverheels' favorite dessert.

"Whoopee," Brad Connors yelped, leaping over

the same hedge Dennis had crossed. "Looks as if we'll just have to help you move things along so we can get around to eatin' it."

Smitty lingered for a moment on the walk, then dropped the knapsack he was carrying and joined his friends next to the garden. "What do we have to do?" he asked, eyeing the neat rows of vegetables with mistrust.

Brad slapped his shoulder. "Great farmer you'd make." He bent over and pulled out some weeds, then slapped the clump into Smitty's hand. "We don't eat this stuff, so we gotta get rid of it. Just go along this row and every time you see a sprout like this one, pull it up. Just don't pull up the bean plants."

"Didn't ever say I wanted to be no farmer," Smitty grumbled, but he started walking along the edge of the garden, carefully inspecting each bunch of green.

Jennie smiled. "I can't believe you boys have enough energy left to help in the garden after a long day at the mine."

Dennis squatted down and began picking beans. "I reckon we've got just as much left as you, Miss Jennie. You'd already been up for hours this morning before these two princesses crawled out of their feather beds."

Brad grimaced and threw a bean at him. "And I suppose you were out chopping wood before old man Carlton's rooster started crowing."

Dennis grinned. "Hours before."

Jennie felt her spirits lift for the first time all day. She was working hard, but she was so lucky to have found these good-natured, generous men as boarders. If she could find a fourth one just like them, she'd really be happy. "You haven't come across anyone else out at the mine looking for a place to live, have you?" she asked.

Dennis duck-walked over to the next batch of beans and continued picking while he answered, "We've asked around, Miss Jennie, but just at the moment it seems that everyone's got a place."

Jennie sighed. A fourth roomer would certainly help with the expenses.

"Haven't you had anyone respond to your advertisement?"

She shook her head. She'd put a sign out front of Dr. Millard's office, but no one had come to see her about it. She hadn't really expected it to bring results, the way people still felt about her in town. She'd been hoping to take on another miner who wouldn't know anything about local Vermillion squabbles. "I don't think anyone from town wants to live here," she said.

"You may be wrong about that."

Jennie whirled around to find Carter walking toward them. She'd been so focused on the miners' antics with the garden that she hadn't even seen him approach. He looked dapper in a gray suit and purple waistcoat that was a little too elegant to fit with Vermillion standards and too hot for the late afternoon sun. She could feel her spine stiffen. He was waiting for some kind of greeting, and she reckoned the miners would think it odd if she didn't offer one, so she finally said, "Good afternoon, Mr. Jones. What can we do for you?"

Carter gestured with his right hand. He was carrying the flyer she'd posted. "I came about the room."

Her skin was damp from perspiration, but Jennie felt a chill run along her arms and legs. "Is there a problem?" she asked. "You did say that I could have four boarders, isn't that right?"

Carter smiled and whisked that Eastern narrow-brimmed hat off his head. Somehow it would be easier to talk with him if he at least *looked* like the other men in town. "Oh, that's correct. Four boarders. I've got the papers right here." He pulled them from a pocket inside the silk waistcoat and offered them to her.

He was a yard or two on the other side of the hedge. Reluctantly she walked around to take them. "It was nice of you to bring them by."

"Oh, I didn't come to bring the papers. I came to get a room. The sign says you're looking for a tenant."

A second chill chased the first, this time making the wispy hairs stand up on her neck. "*You* want a room? For yourself?"

Carter grinned. "I bet you thought I lived in a cave somewhere." He appealed to the three miners, who had continued their gardening while listening to the exchange. "What do you say, guys? Are you willing to have me as a housemate?"

Dennis looked up with a shrug, while Smitty said, "If ya takes a bath ev'ry Saturday like the rest of us."

Carter shifted his gaze back to Jennie. His expression was serious, but there was a light in his eyes that made her wonder if he was somehow laughing at her. Lordy, she'd take *anyone* but Carter Jones. "I thought you already had a place, Mr. Jones."

"Nope. I've been living at the hotel since I got to town last spring. Mighty tiresome, too. I figure a nice comfortable place with good home cooking would be just the ticket."

She cocked her head and tried to think of something to say.

"I pay my bills."

There definitely was a glint in his eyes. But she could use the money. She spoke in a rush. "With meals it's six dollars a week." The miners were each paying four-fifty a week, but none of them said anything.

Carter took the flyer out from under his arm and ripped it neatly in half. "You've got yourself a renter," he said. Then he put out his hand for her to shake.

After a moment's hesitation, she transferred the court papers to her left hand and let him take her right, forgetting that it was soiled from the weeding. His hand was smooth and clean, his cuff snowy-white, but he didn't seem to mind the dirt. And he held her for longer than was necessary for a simple handshake.

"When are you moving in, Mr. Jones?" she asked, withdrawing the dirty hand and hiding it behind her back.

"Would tonight be too soon?"

Jennie's heart sank. She was exhausted. She missed

her sister. She hadn't started supper. And she hadn't the slightest idea how she was going to handle living in the same house with Carter Jones when every time he looked at her, much less touched her, her insides started to quiver. A year from now would be too soon.

"Tonight would be just fine," she said.

Chapter Six

Moving to the Sheridan house had been an uncharacteristically rash decision. After a week, Carter was still puzzling over it. He'd been perfectly happy at the hotel. And his lodging there was certainly more acceptable to the majority of the townsfolk than his current room at the boardinghouse.

The odd thing was that he himself couldn't explain why he'd done it. He'd seen the notice outside Dr. Millard's, torn it off the door and marched right over to the Sheridan house without taking time for a moment of thought. It had been an utterly foolish and spontaneous impulse. And if there was one thing Carter was not, it was impulsive.

How did the phrase go? Act in haste, repent at leisure. He'd had some time to repent at leisure this past week. Jennie had hardly spoken to him. She avoided his eyes. He knew that she was still angry over the night of the supper that had ended so disastrously. But whenever he tried to broach the subject, she insisted that nothing was wrong. She wasn't angry; she was merely *busy*.

At least the miners had proved to be decent chaps. He'd taken to joining their nightly card game. Poker had always been easy for him, but he'd been careful not to win too often or too much with his new house-mates. And his forbearance had been rewarded by a gradual acceptance over the past few days as "one of the gang." Perhaps he should try a game of poker with Jennie, he thought wryly as he headed down the hallway toward the back of the house.

The evening game had wrapped up and the miners had gone to bed, but he could see that a lamp was still burning in the small office at the rear of the parlor where Jennie often disappeared at night. He didn't know if the time spent at her desk meant that she really had that quantity of work to do or if it was just another way to avoid his company. Several times he'd thought to ask Dennis if she'd gone to her office every night *before* he'd moved in. But he never could quite get the question to come out.

Tonight, at least, she appeared to be working. She was writing a column of numbers in a heavy ledger. He knocked gently on the door frame.

She took her time looking up, which told Carter that she'd known, probably even before he'd appeared in the doorway, that her late-night visitor was her newest and apparently unwanted tenant.

"You're working late," he said when she finally acknowledged his presence with a nod.

"End of the month. I keep adding up these numbers, trying to make them come out right."

Her voice sounded tired and, as he walked into the circle of lamplight, he could see shadows under her eyes. It gave him a peculiar twist through his midsection. "Would you like some help with the summing?"

"It's not the summing that's the problem. It's the sum." Her smile was wan.

"Perhaps I could help with that, then."

She shook her head. "Forgive me, Mr. Jones. I have no business involving you in my problems."

Without being invited, Carter sat in the chair across the desk from her. "Well, at least I can pay my next week's rent." He pulled a money clip from his shirt pocket and counted out six dollar bills, then set them on the desk in front of her.

Jennie sat looking at the money for a moment before she said, "It's really only four dollars fifty cents. That's what I charge the silverheels."

Carter gave half a smile. "I'm not a silverheel."

She still made no move to take the bills. "No, it's only fair. Four-fifty."

Carter gave a snort of exasperation. "We made a bargain, Jennie. I'm perfectly happy with the rate we agreed upon. Let's just leave it at that."

Jennie's chin went up as she reached to take the money. "That's generous of you, Mr. Jones."

Carter's neck prickled as the steam rose. "Darn it, woman, how much longer are you going to be mad at me?"

Jennie blinked in surprise. "I told you—"

Carter staved off her denial with an upheld hand. "That you're not mad at me. I know. I've heard you. But then how come you won't call me Carter anymore? And how come you hide yourself away in here like a little mole until after everyone else has gone to bed? And how come you dart those beautiful brown eyes around every which way except toward me when I come down for breakfast in the morning?''

Jennie was silent, unable to answer. She held the dollar bills tightly in her right hand.

''Jennie, I had to back up the sheriff that night. I'm the public prosecutor. It's my job. They had an order signed and sealed by the court. I'm sorry it caused Kate to collapse that way, but I'm sure no one intended for it to have that result.''

''I wouldn't put it past Henrietta Billingsley to have planned things that way.''

Carter brushed the back of his hand against his chin. It was hard to hear the bitterness in her voice. He'd seen the sunny side of her—as she gently taught Barnaby about some household task, as she laughed with her sister, as she bantered with the miners. This brittle resentment seemed to go against the very essence of Jennie Sheridan. ''I think you're wrong, Jennie. Those women are misguided, but they're not evil. No one is wishing harm to your sister.''

''Can you tell me that there wouldn't be rejoicing in several Vermillion homes if Kate lost this baby?''

If it had been any other cause than defense of her sister, he was sure that Jennie would have softened her tone and her rhetoric. But where Kate was concerned, she seemed to find no room for compromise. For a moment he felt a pang of envy. It was a kind of loyalty he'd never experienced. His mother had been his only family, and he'd not been close to her.

"You're overreacting. No one wants that to happen."

Jennie let out a long sigh. "Maybe you're right. But all the same, it was a terrible thing to do to us...to do to Kate in her condition."

"And you blame me."

She sat studying him across the table a long moment. In the dim light her hair had a rich mahogany gleam. He'd never seen it combed out like that, hanging loose around her shoulders. Finally she answered him, the hardness gone from her voice. "I guess I did blame you. You'd told me that you wanted to be our friend."

"And earlier that evening I'd kissed you."

Her long lashes fluttered down, shuttering her eyes. With some fumbling, she opened the center drawer of the desk and put Carter's rent money inside.

"You do remember that?" Carter asked with a touch of irritation.

Suddenly she was looking at him again and he could see without hearing her answer that she not only remembered that kiss, she still felt the traces of it on her lips, just as he did.

"I'd prefer not to remember it," she said quietly.

He sighed, then stood abruptly. Sometimes sheer recklessness was the only way out of an impasse. In two long strides he was around to her side of the desk and hauling her up out of her chair. "Remember this one, then," he murmured, and bent his head.

Unlike the chaste kiss they'd shared in the kitchen, this one was liquid heat from the first touch. It was as if some kind of pressure had been building since the other night and now it was being released in an almost violent rush. He seized her up against him and she went willingly, her arms creeping unconsciously around his neck. His lips opened hers, then their mouths mated, moist and warm and passionate.

He was aroused in seconds, his head swirling while the blood rushed into his engorged manhood. It was nothing like the methodical, carefully orchestrated seductions with which he'd been so successful back East.

She gave a sexy whimper at the back of her throat as he pulled back and slowed the kiss to gentle nips. He tried to get the red haze to clear from his mind, overruling the strident demands of the lower portion of his anatomy.

Her eyes were wide, unfocused. A telltale flush stained the lower portion of her face. There was no doubt that she'd been as powerfully affected as he. But he knew even before he felt her stiffen in his arms that she would never admit it. This latest physical encounter would be counted against him as yet another transgression.

He pulled away, carefully keeping her from losing her balance as she sank once again to her chair. As he had suspected, the warmth in her eyes was turning to ice as quickly as the flush was fading from her face. He took a deep, steadying breath. He'd already learned that in life, as in politics, there were times when bravado in the face of adversity was the only good policy.

"You'll remember that one, I wager," he said with a deliberate grin.

The ice was turning to fury. "How dare you?" she sputtered.

Carter stepped back, safely out of range of her pointed-toe shoes. "Oh, I'm a daring fellow. But before you get too self-righteous, Miss Sheridan, I'll be ungentlemanly enough to point out that for a moment there, the lady appeared to be willing."

She made no denial, but when she answered she sounded discouraged. "I'm afraid this arrangement is not going to work out, Mr. Jones. I won't put you out in the middle of the night, but by tomorrow, I'd appreciate it if you would take your things and leave."

She opened her desk drawer and withdrew the money he'd given her earlier, then held it out to him, her hand shaking slightly. More than anything else, the regretful way she looked at the money she was returning made him feel like a cad. He held all the cards in this game. Jennie was broke, overtired, most likely innocent in sexual matters. He was a scoundrel for taking advantage of her.

"I apologize," he said, now honestly contrite. "This was poorly done." He shook his head to refuse the money she offered. "Keep it. Even if you still want me to leave. But I'd like to stay here, Jennie. I'll behave myself."

She looked skeptical and a little lost.

"I promise," he insisted, giving her his most winning smile. He had little doubt that he could convince her to let him stay, but part of him wondered if it was the wisest course. He was promising to behave himself, something that had never been a problem for

Carter, but he'd never felt quite like he had a few minutes ago when she'd melted against him.

Jennie turned the bills over in her hands, then turned them once again. "Just because everyone in town is saying that my sister and I are fallen women, doesn't mean that we are," she said finally.

Such an idea had never even entered his head, but he could see how his impetuous action might be interpreted in that light. Guilt swept over him. His grin died and he said gravely, "Jennie, I think you have more spirit and more brains than any woman I've met in this town. If my actions implied that I hold anything other than the highest respect for you, I'm truly sorry."

She seemed impressed by his serious tone. Her expression softened. "If we can both forget about this incident, you may stay, Mr. Jones. Goodness knows, I need the money, and it doesn't appear that people are beating down the door to rent rooms here."

He nodded. "That's settled, then. Put that money away and if you need more..." He held up a hand as she began to bristle. "If it would help you to have me pay some weeks in advance, I'd be happy to do so."

"Thank you, but I'll manage, Mr. Jones."

He shook his head. "We need to agree on one other matter."

"What's that?" she asked warily.

"I won't refer to this...um...*incident,* as you call it, if you'll agree to one condition. It's a simple request."

She already knew. "Carter, then," she amended.
He flashed a quick grin. "That's much better."

Jennie was tired, and she knew that her predawn
wake-up would come hurtling at her without mercy
tomorrow, but she couldn't get herself to go up to
bed. Carter had left her office over an hour ago. For
a while she'd deliberately stalled just to avoid any
risk of running into him upstairs as they both prepared
for bed. She didn't think she was up to another encounter tonight. But all had been quiet upstairs for a
long time. She was sure everyone else in the house
was asleep. And still she sat, staring at the flicker of
the whale oil lamp on her desk.

The money Carter had given her was still lying on
the desk in front of her. She ran her fingers over it.
The devil's tool. That's what her mother had called
money. Francis Sheridan had never had much interest
in wealth or luxuries. Neither had Jennie's father,
John, for that matter. From all accounts the two had
had a happy, simple life up in the mountains until
their responsibility to their young daughters had convinced them to move down into town where John
began making his living building houses to keep up
with the increasing demands of the silver boom. Jennie wondered now if her parents had ever been as
happy here in Vermillion as they had in those early
days. They'd never quite fit in with the rest of what
might be called Vermillion society, which was probably part of the reason it had been so easy for that
society to turn against their daughters.

Jennie herself had never cared about social status.
She was content to have the four Sheridans together

in the big, comfortable house her father had built for them. It had been all she ever needed or wanted. Life had been perfect until last spring.

Now all at once, she couldn't seem to decide what it was she wanted. Kate healthy and home again with a healthy baby, of course. But things would never be the way they'd been before. Her parents were gone. The house was no longer a private Sheridan haven. There were strangers living here now—one particular stranger who made her nervous and uneasy, but who at the same time kindled sensations and emotions that she'd never known before.

Once again she felt that peculiar roll of her stomach as she thought about their kiss. She'd never even imagined such a feeling. Was this what had gotten her sister into such a mess? Had Sean Flaherty kissed Kate the way Carter had kissed her tonight? Had he made her sister's limbs go weak and her blood race the way Jennie's had when Carter's mouth had descended on her?

"Why are you still awake, Jennie?" The small voice from the doorway made her jump.

"Barnaby! What are you doing up?"

"I can't sleep."

Jennie gestured for him to come in. He hesitated. They had an understood rule that he wasn't to bother her when she was working at her desk. Finally he seemed to conclude that at this odd hour rules didn't apply, and he walked over to her. There were circles under his eyes. His hair sprouted every which way like badly stacked red hay.

"Is your stomach hurting?" she asked him. For

weeks after he'd first come to them, he'd complained of stomachaches, but as he'd settled into life at the Sheridan house, the symptoms had disappeared.

"No. I don't get those anymore. I just couldn't sleep, that's all."

He was hiding something. Jennie held out one arm and, after another moment's hesitation, he walked over next to her and allowed her to put her arm across his shoulders. "What's the problem? Tell me about it, Barneyboy."

It had been her mother's special name for him. Jennie wasn't sure if he'd like her using it, but he didn't even seem to notice. She held him against her side for a moment, then released him as she noticed a tear trickling down his right cheek. "What is it?" she asked with some alarm.

He looked embarrassed and gave a half turn away from her, trying to wipe the tear without being obvious. "Nothing," he mumbled.

Jennie twisted in her chair and grasped his shoulders, turning him to face her. "It's not 'nothing' if it's keeping you up all night and making you cry."

He wouldn't meet her eyes. "It's just…the other kids."

Jennie felt a surge of anger. This town again. This unforgiving, holier-than-thou town. "What did they say? Were they saying bad things about Kate?"

He shook his head, leaving her a bit confused. She was sure he'd meant that the children in town had been taunting him about Kate's illegitimate child. She waited while he appeared to struggle with the decision to open up to her. Finally he said, "They said bad things about me."

"About you? What kind of bad things?"

Barnaby lifted his head a little to take a hard swallow. She could see that his Adam's apple was beginning to grow prominent in his still puny throat. Barnaby was on the verge of manhood, but he was still enough of a child to be hurt by the cruel words of others. And weren't they all? Jennie thought, her mouth twisting with irony.

"Frankie Sullivan called me a...bastard. And then all the boys were saying it."

Jennie gasped. "Where was Miss Potter when this was going on?"

Barnaby shrugged. "I reckon she heard them, but she didn't do anything. I reckon she thinks she can't punish the boys for saying something that's the truth."

"That's a terrible word, and they have no right to call you that, Barnaby. I'll speak to Miss Potter tomorrow."

The expression in his eyes went from misery to fear. "Please don't, Miss Jennie. I'm sorry I told you."

She rubbed her hands up and down his small arms. He felt cold. "Don't worry about it. I'll be sure those boys won't be able to hurt you for telling the truth."

"It's not that...I just... Please, Miss Jennie. I just want to let it rest. I'll stay away from those boys, and I won't get sad about what they say. They're a stupid bunch of ninnies, anyway."

"That they are, honey."

"But you won't go to Miss Potter?"

"Not if you don't want me to."

He nodded, still leaning against her shoulder. Her support seemed to be all he needed to banish the haunted look from his eyes. Jennie felt a wave of love. The happy family of four she had grown up with was gone, but they were still a family—she, Kate and Barnaby. And soon there would be a new member to love and protect from the occasional cruelties of the outside world.

"I think I can go to sleep now," Barnaby said. His eyelids were already drooping.

She gave him a final squeeze. "Run along, then. And have only happy dreams."

He pulled away and walked slowly toward the door. When he reached it, he turned. "Jennie?"

She looked up and smiled.

"I love you," he said.

"I love you, too, Barnaby."

He bobbed his head, then disappeared up the hall.

Carter had always avoided menial tasks. He'd sworn, as he watched his mother grow old before his eyes, scrubbing and cleaning and polishing, ridding homes of other people's dirt, that he would survive on brains, not brawn.

But the silverheels had taken on the vegetable garden as their own personal project and it seemed churlish not to help out. Which was why he found himself in perfectly good blue wool pants, kneeling in the mud to harvest carrots and potatoes.

The first evening he'd accompanied the miners in

their gardening venture, Jennie had come out to join them, and he'd found the sight of her petite, shapely body bending and straining over the rows of vegetables to be sufficiently entertaining to make him oblivious to the tiny nettles that had lodged in his hands and the bothersome gnats that swarmed around his head. But tonight Jennie was nowhere to be seen, and the endeavor was not nearly as much fun. In fact, he was using his best lawyerly skills to work out a foolproof reason as to why he should be excused from further duty.

"You're ruining them swell Eastern duds of yours, Jones," Smitty observed.

"Never figured you'd be willing to get those soft hands all dirty," Dennis agreed.

Their banter had a teasing tone. In spite of their differences, the three miners had accepted Carter as one of them, or as near to it as to be of no importance.

"These soft hands have pulled twice the harvest yours have," Carter shot back, tipping his basket so Dennis could see that it was nearly full.

Brad poked his head around the cornstalks to taunt Dennis. "So who's the softie, Kelly?"

"Well, now, I didn't know it was supposed to be a contest." Dennis made an exaggerated show of pushing up the sleeves of his denim work shirt. Then he hitched up his trousers, planted his feet wide apart and faced Carter. "Hold on to your bucket, there, Carter, 'cause you're about to get whupped by a better man."

Carter grinned. He'd never in his life engaged in this kind of tomfoolery with male friends. He'd grown up a loner. During his years at school, he'd been plenty popular, especially with the visiting ladies, but he'd always been conscious of keeping his concentration on track to come out ahead of the next guy. And it had been pretty much that way ever since.

He found it relaxing and enjoyable to be with the three miners—working, teasing, playing cards—to be part of their easy camaraderie without having to look over his shoulder to see if one of them might get a better grade or pass him up for an important post. Simply speaking, he was having fun.

He'd let Dennis catch up a little to make the competition more even, then he started in earnest. Just because he wore a white shirt and tie to work every day didn't mean he had to sit back on his haunches and get shown up by a burly son-of-the-old-sod miner.

Dennis's basket was three-fourths full and he was going up and down the rows furiously pulling at anything that looked half-ripe. Carter cradled his own basket in his right arm and called out, "I thought I'd rest awhile, Kelly, to give you a fighting chance, but if I let you keep on dawdling like that, it'll be hard on winter before we get this crop in."

Dennis lifted his head and shot Carter a grin. "What you're saying is you're plumb tuckered after a day pushing papers and you've lost the stomach for this match."

Carter bent and began picking once again, a smile on his face.

From inside the parlor window, Jennie watched the foursome. They were wreaking havoc with her neat garden, but it appeared they were getting the job done…and enjoying it, as well.

Other nights she'd joined the miners in their labors, but when she'd seen Carter with them tonight, she'd stopped, though it was silly to linger here behind the window like an adolescent schoolgirl spying on the handsome schoolmaster.

What she should be doing was getting supper on the table. The men would be hungry after their extra work. But instead she stood at the window, staring, her mind drifting, watching Carter's broad back as he worked in his white dress shirt. He'd taken off his jacket, but wore his suit pants. She shook her head. What a fine mess that would be for the next laundry day.

She straightened up away from the window. This was silly. She and Carter had to live together in the same house for the next few weeks. In spite of what had happened last night, she'd have to learn to be comfortable around him. He'd promised to be on good behavior, as long as she remembered to use his given name. She'd hold him to his word, turn away at the least hint of impropriety. It wouldn't be that hard. Especially with her silverheels around. Unbeknownst to them, they'd be her protectors.

Slowly she tied her apron, pulled on her gardening gloves and headed toward the front door. The only problem was she wasn't entirely sure she wanted to be protected.

Chapter Seven

"Here comes Miss Jennie," Brad shouted as she came out on the front porch. "She can judge your bloody contest and give the prize to the winner."

Dennis and Carter looked up at the same time. Dennis grinned and said, "You can be Queen of the May, lass, and bestow laurels on the victor. Which means me."

It was always a little shock to hear Dennis's speech which still held the hint of Ireland, though he'd come over with his family as a boy. It made him sound like a play actor or even a nobleman. A refined kind of sound that didn't fit the picture of the tough, heavyset miner. The words he used weren't typical, either. Queen of the May, indeed. As if anyone in Vermillion had ever heard of such a thing.

Carter had stopped picking and straightened up to look at her. "Ah," he said. "I didn't know the stakes were to be so high."

"I'm afraid I don't have any laurels to bestow," she said lightly, trying not to let the warmth that had lit Carter's eyes affect her.

"It'll have to be a kiss then," Smitty said with a wicked smile. "A kiss to the winner."

"Hell, for that, count me in, too." Brad threw the spade he'd been using to dig weeds to one side and reached for an empty basket.

Dennis sent him a disgusted glance. "There's no way you can catch up, Connors. You might as well join with the winner. Take this basket over to the porch and give me that one."

Brad pulled the empty basket away from Dennis's reaching fingers. "Hold on there, partner. I'm not joining with anyone. There's only going to be one winner and one kiss as far as I've heard. Unless you want to give kisses to all the entrants, Miss Jennie?"

"I'm not going to give kisses to anyone," she protested, her eyes sliding involuntarily to Carter who, of course, was watching her with that half smile of his. She'd been right in the first place—she should have gone in to put on the supper.

"Listen, this was between Carter and me," Dennis addressed Brad. "And Miss Jennie doesn't have to do anything she doesn't want to. But it would be a fitting end for such a noble competition," he added, his green eyes twinkling.

All four men seemed to be waiting for her to answer. To his credit, Carter had not added his urging to the request. Of course, he hadn't said it was a bad idea, either. She put her hands on her hips. "On the cheek, then. The victor gets a kiss on the cheek. A little one."

Dennis let out a whoop and went back to his picking. Brad started filling his, but soon realized that

Dennis had been right. There was no way he could catch up with the first two participants. Smitty ambled over to the front porch and sat down. "I'll be the referee," he said. "First one to the top of his basket gets the prize."

Jennie could see that both men's baskets were nearly full. She offered up a little prayer that Dennis Kelly would be the winner. She wouldn't feel the least bit self-conscious about kissing the big, amiable Irishman. Kissing Carter would be another story.

"Done!" he said with a shout of triumph. From his stairway post, Smitty nodded agreement. "Carter wins."

"I'm done, too," Dennis protested. "No fair. I was done, too, only I didn't know we had to bellow it out to the end of the street."

"He *was* done," Brad agreed.

Both men looked over at Jennie, who looked from one to the other in confusion. "Smitty decides," she said weakly.

All eyes turned to Smitty, who stood to take full advantage of his sudden importance. "I rule…" He left a long, dramatic pause. "I rule that it's a tie. You'll have to kiss them both, Miss Jennie."

"Yes, sirree, Smitty. I do like the way you think," Dennis chuckled. He set down his basket, took a giant step over the hedge and offered Jennie his cheek. "I'll never wash my face again, lass," he told her with a wink.

She went up on tiptoe, balancing herself on his big shoulder, and gave the promised peck, which landed somewhere on the edge of his muttonchop whiskers.

To her surprise, when she pulled away his face was turning bright red.

"He's blushing!" Smitty yelped.

"Am not," Dennis muttered, turning away toward the street.

"What's the matter, Kelly?" Brad taunted. "Haven't you ever been kissed before?"

"Shut up, Connors."

Carter stepped in front of the embarrassed Irishman, drawing the attention of his tormentors. "My turn," he said softly.

He was taller than Dennis. Even on tiptoe, Jennie knew she'd never reach his cheek. She waited a moment to see if he'd stoop down to her level, but when he remained standing straight, she had no choice but to put her arms around his neck and pull him toward her. Their bodies pressed together for the barest instant. The kiss was over within a second, but his warmth still engulfed her and the feel of his skin lingered on her lips.

"Hey, no fair. I didn't get a hug with my kiss," Dennis observed, now more or less recovered from his flush.

He made a move toward her but she waved him away. "That wasn't a hug. I just had to haul on his neck so I could reach the cheek. So now that's finished. No more kisses or hugs or anything."

There was no longer laughter in her voice and Dennis grew immediately serious. "I'm sorry, lass. We're just teasing you."

She tried to reassure him, though she knew her

smile was shaky. "I know. It's all right. I really do appreciate the help you all have given me."

"We'd do more if we didn't have to be working all day," Smitty said, giving her a smile. "You're a right admirable woman, Miss Jennie. You and your sister both."

She let her gaze move from Smitty to the other two miners, doing her best to skip over Carter who stood among them. He had not said anything since the brief kiss, and, though she tried to avoid noticing, she could see that he was watching her with that intense look in his eyes. "You do plenty. All of you. I'm the luckiest landlady in the world."

The three miners beamed. "And we're lucky to be here, Miss Jennie," Dennis said.

She was looking at the miners, but it was those other eyes she could feel. "Well, you won't keep feeling so lucky unless I get some food on the table," she said briskly. "It's past supper time."

"Kelly and Jones have picked our supper," Smitty joked, pointing to the full baskets.

"But you wouldn't be too happy if we were the ones to cook it," Dennis retorted.

"No one can cook like Miss Jennie," Brad added.

"Now, you've got that right," Smitty agreed.

"Ah, boys," Jennie said, "Dennis has been teaching you some of that blarney of his. It's not necessary. I have every intention of feeding you tonight."

They all laughed and Jennie felt a surge of affection. She *was* the luckiest landlady to have found these three kind and gentle men. If only her sister were here with her—here and healthy—life would actually be rather nice. Of course, if her sister was here, they'd still be battling with the townsfolk, a battle that could start up again when Kate returned to Sheridan House with the baby. She sighed as all the problems came flooding back. "If you men will bring those baskets into the kitchen I'll get Barnaby to start scrubbing them. And I should have supper on in forty-five minutes."

They followed her in a single line into the house, their teasing ended at the change in her voice. Once in the kitchen, they deposited their harvest and turned to go get cleaned up. Carter was at the end of the line. He still hadn't said anything since the prize kiss.

Jennie's attention was on the vegetables. It was a wonderful fall harvest—five baskets, two of them completely full. But it meant she'd be awake hours after supper scrubbing and cutting. She looked up in surprise as Carter spoke softly from the doorway. She thought he'd left with the others.

"Thank you for the kiss," he said.

Jennie bit her lip. "It was just a game."

"Yes."

He made no move to leave.

"It *was*," she insisted. "Just a game."

His smile was a touch devilish. "I know. It usually is when you first start out." Then he turned around and left her standing amidst the vegetables, her mouth open.

Jennie had sold her father's old buggy to pay the funeral expenses, and, anyway, she wasn't sure Scarecrow could make the trip to Virginia City. The old

horse, who as his name implied had never been much
of a beauty in the first place, was growing increasingly infirm. But Dr. Millard had offered to let her
borrow his carriage for the trip on the condition that
she find an escort. Which meant she'd have to wait
until Sunday when the silverheels didn't work. Either
that or spend a long day alone on the road with Carter,
which she'd decided was a little too much to ask of
herself the way her nerves were these days.

Dennis could take her this Sunday. It was four days
away, but she'd just have to hold on until then. She
couldn't remember ever having been separated from
Kate for this long. At night after she climbed into her
bed, she'd picture her sister, lying alone in the stiff,
starched sheets of that hospital bed, cared for by
equally stiff, starched nurses. Some nights she'd
squeeze her eyes shut trying to blot out the picture,
but she'd continue to see Kate's pretty blue eyes looking at her, miserable and accusing.

Of course, this last vision was all in Jennie's head.
Kate had never been accusing in her whole life. She
couldn't even muster enough resentment to blame the
scalawag who had gotten her into this mess, leaving
her pregnant and nearly broke to face the enmity of
an entire town. Once Jennie started thinking about
Sean Flaherty, she'd feel better. Justifiable anger was
easier than the empty ache she had every time she
thought of Kate. So she'd let her thoughts drift to
Sean, and then, inevitably, from there they would
shift to Carter Jones, who also had proved to be un-
dependable at the time when she'd needed him most.

Yes, she'd wait until Sunday and let Dennis take

her to visit Kate. Dennis was still a male, but he was a big bear of a male, kind of like an older brother. He didn't make it harder for her to breathe or do crazy things to her insides. She'd wait until Sunday.

"I hired it for the day," Carter told her as she looked out the front door in wonder at the shiny black buggy sitting at the end of the front walk. "You've been fretting about your sister all week, so I decided to take the afternoon off and drive you over to Virginia City to see her."

Jennie hesitated. "I was going to borrow the doctor's rig on Sunday."

"Well, now you don't have to wait. Go on, get your shawl or whatever you need. Time's a-wastin'."

"Would we be able to get back by supper? The miners will be coming home hungry."

Carter tapped the buggy whip impatiently against his thigh. "We'll try to get back by dark, of course. But supper's all taken care of. I've asked Dorie Millard to stop by and help out the miners."

"You've talked to Dorie?" she asked, not sure why the idea made her a little uncomfortable.

"She'll make sure everything's running smoothly. She's that kind of woman."

"Yes, indeed." Jennie tamped down the little worm of jealousy. Why should she care what Carter Jones thought of Dorie? In fact, the two of them would probably make a splendid match. Carter's ambition would go well with Dorie's assertiveness. "It was kind of her to agree to come."

"She's offered to help before. I don't know why

you're so all-fired resistant to letting your friends give you a hand now and then.''

Jennie shrugged, pretending indifference. How did Carter know that Dorie had offered to help her? Just how much was he seeing of the attractive blonde? Well, it was none of her business. ''I just don't want to be a bother. My parents taught Kate and me that a family stands on its own.''

''Unfortunately, your parents aren't around any longer. But if they were, I'm sure they would say that it's just fine to lean on the people close to you at times when you need some support.''

''You're probably right.'' She gave a sigh so big that Carter started to laugh.

''It's not the end of the world, Jennie. I'm just offering to give you a ride. I don't intend to make nefarious demands to exact payment for my services.''

''Make what kind of demands?'' she asked with a frown.

''Nefarious. You know, *wicked.*''

''I guess I wouldn't be able to tell if you were making them, Carter. I don't always understand you when you talk that highfalutin Eastern lingo.''

''*Nefarious* isn't Eastern, it's just…oh, never mind. Are we going to get going or am I going to have to take this rig back to the livery and waste my one free afternoon?''

''No!'' Now that she had it in her head that she might actually be able to see Kate—to see her *to-day*—she couldn't bear the idea of waiting another minute. ''Just give me three minutes to change and

I'll be ready to go. Oh, dear…I have to wait until the applesauce is boiled.''

Carter took her elbow to gently turn her around and steer her toward the stairs. ''You're an intriguing woman, Jennie Sheridan—the only one I've ever met who can actually change clothes in under an hour. You go on up and get dressed and I'll leave a note for Barnaby about the applesauce.''

She shot him a grateful glance then started up to her room at an unladylike pace, two steps at a time.

The fabulously rich Comstock strike had turned Virginia City into a bustling boomtown twenty years earlier, and it retained its look of prosperity even though some of the mines were beginning to play out. Growing up in Vermillion, Jennie found the larger town a marvel. When she'd visited with her family, she remembered how fascinated she and Kate had been by the hydraulic elevator in the elegant brick International Hotel. The hotel restaurant claimed to have the best food between Chicago and San Francisco.

She recalled that her parents had hurried the two sisters past the rows of saloons, rumored to be more than a hundred, but she and Kate had secretly taken peaks behind the swinging doors, now and then rewarded with a glimpse of a real live painted lady.

Today she scarcely noticed her surroundings as they made their way past the maze of mines and into town. The hospital was on the southern edge at the base of one of the hills. Half the town seemed to be stuck into a hill. The streets were perilously steep, and Jennie grasped the side railing of the carriage as they descended the final block.

"This is it?" Carter confirmed.

She nodded, suddenly nervous. The last time she had seen Kate, she'd looked so...white. Carter seemed to understand. He reached for her gloved hand and gave it a squeeze.

"Your sister's going to be so glad to see you," he said.

"Yes. I just hope she's getting better. I'd expected them to send word or..." Her voice trailed off.

"Well, that's probably a good sign. If she had gotten worse, I'm sure they would have notified you."

"Maybe you're right." His reassuring tone was helping her jitters.

"Do you want me to go in with you?"

She hesitated a moment. She wanted to see Kate privately, but she had the irrational feeling that Carter's presence would serve as some kind of charm. "If you wouldn't mind," she answered.

He dismounted from the carriage, tied the horse to a hitching post, then walked around to help her down. "I'll go in with you until we find your sister, then I'll leave you two alone for a little chat. How would that be?"

She answered him with a grateful smile and left her hand in place when he tucked it into his arm to walk into the hospital.

Mercy Hospital was an impressive facility for a frontier town. It had been built with silver fortunes, some of which had now disappeared, leaving the donors as poor as when they had first come West twenty or thirty years ago. But their legacy—the hospital, the opera house, the International Hotel—remained as evidence of their former glory.

After consulting on two different floors, they were sent down a long hall to Room 63…and Kate.

She was sitting in a chair next to a window, her legs covered with a small blanket. Her face was still pale, and over the top of the blanket her stomach protruded in a bulge that seemed to have grown twice the size since Jennie saw her last. Jennie gave a cry and ran across the room to throw her arms around her.

"Jen!" Kate exclaimed. "My darling sis!"

Carter turned his head discreetly as the girls embraced. Tears were running down Jennie's cheeks. After a moment, when she could finally speak, she drew back and exclaimed, "You're so…big!"

Kate laughed and put both hands on top of her big belly. "I guess there's really a baby in there, sis. Did you think it might all be a joke?"

Jennie smiled and teased, "You always were one for pranks, Katie."

Kate gave another merry laugh. "Some prank I'm pulling this time, eh?" Then she reached out and seized Jennie's hands. "How are you, Jen? You look tired."

"Me? I'm fine. How are *you?* That's the question. What are they telling you? You're still pale, but you look…I don't know…radiant."

"I probably look happy. And I am. It's the baby, Jennie. I can feel her almost all the time now. She wants to come out and join the world. My own dear, wonderful baby.''

''She?''

Kate looked down with a little blush and rubbed her stomach again. ''It's just that I have this feeling.''

''Oh, Kate!'' Jennie and her sister had always had a special bond, a special ability to feel each other's sorrows and joys. Now, though Jennie couldn't imagine how she would feel if *she* were about to have a baby, she could feel something of Kate's joy.

Over by the doorway, Carter cleared his throat. ''I'll just go on out to the carriage…'' he began.

''Oh, Carter, I'm *sorry*,'' Jennie said quickly, her expression guilty. ''Kate, Mr. Jones hired a carriage to bring me today.''

Kate looked over at their former adversary with a sweet smile. ''That was very kind of you, Mr. Jones.''

''Carter, please. It's good to see you looking so well, Miss Sheridan.''

''I guess you'd better call me Kate, since you've done the Sheridan sisters such a good turn today. And since I'm receiving you in my nightgown,'' she added with an impish grin.

Carter grinned back. ''I'd be honored. And now I'll just leave you two alone to catch up.''

But as he turned to leave, he almost ran into another visitor.

''Lyle,'' Jennie said in surprise, glancing sharply at her sister.

Lyle Wentworth looked at Carter with some displeasure. ''What are you doing here, Jones?'' he asked.

Carter spoke calmly. "I'm escorting Miss Sheridan here to visit her sister, Wentworth."

Kate spoke up. "Lyle has been staying at the hotel here and visiting me every day."

Jennie looked from Lyle to her sister in amazement. "Why?" she asked bluntly.

"I didn't like the idea of Kate alone here with no one to watch out for her interests," Lyle answered. "I wanted to be sure they were caring for her properly."

Kate made no comment. After a moment Jennie said, "Well, that's very nice of you, Lyle, but don't you have...*work* to do back home?"

Lyle shrugged. "I told my father I'd be back at the bank when I was good and ready. He wasn't too happy about it, but what's he going to do? Fire me?"

Carter had not bothered to hide his dislike for the banker's spoiled son, but he said with something sounding like approval, "I'm sure it makes a difference to have the staff know that Kate has someone here."

"And that someone should be me," Jennie added, not sure how she was feeling about this latest development. Lyle had defied his parents and risked town scandal to be near Kate as she lay ill and very pregnant with another man's baby. It simply didn't sound like the arrogant, rich boy she and Kate had known growing up.

Kate reached for Jennie's hand. "You're doing enough already, Jennie, running the boardinghouse all by yourself to earn the money to pay for me to be here. I wish I wasn't such a problem to everyone."

Jennie forced a smile. The truth was, even with Carter's extra rent, there was barely enough money to cover the expenses of the big household. She had no idea how they were going to manage a hospital bill in addition, but she certainly wasn't going to burden Kate with this knowledge.

"I can come back later, Kate, to give you some time alone with your sister," Lyle said.

Jennie looked at him in amazement. She'd never known that sensitivity could be part of Lyle's makeup.

"I was about to leave myself," Carter agreed.

Kate sent both men a grateful glance. "We'd appreciate it. You're both wonderful to be helping us this way. People like you make me hopeful that I'm bringing this little one into a better world than it seemed when the whole town came down on us weeks ago."

"We'll be sure your baby is properly cared for, Kate," Lyle said.

The note of proprietorship in his voice made Jennie uneasy, but Kate merely smiled at him again and said, "Why don't you come back in an hour, gentlemen? There will still be time before visiting hours end."

Lyle and Carter agreed and, with just a touch of awkwardness between them, turned to leave together. When they were gone, Kate gave a clumsy little bounce in her chair and said, "Now, tell me everything that's been happening. How's Barnaby? And the silverheels? And, especially, sis—" Kate cocked her head and gave Jennie a sly smile "—what's going on between you and the dashing Carter Jones?"

* * *

The minutes were not enough. Lyle and Carter returned, then left again, Lyle saying he would return in the morning, and Carter telling Jennie he would wait for her out at the carriage. In the end, one of the older nurses, a portly woman who looked as if she could enforce whatever rule she chose, had to suggest none too gently that visiting hours were at an end for the day.

The sisters hugged goodbye. This time Jennie forced herself to keep the tears at bay. She promised a return visit soon, gave her sister's belly a last good-luck pat, then turned to make her way out through the maze of dark, narrow halls that smelled of ether and illness.

It had grown dark outside, though it surely wasn't sundown yet? She'd been too absorbed in her talk with Kate to pay much attention. But the minute she opened the big front door of the hospital and scanned the western sky, she realized that it wasn't sundown that was causing the darkness. It was the approach of a storm.

Carter was standing by the carriage, also eyeing the clouds with a worried expression. He called to her as she approached. "Thunderclouds are rolling in."

"I can see that. We'd better hurry." She reached the far side of the carriage and hiked her skirts to scramble up without waiting for his assistance.

He watched her with a glint of amusement. "Hurry where?" he asked.

She frowned. "Hurry home. We're apt to get drenched."

Carter climbed more sedately up on the other side of the carriage and swung into the seat next to her. "Jennie, look at that sky." The entire western horizon was an ominous black.

"I know. We're in for it. So why are we sitting here?"

"Have you ever driven a carriage through the mountains in the middle of a gullywasher?" Carter asked with some exasperation.

"No."

"Well, neither have I. And I don't intend to start today."

Jennie felt a chill as the approaching storm gave a sudden spike to the wind. "Are you saying that we can't get home?"

"That's what I'm saying."

They sat looking at each other for a long moment. This particular development had never entered her mind. With sudden suspicion, she wondered if it had entered Carter's. "Did you plan things this way?"

He laughed, breaking the tension. "Now, that would be a useful talent for a public servant. Vote for Carter Jones. He can even control the weather."

The absurdity of it made Jennie laugh in return, but she quickly grew serious again. "Carter, I can't stay here. What about the miners? What about Barnaby?"

"I'm sure the boys can fend for themselves for one night. We'll send a wire."

Jennie continued staring at the black sky. "What will people say?" she asked finally, her voice small.

Carter picked up the reins and jerked them to start the horse moving. "Knowing the good people of Vermillion, if they find out about it, they'll say all manner of things, but that doesn't mean you have to let it bother you."

Jennie sighed. "I guess not. They already think Kate's wicked. They might as well think I'm wicked, too."

Carter grinned. "Well, if they're going to call you wicked, you might as well do something to deserve the honor."

She hoped he was joking. "Something like what?"

Carter waggled his right eyebrow. "How about indulging in a nice hot bath, followed by the International's very biggest steak and a glass of brandy?"

After the life Jennie'd been leading lately, a whole evening of pampering just for herself *did* sound wicked. Delightfully so. It also sounded expensive.

"I might have to ask if they'll let me stay somewhere back at the hospital," she said uncertainly.

Carter ignored her and continued directing the horse down Virginia City's prosperous main street. "Or you could have wine instead of brandy, if you prefer."

She put her hand on his arm and blurted out, "Carter, I don't have the money."

Carter gave her hand a pat and smiled down at her. "I know. You'll be my guest tonight." When she started to protest he added, "In your own private room, of course. We'll see if they have apple pie for dessert."

It sounded heavenly. "Carter, I can't accept. That really would make people talk."

They were nearing a six-story building with the

sign International Hotel over the front awning. "They'll talk anyway. We've already established that. So what difference does it make if you're suffering on a cramped cot in that dark hospital or enjoying yourself here?"

She looked up at the elegant brick facade. It *would* be fun to ride the elevator again. The carriage had stopped and Carter was waiting. She bit her lip. "All right. As my mama used to say, in for a penny, in for a pound."

Chapter Eight

If Carter *had* been able to control the weather, he was not at all sure he would have ordered up the thunderstorm that rolled over Virginia City shortly after he and Jennie arrived at the hotel. It had been pleasant and mildly stimulating to spend the afternoon with her—putting his hands around her firm waist to help her in and out of the carriage, listening to her laugh at his sallies, noticing how more and more wisps of her hair curled around her slender white neck as the day progressed. But an evening…and a night. That was another matter.

Lyle Wentworth was probably lodging at the International. Neither he nor Jennie suggested looking him up, but the thought of his presence there could help keep Carter's less virtuous impulses under control. Jennie had enough problems in her life. And Carter, himself, was not about to risk his political future for a scandal, in spite of the casual way he'd greeted Jennie's fears on the topic.

When they returned to Vermillion it would be easy enough to explain the impossibility of returning in the storm. He'd make a point of letting the influential people in town, starting with Henrietta Billingsley, know that any suggestion of impropriety between him and Jennie Sheridan would be treated as actionable slander.

All that remained was for him to endure until morning without giving in to the feelings that had raged with various intensity throughout the course of the day. And Carter was used to that. From the time as a small child that he'd realized that he was "different," he'd kept his feelings under constant control. No matter how sad or how angry he got, his demeanor would stay calm.

He'd rely on that control tonight, he decided, as he watched Jennie tackle the International Hotel's huge steak with delightful enthusiasm. Her brown eyes sparkled like the twinkling sconces that lined the restaurant walls. She'd repaired her hair, which was piled in rich ringlets on top of her head.

"You're not eating," she said as he sat watching her. "You'll make me feel like a glutton."

"I enjoy seeing a woman with a good appetite."

"It's so *good*," she said, rolling her eyes in ecstasy.

Carter laughed. "We can order you another, if you like."

Jennie almost choked on the piece of steak she was chewing. "No one could eat two of these."

"In the early days of the strikes, I'd venture to say they had lucky prospectors who'd order them half a dozen at a time."

Jennie sat back in her chair and put her hands

across her stomach. "Well, not me. I can't eat another bite." She looked wistfully at the piece left on her plate. "Do you think I could take it with me?"

"Why don't I buy you another one for breakfast instead?"

Jennie giggled. "I'll be so fat your horse won't be able to pull me back up the mountain."

Carter's eyes moved over her, lingering a moment on where her hands rested, just at her tiny waist. "Oh, I think he'll manage."

Jennie shook her head. "We'd better not risk it. I'll be as big as Kate and without her excuse."

He was relieved to hear her joking about her sister's condition. It had done her good to visit Kate today and see for herself that her sister's health was improving. "I suppose it's not correct for men to notice such things, but it was rather obvious that Kate's getting…ah…that she…"

"That she's about to have a baby," Jennie finished happily, not the least bit self-conscious. "I can hardly wait."

Carter looked surprised. "I thought you weren't too pleased with the idea."

"Certainly I'm pleased. I mean, I was worried about the way everyone was acting in town, and I was scared to death when Kate got so sick. But I'm thrilled about the baby. Kate will be such a good mother."

All at once Carter didn't feel like finishing his steak, either. "It takes more than a good mother to raise a child."

"Well, of course it does. A child should have a

father, too, for one thing. But since this one won't have that, it will be extra important to make it know that it's surrounded by people who love it—or love *her,* if Kate's instincts are right.''

Carter's mother had loved him. Or at least, he'd always told himself she had. It hadn't been anywhere near enough. ''And who will those people be?''

''Her Aunt Jennie, for one. And brother Barnaby.''

''What about when Aunt Jennie wants to have a life of her own—goes off to get married and raise her own family?''

Jennie dismissed the notion with a wave of her hand. ''Oh, that won't happen. Kate and I will be perfectly happy together at Sheridan House.''

Carter looked skeptical. ''Most girls want to get married.''

''Not me.''

He pushed away his plate. ''Why not? Because of what happened to Kate? Do you think all men are that unscrupulous?''

''No, I suppose there are a few good ones here and there. My father was a good man. I'm just not interested.''

''What if Kate wants to marry?''

''She won't. She's learned her lesson.''

Carter shook his head with a smile of disbelief. ''She didn't seem too unhappy to have Lyle hanging about. And Lyle talks as if he's going to have something to say about Kate's future and the child's, too.''

''Well, he's wrong.'' He could tell the direction of the conversation was beginning to irritate her, which was not what he wanted. It had been too much fun to see her relaxed and enjoying herself. He wouldn't spoil it by starting up an argument. "Perhaps you're right," he said, ending the topic. "Now, how about that brandy I promised you?"

Jennie's expression lightened. "You've lured me into wickedness enough for one evening," she said with a laugh.

Her innocence made Carter feel protective. He suspected that she had no idea the degree of wickedness he'd be able to lure her into if he didn't have a conscience and a political future to temper his more immediate desires. "Just a glass. One glass each to warm us before we go up to our rooms."

"I've never drunk brandy in my life," Jennie admitted.

"Oh, come now. Not even at Christmas?"

Jennie shook her head. "Papa drank it sometimes, but my mother never did. She said it was too dear."

"Well, you're not paying for it tonight, so you might as well take advantage of the opportunity. Think what a story it will make for the miners. You can tell them that you drank me under the table."

Jennie flushed. "I wouldn't dare tell anyone. It's bad enough that we're here alone together."

Carter looked around at the room full of diners. The storm had filled the hotel. "It doesn't feel very alone to me. Come on, give it a try. What happened to the spirited young lady who threw me out of her house the first time I met her? I thought it was in for a penny, in for a pound."

Jennie grinned. "You're right. I love the smell of it, and I always did wonder what it tasted like."

Carter signaled to the waiter. "It tastes a mite stronger than it smells. You could be surprised."

But Jennie appeared undaunted by the warning. She gave a happy sigh and said, "I love surprises."

In the end they'd had *two* glasses each. After choking on the first taste, the fiery liquid had gone down more and more smoothly with each sip, creating a pleasant glow right in her center. Jennie found it lovely. She was more relaxed than she'd been for months. Carter had behaved like a gentleman all evening. He'd made light of paying what seemed to Jennie an outrageous sum for their two rooms. He'd accompanied her without teasing when she wanted to ride the elevator an extra time between the lobby and their rooms on the fourth floor.

Except for those few moments when he seemed to be suggesting that she and Kate were destined to have a man in their lives, it had been a thoroughly pleasant evening.

But suddenly, as they walked down the carpeted hallway toward their adjoining rooms, she was finding his presence oddly disturbing. She was having memory flashes of that night in her office when he'd kissed her. He'd promised her that there would be no repetition of the incident, and she'd tried to put it out of her mind. But now that she was alone with him in the dark hallway, the brandy making a pleasantly warm muddle of her brain, she found the memory wouldn't let her go. Could it be she was wanting him to kiss her again?

Honesty had always been one of her virtues. If she

was walking down the hall hoping that at the end of it Carter Jones would kiss her, she wanted to be able to admit it, at least to herself. She licked her lips, tasting brandy on them, and noting that they felt extrasensitive.

"Perhaps it's just the brandy," she said aloud.

Carter looked down at her in surprise. "Perhaps what is just the brandy?"

She made a little twist with her mouth. "Nothing. I'm just tasting it."

"Oh."

In a minute they would be at their rooms. He would open her door and say good-night like the gentleman he promised to be. Suddenly she blurted out, "I was wondering if it was the brandy that was making me remember the night you kissed me."

She could feel him stiffen beside her. It had been a terribly forward thing to say, but it was something of a relief to have let it out. Now he'd probably laugh and tell her that she was perhaps a little tipsy, and then they could part and get some sleep.

Instead he said in a voice that had grown slightly hoarse, "I haven't needed brandy to remember it, Jennie."

They'd reached her room and stopped. The odd flashes of memory that had been seizing her since leaving the dining room blended with the present moment. His gray eyes looking down at her held the same slightly hooded look. His nostrils had a predatory flare.

Instead of frightening her, his expression seemed to release some kind of liquid feeling straight through her middle. Her hand gripped his wool sleeve. Her first attempt to speak came out as a dry crack. She started over. "I guess I wouldn't mind if you did it again. Just one kiss."

Her beautiful eyes were trusting and slightly unfocused from fatigue and brandy. Carter gave a silent groan and looked up and down the hallway. It was empty at the moment, but there was no guarantee it would stay that way with the hotel so full. He plucked her key out of her hand, opened her door and drew her inside, shutting it behind them.

This would not help his campaign to get safely through the night and back to Vermillion with Jennie's virtue and his career intact. But his body was past listening to the voice of reason. "One kiss, then," he murmured, and turned her so that she was against the door.

Her mouth opened to his immediately. It was brandy flavored and hot. It seemed as if his entire body grew hard against the softness of her as he pressed her gently into the door. She turned her head, allowing his tongue to explore her mouth, her lips and then the soft underside of her jaw and her long, exquisite neck.

"Ah, Carter," she breathed, and her voice had the throaty sound of a woman in the midst of sensual pleasure. It triggered an inner smile of male pride. She might be innocent, but she was quick to respond to his passion. He turned his attention once again to her mouth. One kiss, he'd said. He'd intended. It was already considerably more than that.

With a feeling somewhat akin to drowning, he

reached around her and lifted her in his arms. She made no protest as he carried her across the room to the big walnut bed. Beyond the lace curtains, rain still lashed the window, transmitting some of the storm's violence to the turmoil that was raging inside him.

He leaned over to place her in the center of the bed, then followed her down into the downy feather bed. It was silky and cold, whereas every inch of her was warm. He gathered her up against him, the lengths of their bodies melting together.

Her mouth sought his, still brandied, less tentative this time as her tongue began to explore just as his had done. Its soft trail over his lips was exquisite agony. For a moment he let himself revel in the sensation. At one time in his life there had been many such encounters, but he'd gotten bored with the chase. It had been a long time. It was as if he'd been saving up, waiting for this exquisitely right woman, waiting to discover an experience that went beyond mere mating.

The room was in almost total darkness. He couldn't see her face. But even without seeing it, he could sense when she began to withdraw, though his thundering body took several seconds to let his mind convey the message. He pulled his head back. There was no doubt about it. She'd grown stiff and uncomfortable beneath him, the intimate entwining of their bodies suddenly embarrassing for them both. He rolled off her.

Keeping his voice deliberately light, he tried to defuse the tension with humor. "Well, now. That ought to teach you about drinking brandy in strange hotels."

To his relief, when she finally answered him, her voice, though trembly, was not accusing. "I did ask, I guess."

He sat on the edge of the bed and reached a hand to pull her to a seat beside him. "Yes, you did, Miss Sheridan. A thoroughly wicked request by the standards of Vermillion womanhood."

Jennie gave a shaky laugh. "Which will never be my standards, as you know."

"Should I apologize?"

"No. Except maybe for the brandy. Did you do that deliberately?"

Carter shook his head and teased, "How was I to know that a little bit of brandy would turn you into a hussy."

Jennie sat up straighter on the bed and rearranged her disheveled skirt. "Oh, dear. I was, wasn't I? Don't tell Kate."

"I won't tell anyone. But I do intend to get out of here before I decide that your lesson isn't quite over with."

"It was kind of nice." She sounded wistful and unintentionally provocative.

Lord. Carter stood and rearranged his trousers. Sleep would be a while in coming tonight, he predicted. "Will you be all right here now?" he asked.

"Yes. Thank you for everything—for dinner and…all."

He grinned. "It was my pleasure, ma'am. Anytime you decide to be wicked again, you let me know."

He touched her cheek with his hand, then stood and walked across the room. As he started out the door, he turned back. In the darkness, he could just barely make out her form, sitting on the bed. He thought of several things to say, but finally said simply, "Lock the door after me, sweetheart." Then he slipped into the hall.

Moments after Carter had left, Jennie still sat on the bed without moving. He'd called her sweetheart. The endearment had affected her almost as much as the kiss. The *kisses,* she amended. It had definitely been more than one. She'd lost track.

For a while, in fact, she'd lost track of everything except the feel of Carter's mouth on hers and the peculiar *yearning* inside her. She suspected that she'd been quite close to finding herself in the same kind of predicament Kate had with the unscrupulous Sean. If she hadn't used every ounce of will she could muster in her brandy-fogged brain, she'd have let Carter have his way with her, regardless of the consequences. Part of her wished he was still back here on the bed with her.

Thank goodness for sanity. And, she felt obliged to add, for Carter's restraint. If he'd continued his devastating onslaught of her senses instead of pulling away at her slight demurral, she didn't know what might have happened. Sean Flaherty had obviously been less principled than Carter, and look where it had put Kate.

Slowly she stood and made her way over to the marble-topped dresser to light the lamp. Her body was still oddly sensitive as she removed her clothes and prepared to sleep in her shift, since she didn't have any nightclothes with her. By the time she'd washed her face and neck at the carved nightstand, embarrassment had begun to set in. She would have to face Carter tomorrow in the cold light of day with memories of their heated encounter fresh in both their minds.

He'd been a gentleman, yes. This time. But drawing from her sister's example, she'd be a fool to trust his restraint a second time. His or anyone else's. She'd better concentrate on running Sheridan House and comforting Barnaby through his childhood heartaches. Men and love and kisses were for other women, not for her.

She'd learned a lesson Carter had said. Yes, indeed.

"So am I going to order you that steak?" Carter said as they sat down in the hotel's now sunny dining room.

Jennie smiled. The meeting had not been as awkward as she'd feared. Thanks, once again, to Carter. He'd made no mention of how they'd parted last night. He'd escorted her to the dining room with his usual courteous charm, offering with a grin to ask the elevator attendant to let them ride up and down again.

"No steak, thank you. I'm not sure I want anything to tell you the truth."

Carter quirked an eyebrow. "Are you a little under the weather today, Miss Sheridan? Could this have anything to do with the imbibing of a certain alcoholic beverage?"

"Don't remind me, please."

"A plate of eggs will fix you up."

Jennie's stomach rolled. "I don't think so."

"Porridge, then. You can't ride all the way back to Vermillion on an empty stomach."

The waiter came and Jennie made no protest as Carter ordered eggs and ham for himself and porridge and honey for her.

"Can we stop to see Kate again before we start back? I mean, do you have the time? You didn't intend to take two days off."

"Of course. Spend as much time as you like. I'm sure you have a lot to talk about."

She couldn't tell if he was referring to last evening. "We always do," she said simply.

When she didn't rise to his bait, he evidently decided to be more direct. "What will you tell her about your night at the hotel?"

Jennie hesitated before answering. She wanted to be fair. Carter had certainly been a gentleman. He'd had an opportunity to take advantage of her and he'd not pursued it. But she'd lain awake a long time last night cementing her resolve that this would not happen again. "I'll tell her that I rode the elevator, that I had a wonderful dinner, that I drank two glasses of brandy, that I asked you to kiss me and you did."

Carter looked surprised. "You'll tell her that?"

"Kate and I usually tell each other everything. Which is why I'll also tell her that I've now learned my lesson and I don't intend to play with that kind of fire ever again."

The waiter arrived with their breakfasts, giving Jennie's words a chance to sink in. When he'd left, Carter asked with a touch of irritation, "Play with fire? Does that mean you never intend to let a man kiss you? Or just that you never intend to let *me* kiss you?"

"You're the only one I'm worried about. No one else has ever asked."

"That doesn't mean that they won't ask, Jennie. You're talking crazy—a beautiful woman like you is going to have men wanting to kiss her."

"Well, they'll be disappointed."

Carter took an angry stab at one of his eggs. "You've let one scoundrel sour you on the whole male gender."

"Maybe so. But I've got a family to think about and a new baby to prepare for. I don't have time for hearts and flowers foolishness."

"Did you ever think that a man might be a help to you in taking care of that unusual family you're planning?" Then Jennie laughed, almost spitting out her bite of porridge, as he added in a horrified voice, "Not me, of course."

"Don't worry, Carter. I won't demand that you make an honest woman of me after our tryst last night. And if it will make you more comfortable, I won't tell Kate anything about it."

"That might be best," he said, sounding relieved.

They lapsed into silence, lost in their own thoughts. Carter may be more of a gentleman than Sean Flaherty, but he was still a man, cut from the same cloth. He didn't want anyone to know that he'd been kissing one of the notorious Sheridans. His life and his ambitions would always be more important to him than any woman.

She'd learned more than one lesson on this trip, and she didn't intend to forget them.

Chapter Nine

Carter had told the livery owner only that he'd decided to keep the rig an extra day. The miners didn't talk much with the rest of the people in town, so there was a good chance that no one else would ever have to know that he and Jennie had spent an unchaperoned night in a hotel.

After they'd arrived back at midday, Carter had spent the rest of the afternoon in his office, cleaning his desk and moving papers from one pile to another. He accomplished nothing, and by the end of the day, stopped pretending that he might.

What he needed to do—urgently—was move out of Sheridan House. The situation was simply untenable. He never should have moved there in the first place. He'd convinced himself that the decision was due to a real desire to help Jennie out and also to his boredom with the hotel menu. But deep down he'd known that the move had really been due to his desire to be near Jennie.

The encounter in Virginia City had left him shaken. He'd acted with uncharacteristic recklessness. What would have happened if Jennie hadn't had that slight hesitation? Would he have continued his seduction of her, taken her virginity? Perhaps left her with a bastard child? Like father, like son, he thought bitterly. He grabbed three sharpened pencils from the box in front of him and cracked them in two as if they were toothpicks.

It wasn't going to happen. He was a better person than the unknown man who had left his seed to grow inside Carter's mother and then disappeared from her life. Carter had always taken care in his sexual encounters to avoid that possibility. And he'd never, ever touched a virgin. Until now.

He'd be late to supper. He stood and stuffed some papers into his briefcase. After doing no work for two days, tonight he'd tell the miners that he was too busy to join the card game. He'd sit in his room and use his work to keep his mind off the fact that Jennie was alone in her room just three doors down.

Tomorrow he'd pack up his things and move back to the hotel.

There'd been a bit of teasing by the miners at supper over the overnight stay, but when neither Jennie nor Carter seemed much in a mood for raillery, the subject was dropped. The miners had taken to offering to help with the cleanup after supper, but tonight Jennie insisted that she could handle things. She even sent Barnaby off to do his schoolwork. She wanted to be alone.

Carter hadn't offered to help. He'd disappeared the instant supper was finished, which was just as well.

Twenty-four hours had only heightened the embarrassment she was feeling about the previous night. She'd had trouble meeting his eyes when he'd come in late to supper. He seemed to be feeling the same way. He hadn't addressed two words to her.

It was obvious that Carter Jones was not about to sully his reputation by letting anyone know that he had developed some kind of affection for "one of those Sheridan girls." Or perhaps that was putting things too favorably. She'd heard that men had sexual urges that were not necessarily connected with feelings. It could be that Carter's kissing her last night had had nothing to do with affection.

She sighed and reached to put the last of the clean plates in the cupboard. Well, heck. Perhaps it had been purely physical on her part, too. She'd wanted another one of those kisses. As an experiment. It could have been any number of men doing the kissing.

But as she slowly walked out of the kitchen and up the stairs to her room, she was forced to admit that that was a lie. It wasn't the kiss she'd wanted. It was *Carter*'s kiss. And for all her sane and sensible arguments, she *still* wanted it.

She might have predicted that he'd be there at the top of the stairs, a towel in hand, heading toward the washroom. That seemed to be the way fate had decided to treat her recently.

He could have continued on his course, but he stopped and said, "I forgot to thank you for supper."

"You seemed to be in a hurry."

"I've got a lot of work to do tonight. I got behind."

Jennie bit her lip. The hall was lit only by the light coming from downstairs and from the open door of his bedroom, but in the dimness she could see that his starched white shirt was unbuttoned, hanging open to reveal a sculpted chest, lightly covered with hair. Jennie's stomach plunged.

"You got behind in your work by doing me a good turn. I thank you again."

"It was nothing."

They stared at each other a long moment. They both knew it had been considerably more than nothing.

Finally she said, "Well, I appreciated it all the same."

He nodded. "If you feel the need to go again, let me know. I'll arrange it. On a sunny day," he added with the ghost of a smile.

"As I told you, Dr. Millard's offered to loan me his rig. I can probably get Dennis to take me."

"Fine." The flicker of smile disappeared. "I... ah...wanted to let you know that I'll be moving out tomorrow."

Jennie gave a start of surprise. "You're leaving?"

"I thought it would be best."

She felt a swift pang of sadness, followed closely by anger. "I can assure you that's not necessary, Carter," she said stiffly.

"Not necessary, but easier on us both."

"If that's what you want."

The anger in her voice was now clear. But he misinterpreted its cause. "I'll pay the next week's rent and you can keep the rest of this week's, as well, since I didn't give any kind of proper notice.''

She shook her head. "I'll see that you get back the money for any unused days.''

"I won't take it. It's not fair,'' he protested.

"You'll have no choice. This is my business, after all. I'll send Barnaby to your office tomorrow with the money.'' He looked as if wanted to continue the argument, but she turned away and started walking toward her room, saying over her shoulder, "If you need any help with your packing, let me know.''

The wire had come Tuesday, and she'd resisted going to town for two days, but in the end she had to face the fact that money was not going to suddenly start growing in her vegetable garden. She'd have to find a way to earn it. Kate would not have sent the wire if the situation were not serious.

Hospital needs payment. Lyle offered but I said no. Please advise.

She'd read the words over and over, and in her weaker moments she was tempted to wire back to Kate and tell her to accept Lyle's offer of help. But that would be tantamount to selling her sister to Lyle Wentworth, which she wasn't about to do.

She'd have to get some kind of job, and she had no illusions that that would be an easy task in this town. The first person she approached was Margaret Potter, not because she thought the old schoolteacher would be among the more sympathetic townsfolk, but because she figured teaching was the job she'd be most suited for. But she hadn't been inside the walls of the schoolhouse more than three minutes when she realized that to come here had been a fool's quest.

"Teachers *and their families* have to set an example for the rest of the community," Miss Potter said, squinting her eyes to look at Jennie through tiny gold-rimmed glasses. Her implication was unmistakable.

"Thank you anyway, Miss Potter," Jennie said through tight lips as she turned to leave. Beggars did not have the luxury of speaking their minds. She couldn't afford to alienate one of the town's leading citizens.

She walked slowly up the shady street from the schoolhouse and headed toward town without much enthusiasm. Her encounter with Miss Potter had left her discouraged. How many of the shopkeepers in town would feel the same way as Miss Potter? If they had nothing against the Sheridans, their wives probably would, which would amount to the same thing.

Perhaps she should try talking with the Wentworths. Harmon Wentworth had not been at all sympathetic when he'd broken the news about the sad state of their finances to the sisters after her parents' funerals. He'd implied that it had been disgraceful for parents to be so irresponsible as to not have provided for their daughters' well-being.

But now the Wentworths' only son was staying in Virginia City to be near Kate. They must realize that he was in love with her. And Lucinda, though she had the reputation of being a bit scatterbrained, had always been a staunch supporter of her baby boy. For that reason alone, she might be willing to support Jennie's request. The Wentworths employed several part-time clerks and Jennie was good with sums. She turned toward the bank.

Her cheeks were flaming as she sat ramrod straight in the high-backed chair and wondered if she dared bend over and bite the tip of the finger Harmon Wentworth continued to jab toward her face as he leaned toward her across his desk.

"...when it has come to this shocking state of affairs. That a shameless girl, already suffering the consequences of her licentious behavior, can entice an honorable young man to reject his family, defy his parents..."

Jennie slowly put her fingertips on the edge of the desk and stood with as much dignity as she could muster. To heck with the consequences, this she would not let pass. The banker's diatribe trailed off as she stood looking down at him. "Mr. Wentworth, in the future I will look more kindly on Lyle, since I now understand that he has been able to turn out to be a more or less acceptable and decent human being, in spite of being subjected to the influences of a father who is a bigot and a blowhard."

Then she turned without haste and made her way out into the afternoon sunshine, tears in her throat and a weight the size of a boulder on her chest. It was hopeless. There was no way anyone in this town was going to give her a respectable job. At least not until the furor over Kate died down, which would probably be months, and which would not help with hospital bills now.

It was one of those moments when she wished with all her might that she could go home, crawl into her mother's lap and cry. Her mother used to croon to her in her pleasant alto voice and tell her that everything was going to be all right. And then it usually was.

She walked aimlessly up the street, heading almost without thinking toward Dr. Millard's office. It was probably some kind of subconscious search for a substitute parent, but as she neared his office she remembered how he was always joking about how he wished he had someone to tidy up after him. She had too much pride to take money from friends, but she wasn't too proud to do some hard work in exchange for pay. And perhaps come of the townspeople wouldn't object to her doing something as menial as cleaning.

She'd hire on with the doctor one afternoon a week and post a notice offering her services. Dr. Millard would let her place the advertisement in front of his office, as she had the notice for the fourth boarder. She'd have to hope she had better luck than she had with that flyer. Her only alternative would be to go house to house asking directly for the work, and after her encounters with Miss Potter and Mr. Wentworth, she didn't think she could quite bear it.

As she anticipated, Dr. Millard was indignant at first, insisting that he would help her without accepting her labor in exchange. But after she patiently explained for the third time her determination to do this on her own, he reluctantly agreed that she could come every Tuesday afternoon.

"But I won't be particular about whether you come or what you do when you get here," he told her.

"I'll come," she told him, "and I'll leave this place spotless. You'll wonder what you ever did without me."

She used the doctor's pen and paper to make up a notice, then left his office, smiling, and crossed the sidewalk to the awning post to tack it up. This might work. If she could find two or three more places, she'd start bringing in enough extra to send the required payment.

"What in the devil's name do you think you're doing?"

Her bubble of optimism burst as she heard Carter's voice behind her. She closed her eyes as if hoping it would make him go away. "I have permission from the property owner, Mr. Prosecutor," she said, without turning around. "So take your ordinances elsewhere."

"I don't give a damn about the ordinances. What does that mean—*maid service, fifteen cents an hour, contact Jennie Sheridan?*"

She opened her eyes and turned to face him, the notice still in her hands. Unlike the last time she'd seen him with his chest bare, today he was neatly starched and proper in his most formal attorney garb. She found it almost impossible to believe that those stiff arms had ever been around her. "I think the sign is fairly clear," she said.

"You're not hiring out? Hiring *yourself* out?"

He stepped up on the sidewalk to bring himself level with her, which made her have to look up at him, shading her eyes from the sun. "Yes, I am, if it's any of your business."

He let out a long, angry stream of air through his nose. "It is my business. You're doing this because you wouldn't take my rent money."

"You're not renting from me anymore."

"But I should be. I mean, I *would* be if I'd been able to." He looked up and down the street to see if anyone was in earshot. There was no one, but he lowered his voice anyway. "If I'd been able to keep my hands off you that night. It's my fault."

The more agitated he grew, the calmer she became. "If I recall, I more or less invited you to put your hands on me. So I guess that makes it *my* fault that I no longer have a fourth boarder, which is why I'm planning to earn the money another way."

As she turned again to tack the flyer up, he reached over and ripped it out of her hand, tearing the paper in half. He'd seen her leaving the doctor's office as he left his own office down the street, and, though he wasn't exactly sure why or what he'd say to her, he'd found his feet taking him in her direction. But as he approached, admiring the way her green dress tucked in sharply at her trim waist, he'd caught a glimpse of the paper she held. His blood had begun to boil the minute he'd seen the word "maid."

"What are you doing?" she protested, grabbing the two halves of the paper back from him and staring down at them wrathfully.

"You're not putting up that flyer. And you're not working as a maid." He could tell her a thing or two about maids. About how they picked up other people's messes and scrubbed their dirt and in return were treated as less than sticks of furniture. He'd seen his mother literally shrivel up through the years of backbreaking work and humiliating treatment. He couldn't begin to count the times he'd seen her wealthy employers stare right through her as if she didn't even exist until it seemed by the end of her life that she wondered the same thing herself.

"Don't be foolish, Jennie," he said in a calmer tone. "You're a bright, educated woman. You don't need to do this. Let me help you—just until your sister's out of the hospital."

"Until my sister comes home with her illegitimate baby, you mean. At which time the town denizens will probably try to shut down our boardinghouse again and we'll be in a worse coil than ever."

"Let me help you until we can work out another solution, then."

Jennie folded the torn paper. The flyer was ruined anyway. And the truth was, while it would not be bad to do cleaning for Dr. Millard, she hated the idea of taking that kind of position with people who already thought she was lower than they. "What other solution, Carter?" she asked, her voice depressed.

"Well, for one thing I've reviewed the laws and I think we can get you permission to keep the miners at your house, not as a business, but as a 'multiple residence.' And then we can find you the fourth boarder you need."

"I may need that room soon. Kate and I could room together, but with the baby and all..."

He waved his hand. "That's a ways off yet. We're talking immediate solutions."

His tone had become lawyerly and bossy, and it made Jennie tired. She'd had enough lectures for one day. "Carter," she said, interrupting him. "I appreciate your concern. I'll think about this some more before I decide on the maid position. But now, if you don't mind, I should be getting home before Barnaby starts to worry about where I am."

Carter wanted to continue with his suggestions. It was easier making them than it was dwelling on the fact that his behavior had partially served to put her in the bind she was in. But she looked on the verge of tears. It made something well up inside him beyond the indignation he'd felt when he thought about her working as a maid. It was a mixture of protectiveness and some emotion that he didn't recognize as ever having felt before.

The words slipped from his mouth, "Go home, sweetheart. We'll talk about this later. I'll help you figure it out."

The tears that had been at the base of Jennie's throat all afternoon glazed her eyes. It was that word again. *Sweetheart.* It made her start to lose her hard-fought battle for control. She blinked furiously. "Thanks anyway, Carter, but I can figure things out for myself," she said, and then turned to hurry up the street before the drops could spill on to her cheeks.

"Twenty dollars? Twenty dollars a *week?*" Jennie stared at the three miners as if they had indeed suddenly sprouted feet of silver.

"They don't care about money, Miss Jennie. Those mine owners have more than they know what to do with. You should see some of the mansions they've built over in Virginia City."

"But I can hardly believe they would pay someone twenty dollars a week just to cook dinner once a day."

"Dinner for forty hungry men," Brad clarified.

"Who eat like a pack of wolves after a long winter," Smitty added.

"And don't smell much better," Dennis concluded.

Jennie laughed. "Whose idea was this? How did you know I was going to town today to look for work." They were sitting around the supper table, drinking coffee while Barnaby cleared the dishes and brought out huge servings of crusty peach pie that lopped over the sides of Francis Sheridan's dainty china plates. Jennie already knew how miners ate.

"We didn't," Dennis explained. "But we knew that you'd been worried about finding another boarder, and when the Greaser up and quit after his brother struck it rich down by Elko, we thought, maybe Miss Jennie could come out here every noon and do this."

"You're a sight better cook than the Greaser," Brad said.

Smitty added, "Amen to that."

Jennie could hardly believe it. Twenty dollars a week. It would solve all her problems, or at least all the ones that had to do with money. "The Greaser?" she asked.

"Our cook," Dennis explained. "Greaser Johnson. He left yesterday before the noon meal, and the foreman nearly had a mutiny on his hands. They need to get a replacement quick.''

"But I imagine they expect to hire a *man*," Jennie said, not wanting to get too hopeful, but already making calculations as to exactly how many of her bills she could pay with twenty dollars a week.

"I imagine they do," Dennis agreed with a shrug and a grin. "But once we three tell the others about the kind of fare you've been giving us these past few weeks, they won't settle for another Greaser. They'll want you."

"We could just pack up some of this pie to hand around tomorrow morning," Brad said, shoveling a bite into his mouth. "That'll do the trick."

Jennie's pie was untouched. "You don't think the owners would be upset about a woman being there…I mean, there aren't any other women up at the mines, are there?"

"No, ma'am," Dennis answered. "But you wouldn't be alone. You'd have the three of us for kind of guards—what's that French word?"

"Chaperons?"

"Yeah. We'd be your chap-erons."

"We'd take care of you, Miss Jennie," Smitty added.

Jennie looked around at their three eager faces. They made quite a trio, big, jovial Dennis, then medium-sized Brad and finally the tiny Smitty, who didn't seem brawny enough to be a miner. She felt a wave of affection for each of them.

"Well, how can I refuse the offer of such gallant gentlemen?" she asked, smiling back at each in turn.

"I'll go up with you tomorrow morning after breakfast and apply for the job."

"Oh, you'll get the job, Miss Jennie. We'll see to that," Dennis said firmly. "You just pack up your apron and that little recipe book of yours and plan to stay until the meal. We'll arrange for someone to bring you back home when it's finished so you can get your own work done here."

"Why, it's just the perfect solution," Jennie said happily, pushing back her chair.

"Yes, it is," Dennis agreed. Then he leaned forward and picked up her plate of pie. "If you're not going to eat this, little lady, can I have it?"

It had only taken the foreman of the Longley mine a few minutes to decide that he should take the unprecedented step of hiring a woman to do his midday cooking. The mine provided the big noon meal for the miners as part of their pay. For breakfast and supper they fended for themselves, which, in the case of the men who had less agreeable habitation than the three Sheridan silverheels, meant that they came to lunch at the long pine tables ravenous. The foreman had had two days of trying to get the food prepared himself, and was more than happy not to have to endure the men's complaints a third noon hour.

Of course, his decision had been helped along by the fact that the three silverheels had lined up a contingent of almost half the workers backing their choice of Jennie as the new cook. Against those odds, the foreman had really had little choice.

Jennie had made a quick assessment of the mine's

makeshift kitchen and rather haphazard larder and had thrown together a stew hearty enough to make dead men walk. She served it along with fluffy biscuits and a rice pudding for dessert. The promised pie would have to wait until she had time to cut up that much fruit. But for a hasty first day, the result was more than satisfactory, as evidenced by the compliments and grateful looks of the miners as they cleaned up plate after plate.

One of the men was assigned to clean-up duty, so once the food was served and cleared, Jennie's duties were over. Dennis had been given permission to take her down the mountain in one of the mine wagons each day. In the morning they made the forty-five-minute climb up to the site on foot.

As she finished up her first day, she thought of the apples in her larder. She'd cut them up tonight after supper and bring them with her tomorrow to make apple pies. It would all take a bit of organizing, but she was sure it could be done so that everything would fit into her schedule. She hummed a little as Dennis drove her away from the camp. It was a beautiful late fall day and she felt as if perhaps things were finally going her way for a change.

The mood lasted until they turned into Elm Street and saw Carter sitting on the front stairs of her house, tapping his hat impatiently in his hand.

"Where have you two been off to?" he yelled as the mine wagon approached her front sidewalk.

"We've been up to the mine. Miss Jennie's going to—" Dennis stopped in midsentence with an "oof" as Jennie knocked an elbow rather firmly into his stout side. "We've been up to the mine," he concluded lamely.

"Nice morning for a drive," Jennie said firmly. She'd done some thinking about her new position as she'd kneaded the biscuit dough this morning. The miners all seemed to accept her presence without question. They'd been unfailingly polite, even sweet. But she wasn't so sure what the reaction of the town would be when they discovered that she was going up there every day by herself to work all alone among a group of brawny men. She suspected it would just fuel anew the furor over the wanton Sheridan sisters.

And Carter was the last one she wanted to know. After his reaction yesterday to her attempt to hire out as a maid, she couldn't imagine what his reaction would be to her new job. He'd probably find some kind of regulation against it, she thought with a sniff. Anyway, it was none of his business.

"You went for a drive up to the mine?" he asked, perplexed.

Jennie nodded. Carter had stood up from the porch stairs and was coming toward her, but she didn't wait for him to reach her before she jumped down from the wagon without assistance. "The silverheels gave me a little tour. It was quite interesting. Thank you, Dennis," she added, smiling up at her escort.

He tipped his hat and winked at her. "It was a pleasure, Miss Jennie. Let me know when you want another tour."

"I will." She waved as he signaled to the horses and the wagon pulled away.

Carter stood behind her, waiting. After the mine wagon had turned the corner and disappeared, he said softly, "Now, Jennie. Tell me what you were *really* doing this morning."

Chapter Ten

He'd wanted to come last night, but he'd sensed after their encounter in town in front of the doctor's office that Jennie had a tenuous grip on emotions stretched to a dangerous limit, and he hadn't wanted to push her. Also, night was a dangerous time. They'd already discovered that. He wasn't too sure about his own grip on things when he was around her after dark.

So he'd come over after lunch today. His plan was to offer to help her go over her books and set figures on exactly how much she'd need. Then in the course of the calculations, he'd once again make an offer to supplement her income, at least until the hospital was paid off. He didn't have a lot of savings, but his prosecutor's salary was generous and, as a single man with no obligations, he spent little of it.

But he'd arrived to find the house empty and Barnaby, who'd run home during the school lunch recess, had been oddly evasive about where Jennie might be. So he'd decided to wait.

Now he was more mystified than ever. As far as

he knew there was only one kind of woman who ever went up to the mines. And they went up there for only one thing. In a way, it was the same thing Jennie was trying to do—make money. But it was too absurd to even think that Jennie would be that desperate. Although, she had been willing to hire out as a maid, which in some circles might be put in the same category as those women from Tinkersville who'd head out to the mines every payday.

"I fail to see that it's any of your business how I spend my mornings," she answered, turning up the path toward the house.

He grasped her shoulder and spun her back around. "Damn it, Jennie. When are you going to let down some of that stubborn pride of yours and let me help you? What were you doing with Dennis? Surely the mine doesn't need *cleaning?*"

She pulled out of his grasp and rubbed her shoulder where his hand had been, though he was sure he hadn't been rough. "You might try seeing how proud you'd be, Mr. Jones, if you'd been shunned and called ugly names by half the townsfolk."

Carter hesitated. Yes, he understood that kind of pride. He'd already had a lifetime's share of ugly taunts. His voice more calm, he said, "Those people aren't worth getting upset over, Jennie. Believe me, you have to learn to pay no attention to people who are that ignorant. You need to toughen up that lovely soft skin of yours."

He started to reach a hand toward her cheek as the personal remark slid them both back to the dangerous territory they'd traveled the night in Virginia City. It seemed to keep happening. And Carter was darned if he could figure out if he welcomed it or dreaded it. Jennie's response was less equivocal. Instant anger.

"What makes you such an authority on insults? Did you get some criticism on how well your shirts were pressed at that fancy school of yours?"

Carter sighed. "My life didn't start at Harvard, Jennie. If you'd let down that guard of yours for a moment or two sometime, we might have a chance to discuss exactly how much I might know about insults."

Suddenly the bravado disappeared and once again he saw the scared young woman who was doing her best to tackle a world that had not been particularly kind to her over the past year.

"I'm sorry," she said. "You're absolutely right. You've done nothing but offer to help me, and I always seem to end up railing at you."

Carter smiled. "We do seem to set sparks off."

"Perhaps we should just realize that we have conflicting temperaments, and leave it at that."

"Perhaps." In Carter's mind, it was the attraction that was causing their problems more than the conflict, but he refrained from saying so. Even now, irritated with her as he was, he could feel his body's response to her. He had to shift his gaze away from the slight heaving of her full breasts.

Jennie offered a peacemaking smile and extended her hand. "So, thank you for your various offers of help, Carter, but I think I'll be fine on my own."

The breeze was picking up and he felt chill on the back of his neck, but she had a sheen of sweat at her temple and along the line of her jaw. He tried to blink away the memory of kissing her there. "What about your financial problems? The hospital bills?"

"I'll be able to manage."

He frowned and said bluntly, "How?"

Jennie looked as if she were exerting control to keep from snapping at him, but her voice was pleasant. "Now, see. There we go again. Those conflicting personalities. You can't seem to get this through your head. My financial problems are not the concern of you or any other man. In fact, I don't intend that they ever will be."

"I'm not trying to imply that you're not capable—"

"Good," she interrupted. "Because I am. And now, Carter, if you don't mind, I've had a tiring day and I have yet to get the supper started."

He had no choice but to let her go. He stood at the end of her walk until she'd disappeared inside the house, debating whether he should march after her and demand to know exactly what kind of tiring day she'd had, up there in the mountains. It was none of his business, she'd told him in so many words. Never would be. But it was driving him crazy.

Jennie giggled a little as she shut the door behind her. She'd seen the frustration on Carter's face. He'd wanted to know what she was up to. There'd been that other kind of interest there, too. He'd had the same look she'd seen at the hotel in Virginia City. And she had to admit that it evoked a response somewhere low in her insides. But just because her body had discovered these unruly sensations didn't mean that she was about to begin letting a man interfere with her life.

She was perfectly capable of handling things on her own. Granted, it had been the miners' help that had gotten her the lifesaving job at the mine, but it would be her hard work and skill that would make it successful.

With the energy of one who's found a way around a huge obstacle in her path, she bustled around the kitchen, fixing chops and cabbage for the evening supper and starting to peel a barrelful of apples to take up to the mine tomorrow for pies.

When Barnaby came in from school, she enlisted his help. "It sure takes a lot of apples," he said, perched on a stool to reach the kitchen counter.

"The men eat a lot, because they work so hard."

"You work hard, too, Jennie, and you don't eat a lot."

In fact, she'd lost some weight over the past few months. Some of her clothes were sagging. "I eat my share. And I'm not as big as those men are."

"You're sure not as big as Dennis," Barnaby said, and chuckled. "At school they'd call him a fatso."

"Which would be quite unkind," Jennie chided. "It's never nice to call names, particularly ones that might hurt people's sensitivities."

"Their what?"

"Their feelings. It happens especially when you tease about things that are of special importance to people. Things that they feel deep down."

Barnaby was silent for a long moment, then he said. "Like not having a father."

"Yes. Or being fatter than others or not quite as smart."

"I'm glad I'm not fat or dumb," Barnaby said with youthful bluntness.

"Everyone has weaknesses in one area or another. The important thing is to be kind to all types of people."

Barnaby nodded gravely. "They should tell that to the boys at school."

"Yes, they should. The teacher should and their parents should, too." The way some of the prominent adults around town had been acting, it was probably too much to hope that their children would be growing up to be any more tolerant.

"So I'm not supposed to tell anyone that you're cooking up at the mine?" Barnaby asked. Jennie had told Barnaby of her decision to keep her job secret.

"That's right. It'll be easier to keep it just between us."

"And the silverheels won't tell anyone?"

"No. You know they don't talk much to the regular townsfolk here."

"Did you tell Carter?"

"No."

Barnaby looked surprised. "I thought you'd at least tell him."

"Well...no. Why did you think that?"

"'Cause he's in love with you. Usually people tell each other things when they're in love." He stopped and looked a little uncertain. "But maybe you're not in love with him back."

Jennie didn't know whether her urge to laugh came from Barnaby's attempt to sound worldly with such an adult topic or from her discomfort at his assertion. "Carter's not in love with me," she said firmly.

Barnaby finished peeling the last apple in the pile and sat back with a sigh of relief. "Yes, he is."

Jennie hesitated at the absolute certainty in his voice. "Now you have to chop them," she said, waving at the peeled apples. "Neat pieces about a half-inch thick. Why do you say that?"

Barnaby sat forward again and picked up the first apple. "Well, he looks at you all the time. I mean, *all* the time. And he looks at you the way Chauncy White looks at Susan Hardwick in the back row at school. And they're *sweethearts.*"

Jennie took several furious chops at the apple she was holding, her eyes down. Finally she said, "Well, Carter and I are *not* sweethearts. I'm too busy to have a sweetheart."

Barnaby shrugged. "If you say so." He attacked his apple with careful precision, making each piece exactly the same size as the first. But after a full minute had passed, he looked directly up at her, his young eyes suddenly wise, and said simply, "I wonder if Carter knows that."

The conversation with Barnaby stayed with Jennie the entire evening and into the next morning as she once again went up to the mine and prepared a huge vat of scalloped potatoes and ham, which was sucked clean by the end of the appreciative miners' meal.

She half expected to see Carter sitting on the steps again when Dennis brought her back home. She wouldn't put it past him to check up on her. But the steps and house were empty. Perhaps he'd finally taken her at her word that she wanted to deal with her problems by herself.

Perversely, that thought made her a little sad. Make up your mind, Jennie, she berated herself. You either are going to stand on your own two feet or not. She'd already resolved not to risk getting involved with one of those males who are around when they need you but not when you need them. Just because a particular one of the species happened to have gray eyes that made her breath catch when they looked at her was no reason to change her opinion.

She went into the kitchen to deposit the heavy sack containing two large briskets she'd brought down from the mining camp. She intended to soak them overnight with some of the spices from her own kitchen. When she got used to her new schedule, she'd arrange to get help transporting some of her kitchen supplies and food up the mountain. The mine had its own larder, but it consisted of simple fare. Jennie looked forward to trying some of her favorite recipes on the men. They were so complimentary about the easy dishes she'd tried so far. She loved her job.

Perhaps she should tell Carter what she was doing, after all. It was a perfectly respectable employment. Except for the fact that she was working with all men, she couldn't see how the position could be criticized. And, at twenty dollars a week, she was probably making almost as much as Carter himself. That would steam a pleat or two out of his starchy shirts, she thought with a smile.

She thought about the matter all the while she prepared the briskets for soaking and whipped up a batter of potato pancakes to serve with the leftover chops for supper. Finally she reached a kind of compromise. She wouldn't seek Carter out to tell him about her job, but if he questioned her on the subject again, she'd tell him the truth. It probably didn't matter anyway, she thought, attempting an indifference she couldn't entirely master. After the way she'd snapped at him yesterday, Carter wasn't likely to seek her out, and with her busy schedule, she'd rarely get into town. She might never see the man again.

The silverheels had consumed a frightening quantity of potato pancakes and were in no hurry to move away from the table, so Barnaby ran to answer the knock at the front door. Jennie knew immediately who it would be. Her mother would have said that she'd *willed* him there.

"Hey, Jones—have you finally gotten your senses back?" Dennis greeted him. "Your room's a-waitin' upstairs. I can't understand how you can sit down there in town and eat that hotel food while we're feasting on these." He pointed to the platter where one lonely potato pancake remained as the silverheels' token tribute to table manners.

"I could make up some more in a minute," Jennie offered.

Carter shook his head. "I've had supper, thanks. Though you're right, Dennis, I'm sure it was nothing like yours."

Jennie stood. "Have a seat. I'll just help Barnaby bring out the puddings."

"And then after supper you can join our game, just like old times," Smitty suggested to Carter.

Carter looked around at the three miners, then at Jennie. "Ah…thank you," he said, sitting down at an empty place. "I'd be obliged for the dessert, but then I…" He looked uncharacteristically ill at ease. "I was hoping to be able to speak with you, Jennie."

"Come sparkin', eh?" Dennis said with a wink.

Jennie almost dropped the plate she was carrying. From the doorway Barnaby grinned and mouthed to her, "Told you so."

Without answering, she swung into the sanctuary of the kitchen. So he'd come after all. His curiosity had probably gotten the better of him. Well, she'd satisfy it. When the silverheels started their game, she and Carter could go into her office and she'd tell him all about her new employment. That should settle things. He wouldn't have to feel guilty anymore about the lost rent money, and maybe then he'd leave her in peace.

She put the dishes of butterscotch pudding on a tray, wondering once again why everything suddenly seemed so much more *alive* when Carter Jones was in the vicinity.

"I told you he was sweet on you," Barnaby said

in a stage whisper as he came swinging through the door with the last of the dishes. "You can go sit out on the front porch swing and moon over each other."

Jennie felt the heat of a blush rising around her neck. She wondered what a boy of Barnaby's age knew about front porch swings and such. She was more or less certain he'd be shocked to learn that she'd already been considerably more intimate with Carter than mooning on a porch swing.

"He just said he wanted to talk with me. It's probably some kind of legal stuff."

Barnaby grabbed one of the puddings off the tray. "I don't think so. Can I have this one? It's the biggest."

Jennie nodded and turned to carry the rest of the desserts into the dining room where the miners and Carter were laughing over some story, just as they had the nights he'd stayed here. They had been enjoyable evenings, she thought with a touch of regret. The fastidious Carter was such a good foil for the rough-and-tumble miners. And he always gave as good as he got.

She handed around the puddings, noting that Carter looked especially handsome tonight. He was letting his hair grow longer so that it looked a bit shaggy, making him seem less formal and austere. Jennie was hit with a sudden urge to run her fingers through it, which almost made her drop the dish of pudding she was handing him.

She had trouble concentrating on the conversation, impatient to be alone with Carter and hear what he had to say. But the miners were enjoying the renewed acquaintance with their friend, and it was almost eight o'clock before Carter made a rather deliberate show of looking at his pocket watch. Immediately Dennis got to his feet and said, "C'mon lads. Carter didn't come over here tonight to see our pretty faces."

Smitty and Brad shuffled up more reluctantly and followed Dennis out of the room, as Carter gave him a little salute of thanks.

Barnaby had schoolwork to attend to and had gone up to his own room, which left Carter and Jennie alone at the big dining room table.

"Would you like to go sit back in my office?" she asked, suddenly nervous. He had that look in his eyes again.

"No. I haven't had a chance to tell you that you look lovely tonight."

"Thank you. I was thinking the same about you," she said a little shyly.

"I look lovely?" he asked with a lift of his eyebrow.

She nodded. "I mean…I like your hair longer like that."

Carter laughed. "I haven't had time to visit the barber. I've been too busy thinking about the problems of a certain young lady in town who seems to have cast some sort of spell over me."

"Who is she?" Jennie asked, relaxing. Unlike their abrasive meeting yesterday or their tension-racked encounter at the hotel in Virginia City, this time he was teasing, flirting with her. This wasn't as hard as she'd thought.

"Oh, you wouldn't know her," he answered.

"She's one of those women who spend nights in hotels with strange men."

"A hussy."

"Mmm." His laugh was gentle, his eyes warm. Jennie felt herself sliding once again under the influence of his charm.

"I'm surprised you're thinking about her so much, if she's such a lost cause," she said.

"Oh, I don't know that I'd say she was beyond redemption. I have it on good authority that her reputation as a fallen woman is highly undeserved."

"Ah, the poor thing. Town gossip can be so cruel." It felt good to joke about the scandal after so many months of fighting it.

Carter grew serious and reached his hand across the table toward her. "No one knows about that night, Jennie. There's no reason to worry about it."

She laughed. "I'm not worried, Carter. The only reason I care a fig about my reputation is because I know people like Mrs. Billingsley could make life miserable for Kate and her baby if I'm not careful. Otherwise, I wouldn't care if you published an account of that night in the newspaper."

He took her hand and gave it a squeeze that she felt as a tingle all the way up her arm. "You're a remarkable woman, Jennie Sheridan. I've never met anyone quite like you."

She let her hand rest in his, relaxed and content. In spite of her resolutions earlier to never count on a man for support, the warmth and strength of his fingers around hers felt good. It was purely a physical sensation, she told herself. Nothing more. It changed nothing.

But as she sat listening to his entertaining account of the cases he'd dealt with that day, Jennie realized that there was something about being with him that made her feel more complete than she had since she'd lost her parents all those months ago.

The evening had passed quickly, and she hadn't told him about her job after all. After their other more highly charged encounters, they seemed to have reached an unspoken agreement to keep the mood light and upbeat. Carter had made just one reference to her job search, and she'd told him that for the time being she wouldn't be looking in town anymore. He'd seemed relieved that he wouldn't have to go into his arguments against her maid idea again, and they'd moved on to another topic.

Neither realized how much time had passed when the miners stopped at the door of the dining room to say good-night. They'd already finished their game, and Jennie and Carter had not even moved out of the dining room.

Carter had hastened to take his leave. It appeared that he hadn't wanted to test the limits of their pleasant, innocent meeting by being alone with her when the rest of the household had retired upstairs.

Jennie, too, had been relieved when he left immediately after the miners said good-night. Or at least she told herself she was relieved. But she found the memory of their talk pleasantly stimulating as she worked on the meal the next day at the mine. When she got home, she took the time to take a bath before getting ready for the evening, just in case he might decide to drop in again. And it was not totally a surprise when he did.

That night she told him that if he planned on stopping by to visit "the silverheels" again the next night, he might as well arrive a half hour earlier and take supper with them. He'd clarified that it was not the miners he'd come to visit and then promptly accepted the invitation with the condition that he be allowed to bring some wine.

By the next week, they'd established a pattern, and Carter flat out demanded to pay a weekly sum of three dollars for board alone, no room, which made his visits now expected and no longer subject to Jennie's invitation. She hadn't told him that the extra money was no longer as crucial as it had once been. In fact, she'd never told him about her job at the mine. It was easier having that part of her life be a little secret between herself and the crew of miners she fed each day, all of whom were now dubbed silverheels, much to their delight.

Some evenings Carter joined the card game, but most nights, he'd tell the miners to go ahead without him. "I'll just help Jennie with the dishes," he'd say. "Perhaps join you later."

And then he and Jennie would clean the kitchen together while he entertained her with tales of his life back East and his first couple jobs as a fledgling attorney. He didn't tell her that he'd come West because he'd finally determined that a man with no name would never have real opportunity to get ahead in the old-money, old-society East. In a raw state like Nevada, a man's deeds were more important than his name.

"I'll pay you for another week," he said as they finished up kitchen duty after his tenth day of dining with them. Jennie paused a moment as she reached up to put away a platter. "That is, if the arrangement is working out to your satisfaction," he added.

She put the platter in place and turned around. "It's just that I was wondering if instead of the money this next week, I could ask you to do me a favor."

Carter put his hands on his hips. "Hell's bells, woman. Haven't I been begging you to let me be of some help to you for weeks now?"

He was smiling, but Jennie could tell he was serious. But that didn't make her request any easier to voice. She was enjoying the friendly, less intense pattern into which their relationship had fallen, and she was reluctant to bring up the memory of that time when they both had almost spoiled things beyond repair. "I want to see Kate again," she said slowly. "She's getting near her time, and I have to know she's all right."

Carter's smile died. It was obvious that he, too, was remembering what had happened the last time they'd gone to see Kate together. But that time the storm had *forced* them to stay overnight. "We could pick a day that looks really fair," she said, her voice small.

He stiffened, but hesitated only a moment before answering, "Of course I'll take you. We'll leave early in the morning so that we'll have the whole day to get there, have a nice visit and get safely back."

She nodded. The simple thought of setting out alone in a carriage with him had started her heart pounding. But Carter sounded as if he were anxious not to get trapped again. "I could ask for Dr. Millard's carriage and wait until Sunday, if it would be too much trouble," she said, unsure.

"Not at all. We'll go tomorrow."

His voice was businesslike, controlled. There was no evidence that he was feeling any of the nervousness that was suddenly making Jennie's dinner sit uncomfortably in her middle. They'd been able to maintain a friendly, arm's length relationship these past several days. Perhaps this would work. And she *did* want to see Kate. She'd have to arrange to prepare food ahead of time up at the mine and ask the silverheels to pitch in and serve it themselves. "I'll need a day to get ready. Could we go Wednesday?"

"Wednesday it is," Carter agreed.

They looked at each other across the kitchen, self-conscious for the first time in days. Carter's gray eyes were inscrutable. Jennie couldn't tell what he was thinking. Her own head had suddenly flooded with the memories of the kisses they'd shared at the hotel on their last trip.

"We'll just go early in the morning and be back by midafternoon," Jennie said again, lightly.

"Yes."

"And if it looks as if there might be a storm that day, we simply won't go. We'll put it off."

Carter walked across the room and put his hands on her upper arms, turning her to face him. It was the first physical contact they'd had since the night he'd held her hand across the table. "We won't let anything happen, Jennie," he said quietly. "It'll be just fine."

She nodded, her throat closing. "I hope so," she said. Then she slipped out of his grasp and continued putting away the plates.

Chapter Eleven

Part of Jennie's sour humor was undoubtedly due to the fact that she'd stayed up until past midnight the previous evening getting the meat pies ready for the silverheels to take to the mine with them. She'd arranged with the mine foreman to take the day off, but she'd agreed to send up food that was ready to eat so that she wouldn't lose out on a day's pay. It had meant that she'd had to get Carter out of the way immediately after supper so that she could start in chopping the vegetables and meat and cooking the pies.

She'd awakened still tired. Carter had done his best to lift her spirits, stopping at one point to leap out of the carriage and pick her a bouquet full of wildflowers. But just as her spirits had started to rise, they'd arrived at the hospital and her mood plummeted once again. Kate had looked sallow and listless, her stomach now an impossibly huge bulge under the rough hospital blanket.

Lyle had been there, and this time had not offered to leave to give the sisters a chance for privacy. It had given Jennie an odd feeling. It was as if *she* were the visitor, the intruder, while Lyle was family. She came away with the distinct feeling that the arrogant banker's son had somehow seized possession of Kate while she was too weak to fight any longer for her independence. And there didn't seem to be a thing Jennie could do about it.

On the way out, she'd been accosted by an officious hospital administrator who had demanded to know when further payment could be expected for Kate's bill. It had been a real pleasure to pull out her reticule and plunk forty dollars cash into the man's hand. But that meant her entire hard-earned mine salary was gone. And it had covered only the first installment on the hospital bill. Once the actual birth came, the sum would be staggering.

Carter tried to draw her out as they headed back up the mountain road toward Vermillion, asking the source of her lack of animation, but she didn't feel like burdening him with her troubles. She'd done her duty and seen Kate—though her sister hadn't seemed all that pleased to see her. Now Jennie just wanted to get back home without any further distress.

"Are you cold?" Carter asked. There was a late fall chill to the air. "There's a blanket underneath the seat. Why don't you get it and cover up? Maybe you can even sleep a little."

She gave him a grateful smile. "I'm afraid I haven't been very good company today, Carter. You've been so nice, and I've been something of a grouch."

"You look a little tired. I think you're still working too hard."

"I'm sleepy. It must be the rocking of the carriage."

The small tandem rig Carter had hired was much older and more worn than the one they'd had on their previous trip. It was all the livery had available, he'd explained apologetically when he'd arrived to fetch her early that morning. But Jennie found the back and forth sway of the old carriage oddly soothing.

"Take a nap if you want. It would probably be good for you." He reached under the seat and pulled out a gray wool blanket, then shook it with one hand and tucked it around her. Its warmth was comforting. She pulled it tight around herself.

"You're a nice man, Carter Jones," she said sleepily. "I wasn't so sure when I first met you and you were trying to send my sister away, but I've decided to forgive you for all that because you've been so good to me lately."

Carter smiled. "Perhaps I have ulterior motives."

His voice was teasing, but she answered him seriously. "No. If you had ulterior motives, you would have taken advantage of me that night when you had me alone at the hotel. You wouldn't have…stopped when you did."

His smile had faded. He paused a moment as if deciding whether he dare let the conversation continue in this direction. Finally he said, "I didn't want to stop, that's for sure."

She hesitated as well, then said. "I know. And I almost wished you hadn't."

It was as far as they could take it. Both knew that any further declarations along that line would take them on a path they were determined not to follow. Jennie leaned against the buggy hood and closed her eyes. She was exhausted.

Perhaps she would take that nap after all. It would be better than continuing to think how her sister had looked helpless and resigned while Lyle acted as if he were in charge of her care. And it would be better than continuing to sit close to Carter, wondering what it would be like if he suddenly stopped the carriage and took her in his arms.

This old rig does certainly wobble was her last thought before she drifted off to sleep.

She was awakened by a crash and a sudden jolt forward, then to the side. "Lord 'a' mercy!" she exclaimed, her eyes flying open as she slid down the seat that was now tilting crazily to the right.

Carter held on to the carriage stanchion with his left hand and reached for her with his right. "Damnation!"

"What happened?"

"The blasted thing just fell apart." With his arm still around her waist to prevent her from slipping out of the carriage, he swung his head over the side. "I think the axle's broken clear through."

Now wide-awake, Jennie was suddenly aware that his hand was flat on her soft stomach and that he was holding her against him in a most intimate posture. "I should probably get down," she said.

"I don't want you to fall. Hold on there until I can

lift you down.'' When she had taken hold of the other stanchion, he climbed nimbly over her and jumped to the ground, then reached up and lifted her out of the carriage.

She laughed. "I'm not a rag doll, Carter. I could have gotten down by myself." He didn't smile in response to her laughter, and as he put her down, the reality of the situation began to dawn on her. "Is it really broken?"

Carter was already on his knees looking under the carriage. He stood up, dusting off his hands. "It's really broken. Clear through. If it were a wheel I might be able to fix it, but not this."

"Do you think someone will come along?" She looked up and down the narrow road. It was already darkened by the late afternoon shadows of the trees.

"I don't think we can count on it. This road just goes up to Vermillion, then stops. It never has much traffic."

"So what does that mean? We have to walk home?"

He shook his head. "It's fifteen miles or more. You'd never make it."

She started to bristle. "I can walk as far as you can, I suspect."

For the first time since the breakdown, Carter smiled. "I suspect you can. But those shiny shoes of yours would be a sorry sight after the first couple miles."

Jennie swept aside her skirt to look ruefully down at her patent slippers. What devil's vanity had possessed her to take a cross-country trip dressed as if she were going to a dance? She thought about the serviceable leather boots she wore each day up to the mine. They were sitting neatly at the bottom of her wardrobe back home.

He walked over to the horse, which looked at least as old as the carriage itself and in about the same shape. "This nag could carry you, but not both of us. I could send you on ahead riding her and walk home myself. Could you ride her without a saddle, do you think?"

"I'm not sure, but it doesn't matter because I'm not leaving you," Jennie said firmly.

Carter ran a hand over the horse's flank. "These reins would work, just gather them up and hold them shorter. And we have the blanket to put over her back."

"I'm not leaving you," she repeated.

He sighed. "The only sensible thing to do is go back, hire another rig and start again in the morning."

"Go back to Virginia City?"

"Yes."

They were silent a moment as each had their own thoughts on what it would mean to spend another night alone together in a hotel.

"How far back is it?"

"About four miles, I'd say. Downhill. We'll be back there before dark."

Carter started unhitching the horse. "I'll lead her and you can ride. That way those pretty shoes of yours won't get worn down."

Jennie took another disgusted look at her feet. "I'm sorry," she said, resigned.

"No, I'm sorry that I couldn't get us a better rig today. You're going to start thinking I planned this, just like I planned the storm the last time we traveled together."

Jennie took a quick look at the sky. It was a cloudless day, though not too warm. The sun was already sinking, kicking up a late afternoon breeze. She shivered. "We could rent the rig and travel back tonight."

"In the dark? On this road? No, thank you. One broken axle per trip is enough for me."

He reached to pick up the blanket from the tilting carriage seat, then arranged it over the horse's swayed back. Jennie eyed the setup doubtfully, bit her lip and held her hand out to him. "All right, then. Help me up on the beast."

By sundown, they still hadn't reached Virginia City.

"Are you holding on all right up there? You won't slide off going down this hill?" Carter asked her just before the road changed to a steeper descending grade.

Jennie nodded, unconcerned about the road. "Barnaby and the miners will be worried. I hope they saved some of the meat pies for supper."

"Meat pies?" Carter's mind was obviously on the task of navigating the hill, not on the stomachs of the people who were safely back in Vermillion.

Jennie stretched her back. It *was* awkward perched sideways on the horse this way, holding on to the long carriage reins that Carter had coiled neatly between the horse's shoulder blades. "I'd just as soon walk for a while," she told him.

He reviewed the situation for a moment, then nodded and reached up to help her down. The brief contact as she slid into his arms made them both stiffen. In spite of the friendly evenings they'd spent recently and the polite distance they'd maintained throughout the drive today, that instant heat was hovering just below the surface. Carter recognized it immediately, though in his experience it had never been quite this instantaneous or quite this compelling.

He hoped Jennie was less aware. In particular he hoped that her naïveté would make it unlikely that she would notice his body's all too obvious signs of arousal. He stepped back from her quickly. "Steady?" he asked, keeping his voice light.

She held on to his upper arm just a minute for support, then let go. "Yes. But you're right about these shoes." She kicked one lightly in the dirt of the road.

"Do you want to get back up on the horse?"

"No." She sighed. "I want to be home in bed."

Carter wanted to be in a bed at the moment, too. Or at least, his body did. He lifted his face to the increasingly chill breeze and tried to cool down. He looked down to see that her shoulders were shaking. "Let's pick up the pace," he said. "You're going to take a chill."

Once again Jennie stood in the middle of the plush lobby carpet of the International as Carter secured rooms for the night. There was the same shining mahogany reception desk, the wrought iron torch lamps, the elegant cage elevator. Just like the last time.

Carter walked over to where she was waiting and handed her a key. "My room is next to yours again." He spoke in a rush as if embarrassed. "But it's only because I don't feel comfortable with you alone here. If you should need anything, I want to be close by."

She nodded. He'd proved honorable enough before when, goodness knows, she'd given him enough opportunity not to be. She wasn't going to start to question his motives now.

"And I ordered you a bath," he added, smiling and making a vague gesture at the horse blanket she'd finally pulled around herself when the cold had become too intense toward the end of their walk. It smelled of horseflesh.

"What should I do with this?" she asked, wrinkling her nose in distaste.

He took it from her. "I'll have the hotel laundry deal with it."

He disappeared for a moment, then returned without the blanket. There was something to be said for having a man to take charge of things, Jennie thought. It wasn't that she wouldn't be capable of handling it all by herself, but it was nice to depend on someone else for a change.

She'd better not get used to it though. Tomorrow she'd be back in Vermillion, running the household and cooking for the miners and worrying about her bills. This one night of having a man to take care of her was just make-believe, like the fairy stories her mother used to tell. In those tales, the handsome prince had always taken care of the beautiful princess.

Kate had thought Sean Flaherty a handsome prince, Jennie reminded herself.

Still, she was enjoying her one night of pretend, she decided, as she luxuriated in the warm bath Carter had had sent up for her. Afterward, she donned her same dress, not so unhappy now that she'd worn her blue silk instead of a more sensible traveling outfit. Carter's eyes, when he came for her to go down to supper, told her that her efforts to look renewed and fresh had been successful.

They went down together to take the same corner table they'd had before in the dimly lit hotel dining room. Carter ordered them another delicious meal. This time without asking her, he'd asked for wine— a whole bottle, though Carter drank the larger share. But when he suggested a brandy following dinner, she shook her head. The wine had taken away the last of the chill from their cold walk and left her pleasantly groggy.

"Well, if we're going to get an early start in the morning, I should get you to bed." He spoke loudly, in a businesslike tone that woke her up.

It was the same long, dark hall. She remembered walking down it that last time, wondering if he was going to kiss her. Then she'd all but invited him to do so, and he had. And they'd ended up in her bed on the verge of something that she still couldn't fully imagine.

"So we'll start early," he said again as they neared

her room. His voice was altered, raspy. He was re-membering that other night, too. She was sure of it.

"Yes, I have to get back." She couldn't quite say why she still hadn't told him about her job at the mine. She'd avoided the subject for so many nights that it had become harder and harder to find a way to explain it. Her secrecy would seem to imply that there *was* something wrong in the arrangement.

They were at her door. He hesitated. "So I guess we should say good-night," he said.

The single wall sconce at the end of the hall was the only light, but it was enough to see his eyes, glit-tering gray. "All right," she whispered, forgetting to breathe. "Good night." She held the key in her hand and made no move to open her door.

After a long moment, he took it from her and reached around her to put it in the lock. His arm brushed along her back, almost like an embrace. The door swung open behind her. "There," he said, straightening and holding the key out to her.

"Thank you." The words were barely audible.

"Oh hell, Jennie," he said then, and swept her against him. His lips crashed against her mouth as he picked her up totally and carried her backward into her room. Their lips stayed locked as he kicked the door shut behind him with his foot.

Her arms clung to his neck. The toes of her slippers touched the tops of his boots. "I didn't think you would ever kiss me again," she pulled away to mur-mur. "I thought you didn't want to...I thought..."

"Shut up, sweetheart," he said, then shut her up with his mouth and tongue and lips. His body reacted instantly as it had earlier that day back on the road, but this time he made no effort to hide it from her. He put his hand below her waist, almost to the swell of her bottom and pushed her against him, groaning a little as his hardness pressed into her soft belly.

He tried to dredge some vestige of conscience and reason out of the depths of his wine- and desire-fogged mind, but it was hopeless. He'd wanted her since the day he'd seen her coming toward him with her basket of groceries. He'd lain awake at night in a sweat remembering the taste of her lips. She'd filled his dreams, awake and asleep, for weeks. And now she was in his arms, passionate and wanting.

His hands were shaking. He couldn't remember ever needing a woman this much. He scooped her up and walked over to the bed, like some kind of dream sequence repeat of the night he'd done this very thing in an identical room. They'd stopped that night. They'd been sensible. He pushed the memory away.

He set her down next to the bed and leaned to kiss her neck. "You smell so good," he told her. "Lilacs."

"From the bath you ordered. Better than horse blanket," she said with a low, mellow laugh that made his blood sing.

He continued to place gentle kisses up and down her neck as he began unbuttoning the top of her dress. "I spent the entire hour before supper picturing you in that bath. I wanted to break down your door."

She laughed again. "They would have thrown you out of the hotel, Mr. Jones. Think of the scandal."

Scandal. Carter's conscience tried to surface once

again. Making love to a virgin without the sanctity of marriage would be considered a scandal by most people.

From her neck, his lips followed the trail of opened buttons to the gentle swell of her breast. He could feel it on his lips, but could see little in the dark room. "Shall I turn on a light?" he asked, his voice low and husky.

"No!"

Her panicky response was a raw reminder that she was still innocent. But as he started to pull away, she reached to unfasten the ribbons of her corset, suddenly freeing her breasts entirely to his touch. Almost reverently, he placed his hands over them and felt the nipples swell into his palms.

"Ah, sweetheart, your body is beautiful, ready for loving."

She pulled his head up to her mouth again and kissed him hungrily while his fingers toyed with her nipples. All at once, they were removing the rest of her clothing, then his, and pushing back the bedclothes to fall onto the starchy sheets, bodies entwined.

Jennie had the sensation of falling, tumbling like a boulder crashing down a mountainside. Her breasts had grown hard and incredibly sensitive with the touch of his roughened fingers. Then as she lay back against the pillows, he moved over her and encircled one of her nipples with his tongue. The feeling was exquisite, causing waves of feeling to radiate downward into her groin.

She gave a whimpery kind of groan and could feel

his smile against her sensitive skin. He laved the tip of one breast, then the other as Jennie lay still, too focused on the incredible new sensation to move.

"I thought about these, too, in your bath," he said hoarsely. "These trim, firm breasts, just the right size to fill my hands." He matched the action to the words, and she squirmed with pleasure.

He moved next to her, bringing their entire bodies into contact. As his lips continued their magic on her nipples, distracting her, his hand made circles along the warm skin of her stomach and abdomen, finally slipping between her legs to a place where even Jennie herself had never explored. She let her knees fall open slightly to give him greater access. He synchronized the movement of his fingers with the tugging at her breast, and as the rhythm became quicker, suddenly, without warning, her body exploded in a wild pulsing that made her grip his arms and cry out.

"Hush, sweetheart," he murmured, lifting his head from her breast. "Or they really will throw me out of the hotel."

He pulled himself over her and then inside her. It was odd and a little uncomfortable. Jennie had known that this was what was to happen, but after the magic of that one intense explosion, she felt confused and a little disappointed.

She tried to summon back the magic feelings that had started building at the hotel room door, but as he began to move inside her, the discomfort increased. She hadn't realized that a man was so large and so hard. With the cooling of her ardor, came the realization of what had just happened.

She was no longer a virgin. She'd surrendered part of herself to a man who had promised her nothing more than a ride back home. She was as bad as Kate. No, she was worse than Kate. At least Kate had thought she'd been in love with Sean Flaherty. Jennie had no such illusions. Falling in love was for fools.

Once again, Carter sensed her withdrawal, but this time it was too late. He'd already entered her. He'd felt the tearing, the tightness. The deed was done, and still his body clamored for release. It took only three or four quick thrusts and then he pulled away to finish outside her warmth. It was the only way he'd ever taken a woman. It was his cardinal rule. Someday he might marry and experience the ultimate pleasure of depositing his seed inside his wife's body, but until that time, he was determined not to breed a bastard.

Jennie was ominously quiet beneath him. He rolled to one side and leaned over to kiss her gently on the nose, the cheek, the lips. "I didn't hurt you, did I, sweetheart?" he asked.

She didn't answer, but in the darkness he could see the shake of her head.

He kissed her shoulder. "It's never too easy for a woman the first time, they say."

She still said nothing.

"But, so…are you all right?" He was beginning to worry. And the conscience that he'd held at bay during their frenzied lovemaking was now making its appearance in full battle gear.

She reached to draw a portion of the sheet over her naked body. "You didn't hurt me," she said.

Carter froze at the coolness of her tone. What had

happened to the laughing, mellow-voiced lover of only a few minutes before?

He sat up and pulled the covers around them, folding the tops of the sheets neatly over the blankets. Then he lay back down beside her. "Are we going to talk about this?" he asked.

He heard her sigh in the darkness. "I'm awfully tired," she said.

She was obviously already regretting what had just happened between them. Carter tried to assuage the guilt that was creating an uncomfortable pressure in his chest. He had *not* seduced her, darn it. This thing between them had been building for weeks. Their lovemaking tonight had just happened naturally, like a spontaneous fire in a forest. And it had definitely been mutual. He moved close to her again, sliding an arm under her head so that she lay cradled against his shoulder. "This is new for me, too," he said. "I've never—"

"I find that hard to believe," she interrupted with a humorless laugh.

He continued gently, "What I was going to say is that I've made love, but never with a virgin. It was…a very special gift."

"Do you men take extra pride in that?" she asked.

"That's not fair," he chided. "You act as if I'd planned this in order to…have my way with you."

"Well, you're the one who hired the faulty carriage."

He pulled his arm from behind her and sat up, indignation taking over as the last residue of pleasure faded. "And what? I deliberately broke the axle? You're not even talking sense, Jennie."

She sat up beside him and said a little contritely, "You're right. I'm sorry. You were doing me a favor to bring me here to see Kate, and it's not your fault that we were stranded. But I'm trying to understand what just happened to us here."

He reached for her hand under the sheets. "What happened is that two people who've been attracted to each other for a long time finally found it impossible to refrain from seeking satisfaction for their desires."

She pulled her hand away. "You make it sound very logical."

"It's the truth. You can't deny this has been coming for a long time. We've both felt it."

She didn't try to deny it, but her voice was dispirited as she said. "Well, now we've satisfied our desires, as you put it. I guess we should get some sleep."

"There's more to it than that, Jennie. You didn't give it a proper chance." The moon had risen, casting a ray of light through the open curtains. In its shine on her cheeks he caught the glint of tears. So she wasn't as indifferent as she was sounding. "Aw, sweetheart," he said, reaching to lift her to his lap. "Don't cry. It was beautiful. *You* were beautiful—my sweet, passionate, generous lover. Don't be sorry. Don't spoil it, darling. Let me show you how good it can be."

He started to kiss her again and this time their mouths met with a sensual familiarity. He continued kissing her without any other caresses until he felt her initial reluctance turn once again to interest and then to arousal.

With the edge off his sexual needs, this time he was able to be more deliberate. He lavished attention on all parts of her with his hands and his mouth, from her arched feet to the top of her high forehead, until she was vibrating like a finely tuned orchestra, all its sections harmonious.

She murmured his name and clung to him as he entered her again, unbelievably just as hard as he'd been the first time. But now she was sharing more fully in the experience. There was no hesitancy, no retreat. She arched her back and moved with him, her face in the moonlight a beautiful mixture of revelation and urgency. It set up a thunder throughout his body as they drove together toward completion. Hers came first, but his followed so instantaneously that the pulsing of their bodies merged.

He was reluctant to risk words. It had been such perfection, even without prior experience, she must realize it. He gathered her close in his arms and arranged the covers around them again. They lay pressed tightly together for several minutes, the only motion made by his hand running lightly up and down her arm.

She was the first to speak. "You were right," she whispered. "There was more to it."

He gave a low chuckle. "You're a fast learner, Jennie Sheridan."

"I think I had a good teacher."

"No, it wasn't me, sweetheart."

They were silent for several more minutes, both

drifting to sleep, when Jennie said groggily, "Thank you for not losing patience with me when I snapped at you about the carriage."

He pulled her closer and gave her a light kiss on the nose. "I don't know, sweetheart. If I'd known the outcome, I just might have rigged that axle to give way."

She gave him a sleepy smile. "So I'm right to be mistrustful."

The observation was made in jest, but it made him pause. Hell, yes, she was right to be mistrustful. She was a beautiful, young single woman, alone in the world without protectors, without any family except a sister who obviously couldn't even look after her own welfare, much less Jennie's. Jennie should be mistrustful of every male she encountered, starting with Carter himself. He'd offered her his help, and when she accepted, look where they had ended up.

She felt so good against him, warm and relaxed. He felt a wave of protectiveness. "Yes, you should..." he began, but suddenly he realized her breathing had become deep and even. She'd fallen asleep.

As the minutes stretched out, he went over every minute of their encounter, his body quickening at the memory. It may have been unscrupulous of him to make love to her, but at least in the end it had been good—for *both* of them. Suddenly he frowned. Hell-fire. It had been *too* damn good. For the first time ever he'd been too intensely involved in his climax to think about possible consequences.

He could feel a cold sweat break out on his forehead. His stomach rolled with something resembling fear. He'd been reckless. He hadn't followed his usual custom of pulling away at the end. And that meant that this lovely young woman lying peaceful and *trusting* in his arms could already be carrying his bastard child.

Chapter Twelve

Jennie knew the minute she opened her eyes that it was well past sunrise. What had happened? They'd been going to leave at dawn to get back to Vermillion. Then immediately the memories flooded in and she became aware that Carter was next to her, not touching her but inches away, the warmth of his body palpable on hers.

They'd made love. After swearing that she of all people would never be the type to mess up her life by losing her head and her heart to a man, here she was—lying in a hotel bed, naked and no longer virgin. Possibly already in the same condition as Kate. She shuddered, then looked quickly over at Carter to see if her movement had awakened him. She wished she could slip out of bed, get dressed and find her way back home without ever having to face him.

She wasn't angry, at least, not with him. For a moment last night, she'd tried to be. After their first lovemaking, when she'd been uncomfortable and embarrassed, she'd tried to make herself believe that it was somehow all his fault. But even then she'd known that it wasn't. She'd gone to him willingly. She'd wanted it as much as he had.

She remembered last winter when Kate had become so enamored of Sean. It had felt so odd to see the two of them together, to see the glow on her sister's cheeks when she'd come in after being alone with him out on the front porch. She'd been jealous. She and her sister had always been paramount in each other's lives. She'd felt supplanted by this new interest. But, she admitted now as the morning sun reached high enough to stream in the hotel room window, she'd also been curious and more than a little envious.

Perhaps that was all this was about. She'd wanted to know what it could be like. She'd wanted to know what it was that could make a sensible, shy girl like Kate put aside her reason and her values. Well, now she knew. She'd experienced it for herself.

Snatches of the previous day floated through her head—the way Carter's body had hardened out on the trail when she'd slid into his arms, the electric surge through her limbs as his eyes had met hers over dinner, the feel of his lips on her mouth and neck, and then, wonderfully, gently tugging her breasts. And, finally, that last union, that coming together that had seemed to turn her body inside out and filled her with an indescribable yearning to be one with this man, to belong to him and have him belong to her.

The feeling had been incredible, but was it worth it? Kate had undoubtedly felt that way about Sean before he'd abandoned her without a word, leaving her to come crashing down to the reality of betrayal and lost reputation.

Still, she thought wistfully as Carter shifted nearer and her naked body involuntarily reacted, it had been an interesting experience. Lordy, parts of it had been downright amazing.

Carter moved again. He was definitely waking up. If she wanted to escape, it would have to be now. But instead she found herself moving toward him in the warm cocoon of covers. He hadn't opened his eyes, but his arms came around her and his hard thighs brushed her softer ones. That part of him that had come together with her last night with such astonishing results was once again aroused. All thoughts of leaving fled.

"What a lovely way to wake up," he murmured, his eyes fluttering open. His smile was tender and sensual. Jennie's earlier doubts about the wisdom of what she was doing faded. Carter began to stroke her and drowsily nuzzled her neck, as Jennie gave herself up to sensations totally different from the desperate passions of the previous evening. There was a delicious coziness to their lovemaking this morning. It washed over her like a warm flood, filling her until she was once again tumbling over the edge in waves of sensation.

"Good morning, sweetheart," Carter whispered when it was over and they'd both had several minutes to recover. He was sprawled diagonally across her, his head twisted to look up at her with a heavy-lidded grin.

She grinned back, her resolutions to guard her feelings had disappeared. "Almost afternoon," she said, nodding toward the window.

He pulled himself up beside her, kissed her right earlobe, then drew her more comfortably into his arms. "So who's in a hurry?"

She was. She had forty hungry miners to feed. She was too replete with their lovemaking to try to tell that story to Carter at the moment, but she couldn't afford to lose her job. She said simply, "We need to start back home."

He kissed her forehead, then her lips, lightly. "Pity."

She laughed low in her throat. "Don't you have work to do, Mr. Prosecutor? What are we taxpayers paying you for?"

On top of the sheets he gave her a light swat on her bottom. "They pay me to referee the squabbles of the good citizens of Vermillion." He was teasing, but Jennie's smile died at the reference. Quickly Carter changed the topic. "I thought since we're still here, you'd want to see your sister again this morning."

This didn't cheer her. "She acted as if she hardly noticed I was there yesterday."

"Perhaps she was different because Wentworth was around. I'll ask him to leave if he's there today."

"He didn't seem to want to leave."

"I don't care what he wants. I'll see to it that you get your privacy."

She gave him a grateful smile, then reluctantly slid away from his warmth to sit up. She put her legs over the side of the bed, but then became suddenly shy at her nakedness. "I should probably wash up before we go to the hospital."

He lifted the sheet she'd dragged with her to take a joking peek underneath, but said, "And I'd guess that you don't want me here watching you."

Her face started to flame. She'd let him do incredibly intimate things to her body. It was probably absurd for her to be modest suddenly. But somehow in the broad daylight, it seemed different.

He didn't wait for her to answer. With a quick roll he was up from the bed himself, gathering the clothes that were still scattered around the room. "I'll wash up myself next door," he said with a smile. "Then I'll come by for you and we'll go down for some breakfast."

"Breakfast?"

"Jennie, darlin'," he said, pulling on his clothes. "I don't know about you, but I've worked up an appetite."

In spite of the huge dinner they'd had the previous evening, Jennie was hungry, too. "I guess I could eat something."

He crossed back to the bed with three quick strides and bent down to kiss her hard on her mouth. "That's my girl," he said. "I'll be back in twenty minutes."

It was a brilliant fall day. The sky looked impossibly blue against patches of red sumac scattered up in the hills as they made their way across town. Jennie's spirits were high. That's my girl, Carter had said, and, contrary to everything she'd thought she wanted for her life, Jennie suddenly felt that that was precisely what she wanted to be. Carter's girl. Kate wouldn't believe it, she thought with a giggle—her prickly, independent older sister acting giddy and lovestruck and perfectly content to have a man—a *man*—order her dinner and call her his girl.

But the sight of the imposing hospital building tempered her good mood. She wondered if Kate would be any more receptive today, would appear any more animated. Gracious, how could she go through the distress of a difficult birth and subsequently care for a child if she continued in that apathetic state?

As she'd feared, Lyle was there again in her sister's room. He looked surprised to see them. "What are you two still doing here?" he asked. "Did you spend the night?"

Carter answered, "Our carriage broke down. We were forced to turn back."

Jennie didn't care what Lyle thought about her overnight stay. She was more concerned with her sister, who once again seemed too listless to even care that her sister had come to visit. Trying to push aside the panicky feeling it gave her to see her in such a state, Jennie crossed over to her bed to give Kate a hug. Then she turned to Lyle, who was sitting in the chair by Kate's bed, and asked, "May I sit next to her for a while?"

Lyle looked as if he weren't sure he would relinquish his post.

"In fact, Wentworth," Carter said loudly from the door, "how about if you and I go downstairs for some coffee and let the sisters talk by themselves?"

Lyle stood and motioned for Jennie to take his seat,

but instead of walking toward the door, he walked over to the window well and supported himself on the ledge. "As a matter of fact, it's a good thing that you're here, Jennie. You can help Kate straighten out her thinking on a certain matter that's been causing her some anxiety."

Jennie looked at her sister in surprise, but Kate turned her eyes away. "What matter is that?"

"Do you want to explain it to her, Kate?" Lyle asked. His voice was pleasant, but something in the way he spoke to Kate made Jennie's blood chill. He sounded like a parent talking to a naughty child.

Kate looked down at her hands, folded on the sheet in front of her, and shook her head.

"What is it, sis?" Jennie asked, trying to will some animation into her.

But Kate remained silent as Lyle said, "It's about the adoption."

Jennie's head jerked toward him. "Adoption!"

"The adoption of the child. I've arranged it privately. I didn't want one of those institutional muddles that can come back to haunt you later on. This will be private and quick. The family is impeccable."

Jennie's jaw had dropped open. She stared first at Lyle, then at her sister, whose eyes were still lowered. Utterly at a loss for words, she put her hands on her hips and turned toward Carter, expecting to see her shock mirrored on his face.

Instead, he was watching Kate in the bed. The expression on his face was odd, but it was neither surprised nor horrified.

Jennie turned back to Lyle. "There is not going to be an adoption. Kate is *not* giving away her baby."

Lyle's face didn't change. "I don't think you quite understand, Jennie. I was hoping you'd be more reasonable than your sister's been up to now. I've more or less convinced her that this is her only sensible choice, and I think you're making it harder on her by trying to maintain this illusion."

Jennie jumped to her feet and walked over to Lyle, furious, and interrupted his calm flow of words. "No, *you're* the one who doesn't understand, Lyle Wentworth. This baby is Kate's son or daughter."

"Daughter," Kate murmured. And for the first time in two days, Jennie saw the touch of a smile light her sister's face.

She turned again to face Lyle. "This baby is Kate's daughter, my niece, Francis and John Sheridan's grandchild. She's not going to be adopted. She's not going to live with anyone else but Kate and me, her rightful family."

Lyle pushed himself off the window ledge and stood towering over her, but Jennie was too furious to be intimidated. "It's nonsense to think of raising a child without a father and without a name."

Jennie turned to look at Kate. "Surely, you're not listening to him, Katie?"

Her sister was sitting up a little straighter in the bed and there was finally some color in her cheeks. "Oh, Jennie. I haven't known what to think. There's some truth to what he says. It may be unfair to the child. She won't have a last name. She would have no legal standing."

"Oh, poppycock." Jennie turned to Carter. "You're the lawyer. Tell her that it's perfectly legal for a child to carry its mother's name. What difference does a name make, anyway?"

Carter's expression was grim. "Lyle's right. A name *can* make a difference. If he's really got a good home lined up for this baby, you two might want to consider it."

His words were like a slap across the face. She glared at him, then back at Lyle, who said, "Thank you, Jones. Leave it to a man to be sensible about these things."

Jennie felt as if her head were about to explode. "*Sensible!* We're talking about a baby here, a precious new human being to be cherished and loved, not some kind of puppy dog that can be handed off to any old household in the neighborhood."

"Do you really think we could make everything all right for her, Jennie?" Kate asked, her voice suddenly hopeful.

"Of course, we'll make it all right. Criminy, Kate, no wonder you look so peaked and worn out. How long has he been badgering you with these crazy notions?" She pointed to Lyle as if he were a snake that had crawled into the kitchen.

"Adoption is not a crazy notion," Lyle retorted. The calmness had finally left his voice and it now held barely leashed anger. "It's an honorable and necessary solution for girls like Kate who find themselves in trouble."

Jennie whirled around toward him. "Kate's only

trouble is having to listen to sanctimonious fools like you try to tell her how to run her life.''

"Jennie," Carter admonished from the doorway.

But Lyle wanted to handle his own defense. "I've been here every day taking care of your sister, which is more than I can say for you, Jennie. If it weren't for me she'd have been entirely alone, left up to the whims of this overworked hospital staff. I've been the one here each day insisting that she get the proper care."

Kate's face lost some of its glow. "He's right, Jennie. Lyle's been a big help."

Jennie tried to get her temper under control. "I thank you for all that help, Lyle. It was hard for me to leave Kate here alone and hard for her to be alone. But that doesn't give you the right to come in and tell her that she has to give up her child."

"I'm not telling her anything, I'm merely helping make arrangements for the best solution for everyone."

"Maybe you should calm down a little, Jennie, and listen to what he's telling you," Carter said.

Jennie couldn't tell which man was making her angrier, but Carter's words sliced deeper. After the intimacy they'd shared and the special way she was beginning to feel about him, it was especially difficult to hear him talk so coldly about her sister's baby.

She took a deep, steadying breath and walked over to sit beside Kate on the bed. Taking her sister's hand in hers, she addressed both men. "You know what, gentlemen? I'm going to have a nice, long talk with my sister. A private talk. Carter, if you'd be willing to wait for me, I'd appreciate the ride back to Vermillion later this morning. If not, I'll find my own transportation. And Lyle, it will be up to my sister if she wants to continue to receive you, but please don't come back until after I've left.''

Lyle looked as if he were going to continue the argument, but then Kate spoke up, finally showing a bit of determination on her own. ''Please, Lyle. Jennie and I would like to have some time alone together.''

He hesitated a moment longer, before addressing Kate. ''I'll be back this afternoon,'' he said curtly, then stalked out of the room.

Carter looked at Jennie, his expression grave. ''I'll wait for you out by the carriages. Take as much time as you need.''

Then he, too, turned to leave.

With both men out of the room it was as if a weight had lifted off Kate. She pushed herself up and gave Jennie a squeeze, then took a deep, cleansing breath. ''So we can do this thing, sis?'' she asked, still anxious.

Jennie put her arm around her sister's shoulder and squeezed her back. Her blood was still racing. ''You bet we can, Katie. We Sheridan sisters can do anything.''

Carter's head was in a frustrating and uncharacteristic muddle. It had started last night as he'd lain in bed in the afterglow of making love to Jennie and had realized that he might have gotten her pregnant. No, if he was honest with himself, the muddle had really started the first day he'd seen her. He'd tried to take her side against the townspeople, which hadn't worked all that well. Then he'd found himself renting a room from her and getting involved with her life, which had caused further difficulties. Now he was in about as deep as he'd ever been...with anyone.

They'd driven for two hours out of Virginia City in almost total silence. Jennie had had one of those determined looks in her eyes when she'd come out of the hospital after her visit with her sister. When he'd asked if they'd made any decision about the adoption, she'd fixed him with a cool stare and said, "We've decided not to let anyone else interfere in *our* business." And that was the end of it.

He'd tried to engage her in light conversation but had given up after the first few attempts. They seemed to be even more estranged than they had been on their *other* trip back from Virginia City. Only this time, there was no way he could move out of her house and her life and forget she existed. This time she might be carrying his child.

They needed to talk about it, but he'd be darned if he could see how to broach the subject. The sleepy, sensual lover he'd taken in his arms this morning had been replaced by a silent young woman who looked as if she'd slap the next man who offered friendly advice. Unfortunately, Carter knew that she needed advice badly. True, so far she'd done a remarkable job of taking care of herself and her sister and even the stray, Barnaby. But she obviously had no idea of how difficult it would be if Kate brought home an illegitimate child. And she obviously had not had sense enough to stay the hell away from Carter when he had so recklessly put her in risk of ending up in the same situation.

What Jennie needed, he thought ruefully, was a *man.* And sometime during his long hours lying awake last night, he'd decided that since he was the one partially responsible for putting her future in jeopardy, the man she needed was Carter himself.

He'd been through all the arguments. Up to now, he'd been living a calculated life, planning every step. Jennie Sheridan was definitely not in the plan. He hadn't expected to marry for some years yet. And then it would be to some politically expedient woman who would be able to buy him influence with the important people in the state.

It was definitely *not* in his plan to ally himself with a potential scandal, a feisty, independent woman who cared little for law and less for public opinion and was determined to maintain a household of societal misfits—the same kind of misfit he himself had been.

They'd passed the grove of twisted Joshua trees that marked the halfway point on the road and he still hadn't started in on the speech he'd rehearsed over and over in the dark last night. Before he knew it, they'd be back in Vermillion facing interruptions by Barnaby and her precious *silverheels.* He took a deep breath.

"I'm sorry about the misunderstanding at the hospital, Jennie."

She was staring out the other side of the carriage. "I wish Lyle'd go back to his papa's bank and leave my sister alone."

"But…well, he's right that it's good to have some-one there at the hospital with her."

When she turned toward him, her eyes were glazed with tears. Not a propitious sign for the discussion he wanted to have with her. "I know it is. *I* should be there with her. But I don't know how to do that and also get the money for her to stay there and keep the house going and take care of Barnaby and…"

He reached over and took her chin in his hand. "Sweetheart, you're doing all a person can do, more than most people I know. Your sister understands that. But that's why you should probably just back off a little about Lyle and let him help out."

"And give my sister's baby away against her will."

He released his hold on her and she turned back to look out the carriage away from him. He spoke to the back of her head. "Are you so sure it would be against her will? It seems to me that you're more indignant about the idea than Kate."

"Only because she's too weak to fight her own battles. If Kate were feeling normal, she'd have thrown Lyle out on his ear for even daring to suggest such a thing."

Carter smiled. He could picture Jennie doing such a thing. She'd almost done it to him. But he couldn't picture that kind of vehemence from sweet-tempered Kate. But it wasn't Kate he wanted to discuss.

"I was sorry that it has seemed to cause some dis-sension between you and me after…after what we had together last night."

His breath caught as he waited for her to respond.

When she finally turned around, she was dry-eyed. "Don't worry about it," she said, her voice tight.

Carter gaped at her. "Don't worry about it? Jennie, we made love—more than once. It's not something that you can just forget about."

"No? It seems to me that most men manage to forget about it just fine."

She was no doubt thinking about the man who had abandoned Kate. "Well, not me," he said, sounding a bit lame even to himself. Nothing about this talk was going in the direction he'd planned. For a lawyer, he certainly was making a botch of his case. "Jennie, there may be consequences from what we did," he blurted, realizing at once that this point would do little to improve the tone.

"I realize that, Carter. Which is why I'm going to ask you to stay out of my way in the future. In spite of our differences, it appears that something happens when the two of us are together."

This was more the direction he'd had in mind. He gave her his most persuasive smile. "Yes, sweetheart, something definitely *happens*. And I think we might as well face the fact that it's going to happen again…and again."

She shook her head. "Not if we don't see each other."

Carter's exasperation rose. What a stubborn little minx she was. He considered whether he should stop the carriage, take her in his lap and *prove* to her that there was no way they'd be able to stay apart. It would probably make her so angry that she'd leap out of the carriage and insist on walking home. He considered doing it anyway. The walk might do her good. But it probably wouldn't get his question answered.

"We're going to see each other. I eat supper at your place."

"You can make other arrangements."

"I've already paid up the week."

Jennie wiggled around in her seat, obviously irritated. "I'll refund the balance of your money, Mr. Jones. You'll have it as soon as we reach Vermillion."

Carter relaxed a little. She wouldn't be getting this steamed up if she didn't know perfectly well that the two of them together were dangerous. She felt it every bit as much as he did. And, being a smart girl, she ought to realize that there was only one thing they could do about it. "I've paid for my meals and I'll be there to eat them," he said smugly. "And I intend to take advantage of my evenings there to tempt you into further indiscretions."

Jennie almost sputtered as she said, "Sheridan House is *my* business. I say who will be there and who won't. Granted, I'm an unprotected female who was foolish enough to let my baser instincts get the better of me. But that doesn't mean that I'll let you come into my house and make me your mistress!"

The last word came out with a big huff. Carter sat back to get a little distance from her agitation. Then cautiously he inched forward, placed a hand on each shoulder and turned her to face him. He spoke slowly, willing her to pay attention to each word. "Jennie, I'm not asking you to be my mistress. I'm asking you to marry me."

Chapter Thirteen

Jennie stared at Carter as if he'd suddenly grown an extra nose. He wanted to marry her? She could hardly believe her ears.

In the first place, marriage was for regular people—the kind who intended to settle down behind a picket-fenced house where the wife took care of children and pets while the husband went off each day to a job. Marriage was for people like the people her parents had reluctantly become after they'd discovered that an unconventional life of freedom in the mountains simply wouldn't work.

And in the second place, if Jennie were to ever get married, it wouldn't be to an ambitious, manipulative politician who wanted to arrange her life and keep her sister's child out of it.

The arguments raced through her head in a matter of seconds, but the only word that came out was "Why?"

Carter looked surprised. "I just told you. Because we've made love and now I'm trying to do the honorable thing—"

"To make a decent woman out of me?" Jennie asked dryly.

"Well, no. I mean, you already *are* a decent woman, Jennie. That's why we both need to be concerned with how this looks and what consequences there might be—"

Once again she didn't let him finish his sentence. "It's bighearted of you, Carter, but as I told you before, you needn't worry. The people in town probably already think the worst of me so one more check mark on my list of transgressions won't make that much difference."

Carter hadn't considered that she would turn down his proposal. In fact, he couldn't quite believe that she was turning him down. Women liked to be coaxed. He moved closer to her and put an arm around her shoulders. "No one will ever speak about you that way again once you're my wife, Jennie. They won't dare."

"Well, now, isn't that a comforting thought."

He'd thought it would be, but evidently he'd been wrong. "What I mean to say is that I want to take care of you, sweetheart."

"I can take care of myself very well, thank you. Now if you don't mind, could we get started again? I need to get back up to Vermillion."

"Jennie, I don't think you realize…" She gave an exasperated click with her mouth and glared at him. He decided to give up the attempt…for the moment. She was undoubtedly still feeling strange about the intensity of their night together and was upset about the encounter with Lyle this morning. He'd wait and bring up the subject again tonight after supper when she'd be in a more receptive mood.

"All right," he said, jostling the reins to set the horse in motion once again. "We'll postpone this discussion until later."

Jennie didn't answer. She slumped back against the seat with a big sigh. She wanted to tell him that it wouldn't do any good to postpone the topic. Her answer would be the same. But that would start up the argument again, and she'd had enough conflict for one day.

Carter watched the road ahead as they drove along in silence, giving her an opportunity to study his profile. His words had shocked her, but she had to admit that she wasn't entirely displeased. It wasn't every day a girl received a proposal of matrimony, especially from a man as forceful and striking as Carter. In a way it was too bad that she wasn't the marrying type. If she *had* been, she could do far worse than the handsome prosecutor.

But, of course, the whole idea was absurd. What would Carter do with a wife like her, anyway? He'd be trying to curry votes with the town council while she was at war with them over the latest ridiculous ordinance. He'd be crazy to take on a wife like Jennie. And, she thought sadly as she pushed any notion of romance between her and Carter firmly away, I'd be miserable with someone who was so calculating that he could carry on an entire conversation about marriage without ever once mentioning the word *love*.

The silverheels were already down from the mine by the time Carter and Jennie got back to town. Brad was sprawled on the front steps of the porch while Dennis and Smitty were sitting on the swing. In the wicker rocker at the opposite end of the porch sat Delbert Hammond. He held a glass of whiskey.

"We're entertaining the sheriff while we waited for you, Miss Jennie," Dennis called to her as she and Carter climbed out of the carriage and started up the walk. "Offered him a nip of your spirits."

"You on duty, Sheriff?" Carter asked.

Delbert lifted the glass in a mocking salute. "Well, I ain't seen any bad guys around to chase, if that's what you mean, Jones. I figured a little refreshment wouldn't hurt nothin' while we were waitin' on you folks."

"Why are you waiting for us, Sheriff?" Jennie asked, trying to keep the weariness out of her voice. She'd had enough for one day.

Delbert set the rocker in motion with his foot. "I'm supposed to find out about this overnight trip of yours with Carter. Two unmarried folks staying together in the same hotel is what I was told."

Carter's face grew thunderous. "And what god-damn business is it of yours, Hammond?"

Delbert continued to rock, apparently unconcerned at Carter's tone. "Folks care about things like that, especially when it involves a public servant and someone who was granted a lodging license by the city council. Folks are talking about askin' for a recall of the public servant and rescinding the license."

Jennie's blood was doing a slow boil. It had to have been Lyle. He must have wired the news. How else would anyone in town have found out about their trip so quickly? He probably intended to use the ensuing scandal to pressure her into agreeing to his plan for the baby. Well, he'd underestimated her. Evidently he'd underestimated Carter, too.

"You can tell anyone who wants to know about Miss Sheridan's or my activities to contact me," Carter said, his voice now calm but much more deadly. He walked up on the porch and halted directly in front of the sheriff. "I'll determine if the information is any of their affair and act accordingly."

Delbert stopped the motion of the rocking chair and stood, reaching only to Carter's chin. "Hey, Jones. I just do my job."

Carter reached out and took the glass of whiskey from the sheriff's hand, then leaned to pour it out over the porch rail. "Well, Sheriff, if you don't have any more to occupy yourself than running around spreading town gossip, then maybe I should contact the county to find a better use for their money in this area."

Delbert shrugged. "I can't imagine this is a story you'll want to be telling a lot of people, Jones, but suit yourself."

For a minute Jennie thought Carter might smack the sheriff right in the face. His fists were clenched and the line of his jaw was tight. But then he stepped back to give the sheriff a clear path to the steps. "Get out of here, Hammond," he said with disgust.

The sheriff nodded and ambled across the porch, stepping around Brad to descend the stairs. "Thanks for the drink, Miss Sheridan," he said, tipping his hat as he walked by Jennie. Then he sauntered down the walk and out the gate.

As if her nerves weren't frayed enough from the past two days, the encounter with the sheriff had left Jennie with shaky hands as she prepared a quick makeshift supper. Carter had left shortly after Delbert to go change clothes and check in at his office, but he'd said pointedly that he'd be back to eat with them.

The miners, bless their hearts, had pitched in as usual to help with supper. They'd also taken over the meal at the mine to cover her absence, and then Dennis told her he had sent Barnaby fishing as soon as the sheriff had started in with his insinuating comments about Carter and Jennie.

"I couldn't let the boy see me haul off and hit a man of the law," Dennis said, "which is what I was hankering to do. So I told Barnaby he'd better go try catching us some trout for breakfast tomorrow."

"You're an angel, Dennis Kelly," Jennie told him, and went up on tiptoe to give him a kiss on the cheek, but unlike the last time she'd done so, this time he avoided an embarrassing blush by pulling away before her soft lips could touch him.

By the time the chickens had been quartered by deadly blows from Smitty and fried with a huge pan full of onions and potatoes, Jennie was feeling better. The miners' good humor always cheered her.

Dennis had come in from bringing Barnaby back from the creek. He'd left the boy in the yard cleaning the two tiny fish he'd caught. "By the time the bones are pulled out, there won't be more than a bite of fish left in them critters," he'd told Jennie and Smitty with a wink. "But he's right proud of them and we'll make a fuss tomorrow when we fry them up."

"It's good for Barnaby to be around you three," Jennie told him. "He needs men in his life to look up to."

"He's a fine lad," Smitty said.

Dennis added, "A little too serious for his age. We need to spend some time showing him how to have fun."

Jennie sighed. "I hope they'll let you stay around to do it. After today, they might close this place down for real."

"Don't let them battle-axes in town get you down, Miss Jennie," Dennis said. "The truth is they're jealous of you because you're pretty and you're..." His eyes shyly scanned up and down her trim figure.

"You've got curves the right size in the right places," Brad supplied as he came swinging through the door with an arm full of flowers he'd just cut in the garden. "Unlike most of the town matrons."

Jennie exclaimed in delight at the sight of them. "Oh, aren't they beautiful? What a good idea, Brad."

The usually serious miner gave a sheepish smile. "You looked like you needed something cheery," he said.

She smiled back at him and then at the other two. "You three are all I need to cheer me up. What would I do without you boys?"

"Ah, shucks, Miss Jennie," Smitty was saying as Carter entered unannounced through the swinging kitchen door.

"Something smells good," he said, his eyes going immediately to Jennie.

"It's just chicken," she told him. "If you'll call Barnaby in from out back, we can eat."

Her heart had taken an unwelcome leap to see him again, even though they'd only been apart a little over an hour. He'd washed and changed clothes and looked as fresh as if he'd spent the day sleeping instead of driving through the mountains, whereas she was wearing the same travel-stained dress she'd had on since yesterday morning.

She wished it didn't matter to her. She'd hoped to be able to be more indifferent. Perhaps it would just take time. After all, a mere twelve hours ago she'd been making love to this man. But that had been a fantasy. She was home now with Barnaby and her silverheels. Soon Kate would be back, bringing the baby, and life would return to normal. She could forget about her passionate night in Virginia City and forget Carter Jones along with it. It would just take a little time.

Carter was tired. He had spent too many hours awake the previous evening pondering what he should do about the sudden turn of events with Jennie. The day hadn't been any too restful, either. There'd been the confrontation at the hospital, the long ride home, with Jennie's rejection of his honorable proposal of marriage, all followed by the sheriff's nasty comments.

No one had found out about the first time he and Jennie had been forced to stay in Virginia City, but it appeared that this time they hadn't been so lucky. He didn't know how word had filtered back so quickly, but now that it had, he was sure the Vermillion gossip grapevine would see to it that it was spread to the farthest reaches of town. All of which just made his case more urgent.

But Jennie had said no, and what was more astonishing, she'd appeared to mean it.

It was probably his fatigue that made the miners' antics during supper grate on his nerves. They were obviously trying to cheer Jennie, a goal he should be applauding. But instead, it irritated him. He couldn't help feeling a little pique at the way she seemed to relax in their company and bask in their compliments while treating him with such measured coolness. After all, it had been *his* arms she'd lain in last night, not her precious silverheels'.

Well, he'd set things right when they had their time alone together after supper.

"I'll help Jennie with the washing up tonight," he said loudly as the interminable meal finally drew to a close. "You boys go on with your game."

Dennis stood and picked up his plate. "We've taken over the cleaning from Jennie tonight. The poor lass is weary."

"They spoil me," Jennie said, beaming at the three miners.

"I'm going to help, too," Barnaby said, picking up her plate.

Jennie leaned over and hugged him against her side. "You're always my good helper, Barnaby." The boy seemed pleased and allowed her to squeeze him close without stiffening.

Carter looked around at the volunteer work crew and wondered if he should also offer his services. He wouldn't mind earning her gratitude, or, for that matter, one of those hugs she'd just given the boy, but it wouldn't get him time alone with her.

"What you need is a bit of relaxing," he told her. "How about if we go and sit out on the porch swing?"

"It's a little cold for that, isn't it?" she protested.

It probably was. "Grab a shawl and you'll be warm enough. The fresh air will do you good."

When she'd been thanking the miners for helping, her expression had been warm and animated. Now the enthusiasm faded as she nodded agreement and went to fetch a shawl from the living room settee. Carter felt strangely hurt. All at once he realized that *he* wanted to be the one putting a smile on her face. He'd certainly put one there last night.

It *was* awfully cold to be sitting outside. He felt the evening chill even through his wool coat. But he was determined to talk with her and press his suit. Now that the whole town would be talking about them, it was important to get it settled. He wanted to be able to announce that they were affianced before self-appointed moral guardians like Henrietta Billingsley could begin a campaign to impugn both her character and his.

"I told you, it's too cold to be out here," she said, though she let him draw her down next to him on the swing. She sounded grumpy.

He wouldn't have much time for finesse, and, anyway, when Jennie was around, his lawyerly skills seemed to totally disappear. "So how long do I have to wait before you'll realize that you're going to have to marry me?" he blurted.

Nicely put, Carter, he chided himself. Hell's bells but the woman had a way of twisting up his tongue.

"When the devil's den turns to ice. Would that be soon enough?" She definitely sounded grumpy.

He tried to remember the mood they'd been in when their physical union had seemed so inevitable last night. If he could just recreate that, it might be easier than making his point with words. He slipped an arm around her shoulder. She was shivering. "You're cold, sweetheart. Here, lean up against me."

She let him pull her against his side, but her voice stayed cool as she said, "This isn't going to work, Carter. It's absurd to think of the two of us getting married. Even if I *did* intend to marry someone, you and I would never suit."

Though she seemed unmoved by the sudden proximity of their bodies, Carter was not. He could feel her firm breast against his side and it was all the trigger his body needed to bring the erotic images of the previous evening flooding back. "I think we suited quite well last night and this morning," he murmured, and bent his head toward her mouth.

She was too fast for him, scooting away on the slippery wood of the swing. "I'm sorry, Carter, but this won't do. I'm appreciative of all your help taking me to see Kate, and grateful for the way you stood up to the sheriff for me today, but you must see that it's simply not sensible for us to be alone together anymore. Not after…'' The slight tremor in her voice told Carter that she wasn't as cool about the situation as she was trying to appear. "Not after what happened," she finished.

Her big brown eyes looked almost pleading, giving him a sudden pang of guilt. Her silverheels had been right after all. She was exhausted, much too tired for him to be trying to put pressure on her about a decision this important. Town gossip be damned, he'd have to wait until tomorrow to get this settled.

He stood and offered his hands to pull her up from the swing. "What you need is a good night's sleep, young lady." He tried not to be bothered at her expression of relief.

"Thank you for understanding," she said, taking his hands and standing.

She did look tired. Her face was pale and there were circles under her eyes. But nevertheless he found himself looking down at her with a fierce desire to kiss her good-night. He shoved it away and said lightly, "I guess I'd better go to the office tomorrow and earn some of the salary the taxpayers are paying me, but I'll be back tomorrow night for supper."

She dropped his hands and walked toward the front door. "I'll see you tomorrow then." She sounded as if she were in a hurry to be rid of his company.

Carter nodded and stood next to the swing watching as she opened the front door and went inside. After a moment he heard the sound of her laughing at something one of the miners had said. It gave him an irrational surge of anger so strong that he sat back down on the swing in surprise.

What in hell was wrong with him? he asked himself as his weight creaked the swing into motion. Why should he care if Jennie's miners made her laugh? Because, came the inner answer, *he* wanted to be the one to make her laugh. And he wanted to make her cry in ecstasy as they shared each other's bodies. He wanted to make her happy and safe and loved.

Carter planted his feet on the wooden porch floor to stop the swing from moving as the realization hit him like a gust of cold wind. All of his justifications about why he needed to marry Jennie—a possible child, a possible scandal—were just so many excuses. There was only one real reason.

He gave a harsh laugh. All his life he'd used people for his own purposes. He'd befriended men when expedient to further his ambition. He'd befriended women when the physical urgings of his body required. But something had changed. In the unsophisticated little town of Vermillion, a free-spirited, stubborn, beautiful young woman had unlocked feelings he hadn't known he possessed. Carter Jones—the man born without a name and without a heart—had fallen in love.

The rest of the miners greeted Jennie with cheers when she arrived up at the mine the next day. You'd think she'd been gone a month. It kept her smiling all morning as she took special care in preparing a hearty dinner of roast beef and beans.

She'd tossed in her bed last night for some time

before falling to sleep, but then had finally slept soundly and felt much better today than she had the previous evening. She'd resolved to concentrate on her job and her boardinghouse family and not worry about Lyle's influence on her sister or the town's influence on her own and Kate's future. Trust in the Fates, her mother had always said. Well, it was time the Fates started moving things her way for a change.

She'd also resolved to put thoughts of Carter out of her head, though she was less sure about how successful she'd be in this endeavor. Over and over her mind seemed to want to keep returning to moments they'd shared in the past few days.

He'd been a gentleman last night out on the porch—fortunately. When he'd put his arm around her and looked as if he were going to kiss her, she wasn't sure she'd be able to resist. Every inch of her was wanting to snuggle up against him and feel his lips again. But where would that get her? She had to stop this nonsense and get these ridiculous notions of marriage out of Carter's head—and out of her own.

It was easier to be here, working in the mine's lean-to kitchen on a crisp fall day. Several of the miners found an excuse to break their shift and wander over her way to tell her that they'd missed seeing her the past two days. Her own silverheels had checked in with her at midmorning to see if she needed anything, almost as if they wanted to assure themselves that she hadn't gone missing again. She felt wanted and happy and self-sufficient—the perfect combination for any woman.

She'd been a fool to let her heart get tangled up in

something as complicated and risky as romance. But, as her parents had always told her, she was a smart girl. She'd feed Carter the meals he'd already paid for, then gently suggest that he take his suppers elsewhere.

She'd learned her lesson—that she was no stronger than Kate had been when faced with the onslaught of an unscrupulous male. But she would be wiser than her sister. Definite chinks had been chipped in the wall she'd carefully built around her heart. But before it could tumble, she intended to cement it back together—stronger than ever.

The doyennes had brought male reinforcement. Mrs. Billingsley, Miss Potter and Mrs. Wentworth were once again standing before him, overwhelming the limited space in his office, but this time they were joined by the banker, Harmon Wentworth. Carter wasn't sure why he'd come along, because he had not been able to wedge a syllable into the barrage of words launched by Mrs. Billingsley and Miss Potter.

"We'll go to the county. We'll go to the governor, if necessary," Mrs. Billingsley was saying. "How can they expect a respectable town to uphold its laws if the person they send to take charge is con…tracting…con…"

"*Consorting,*" Margaret Potter supplied.

"Yes, *consorting* with the lawbreakers. Why, you might as well be over there in the jail playing poker with the horse thieves."

Carter was quite sure there had never been a horse thief in the history of the tiny Vermillion jail, but he didn't argue the point. He was finding the conversation enlightening. Two months ago, he'd have been on his feet, bowing and scraping, fearful of offending these key town citizens—worried that they might have some power to cast aspersions on his so-far-impeccable record.

Now he sat back in his chair and viewed the foursome with indifference. It was a surprisingly liberating feeling.

"Are you calling Jenny Sheridan a horse thief, Mrs. Billingsley?" he asked with a quirk of his mouth.

"The principle's the same," she huffed. "Tell him, Harmon. Don't you charge the same kind of interest if you lend out ten dollars as if you lend out a thousand?"

Mr. Wentworth opened his mouth to weigh in on this analogy, but closed it again as Miss Potter took over the assault. "The nature of the transgression is not the point here, Mr. Jones. The point is that you can no longer handle the Sheridan case since you are obviously *involved*, involved in a way that implies questionable morals on the part of both parties."

Carter's half smile died. He sat up straighter in the chair. "Ladies...and gentleman," he added with a nod to the banker. "As you evidently were informed by Lyle, I did Miss Sheridan the favor of escorting her to see her sister who is in a hospital in Virginia City. This trip is no business of anyone in this town other than Miss Sheridan and myself. However, since it seems to have ruffled feathers—" he gave a sardonic glance at the rather ridiculous plumed hats both

Mrs. Wentworth and Mrs. Billingsley were wearing "——I'll add that I can't imagine why it's anything other than perfectly respectable for a man to offer such service to his fiancée."

"Fiancée!" The two feathered women exclaimed in chorus like tamed parrots.

"My future wife. Miss Sheridan," Carter added calmly.

There was a long moment of silence. Then Harmon Wentworth asked, "You're really going to marry the girl?"

"I really am. Now does that clear things up about this trip that you all seem so riled up about?"

Harmon frowned and said to no one in particular, "I can't believe how girls like that can get respectable men to throw over all good sense for them."

He was obviously thinking of his own son. Carter let the comment pass. "Was there anything else today?" he asked pleasantly.

The women were still recovering from their astonishment over Carter's news. For once even Henrietta was at a loss for words. Harmon pulled a watch from his waistcoat. "I've got to get back to the bank," he said gruffly.

He turned to leave and the three women followed with muffled goodbyes. Carter watched them go with relief. That was neatly handled, Counselor, he told himself with a disgusted shake of his head. The way the gossip mill churned in this town, Jennie would hear about their supposed engagement before he even had time to walk up the street to her house.

Perhaps he could press his suit again over dinner

at the hotel tonight. It would be dubious food, but at least she wouldn't have to cook it. But he'd better hurry. If she learned that he'd already announced his intentions to the entire town, she'd slam the Sheridan house door in his face—slam it so hard they'd feel the breeze clear down to the courthouse.

He reached for his hat and headed out, clattering down the office stairs, a grin on his face.

Chapter Fourteen

In the end it was the silverheels who made it impossible for Jennie to refuse Carter's invitation to supper. He'd gotten to Sheridan House just as the miners were arriving home from the mine. Jennie had been in the garden cleaning up what might be the last of the season's harvest.

She'd simply laughed at his suggestion of dinner in town, but then Dennis Kelly had added his encouragement. "We can do up our own supper tonight, lass. You deserve to have a relaxing meal after the long days you've been putting in."

Brad and Smitty had agreed, and Barnaby had come sailing around the corner from where he'd been cutting down the vines from the side of the house to say breathlessly, "Of course you should go, Miss Jennie. I wish I could eat in a fancy place like the hotel."

Carter had stooped down to put his arm around the lad, retrieving the shears that he was waving around with dangerous abandon. "Barnaby, we'll have that fine meal, I promise. In fact, I'll take you down to

Virginia City to have one that's really fine at the International.''

"Is that the hotel where you and Jennie stayed?"

"Yup. And you can ride the elevator, too." Barnaby's eyes widened. "But it won't be for a little while. Tonight I need to talk over some things with Jennie privately.''

This last comment should have told her right away that she was crazy to agree to the evening, but when she'd tried to refuse again, the silverheels kept at her until she would have had to sound downright rude to say no.

So she'd donned her blue silk, which had been hanging outside all day to air after she'd cleaned it yesterday, and they'd headed down to the Continental Hotel, which, unlike the International, did not live up to its elegant name.

"You're going to have to stop doing this, Carter," she said as the waiter showed them to a table in the otherwise deserted dining room.

"Doing what?"

"Coming around, asking me to supper. The silverheels think you're courting me."

Carter grinned at her, his white teeth flashing and his gray eyes glinting with humor. "Smart fellows," he said.

She refused to let his charm soften her. "No, really. It just won't do. Now you've got Barnaby all excited about a trip to Virginia City."

"What's wrong with that?"

"Well, nothing, I suppose if…" She stopped.

"If I actually take him there?" he supplied, his

smile gone. "Jennie, do you think I would offer a special treat to a youngster who's had very little joy in his life if I had no intention of carrying through on it? Do you really have that little faith in me?"

She shook her head and looked down at the snowy-white napkin folded on top of her plate. "I don't know, Carter. I'm confused by all this."

He didn't answer for a moment, but finally he said softly, "Look at me, Jennie." When she lifted her eyes to his he continued, "We're never going to get anywhere until you let down some of that prickly guard of yours and start to trust me."

When his voice was low and intense like that, she'd believe anything he said. "It's myself I don't trust, Carter," she replied.

He closed his eyes briefly. When he started in again, his voice was lighter. "I'm hungry as hell. Let's eat and then we can decide who's going to trust whom about what."

"You're sounding like a lawyer again, Carter."

"I am a lawyer, sweetheart. But don't worry about it, we're not in court. Now here's a little challenge for you—find a dish on this menu that can be cut with something less than a Bowie knife."

She laughed a little and let herself be pulled once again under the spell of his charm. The silverheels had been right. She had been working hard and worrying too much. It felt good to leave everything behind for an evening and enjoy being served food that she hadn't had to plan and cut and prepare. Even if it tasted more like squirrel than chicken.

"What was that fancy name they put on the menu

for this?'' she asked as she cleaned the last bite of the flavorless dish.

"Coq au vin, which is their way of saying chicken that's too old to serve anymore unless we soak it in vinegar. I'm afraid haute cuisine is not one of the Continental's strong suits."

"Hot what?"

"Fancy cooking."

Jennie giggled. "If that chicken was any example, I'd say it's not even a weak suit. In fact, they'd be wise to fold their hand and take up dice."

Carter sat back and watched her with a warm glow in his middle that had nothing to do with the mediocre wine they'd had with their supper. When she wasn't thinking about all her problems and responsibilities, she seemed younger. Her smile was brighter, her laugh happier. He had a sudden fierce desire to keep her that way.

"Have I told you how pretty you are when your eyes sparkle like that?" he asked in a low voice, leaning close to her.

She blushed and looked pleased, but said, "I can't hope to best you in a flirting contest, Carter. I don't have your experience."

He grinned at her. "It's easy. You simply bat your eyelashes and say back to me, 'Oh, Carter, you say such sweet things.'"

She giggled. "That sounds silly."

"Well, flirting is silly. So then I say back, 'I just tell the truth, darlin'.'"

"And I say, that's not what Constance Williams

told me after you kissed her behind the schoolhouse
at recess last week.''

Carter gave a hearty laugh. "See? You do have
experience flirting. Was there really a Constance Williams?''

Jennie grimaced. "Yes. Now *she* had experience
with flirting.''

"And she's now happily married with six
young'uns.''

"Three, but a fourth on the way. She's married to
Jack Foster, who was the one and only boy who ever
made any pretense of courting me.''

"Until me.''

She gave a little sigh of resignation. "Yes, until
you.''

Carter shook his head. "The men of this town are
idiots.''

His vehemence was flattering. Jennie had thought
the same thing herself a time or two. But that had
been back when she hadn't yet decided that she'd be
better off living her life without men. In defense of
her schoolmates she explained, "Oh, I think they had
their reasons. The Sheridan family was always considered a bit odd. My parents lived for years in the
mountains and even after they came to town to live,
they never felt too obligated to do things like everyone else.''

"And their daughters grew up with the same opinion.''

"I guess we did. We were always happy just the
four of us. We never needed the approval of everyone
else.''

"But sometimes it's easier to have that approval."

"I suppose. It's certainly easier if you want to keep a business going in this town in spite of all their stupid regulations."

Carter nodded his agreement, but then his eyes left her face and focused with a frown on a point over her shoulder.

Jennie cranked around to see Harmon and Lucinda Wentworth coming in through the dining room door. She gave an inner groan. Up to now it had been a pleasant evening.

The waiter came to show them to a table, but they detoured on the way to walk over to Carter and Jennie. With obvious reluctance, Carter got to his feet. "Evening, Mrs. Wentworth, Mr. Wentworth," he said.

Jennie exchanged greetings with the older couple, then sat back in her chair as Lucinda said brightly, "So it *is* true, Mr. Jones. I told Henrietta that I didn't think you'd just tell us an outright lie."

Carter looked as if he still had the last piece of chicken caught in his throat, as Jennie asked, "What's true?"

Mrs. Wentworth leaned over and gave her a little pat on the cheek. "Congratulations, my dear. Mr. Jones told us the news this afternoon. When's the wedding to be?"

Jennie looked in horror from Mrs. Wentworth to her husband, who was frowning as usual, to Carter. He looked sick…and guilty. Slowly she got to her feet, folded her napkin and pushed back her chair. "You'll have to excuse me, Mr. and Mrs. Wentworth,

but I have to be getting home. As to the wedding—''
she smiled pleasantly ''—well, now, why don't you
just ask Mr. Jones about that?''

Carter wasted little time trying to satisfy the Wentworths' curiosity over Jennie's abrupt exit. As soon
as he could arrange payment of the bill, he excused
himself and took off after her. It probably looked a
little strange to see the town prosecutor running up
the middle of the street late in the evening, but he
was beyond caring.

He caught up to her just as she was opening the
gate to her yard. ''Jennie, wait!'' he yelled, but she
ignored him and proceeded up the walk after closing
the gate behind her.

Carter was forced to slow down to open the gate
himself, and by that time she was up on the porch.
''You might as well wait for me,'' he called to her,
''because if you go inside I'm just coming after you.''

She turned around. ''We have nothing to talk
about, Mr. Jones.''

He stalked up the path. ''Yes, we do. I'm sorry the
Wentworths blurted that out at the restaurant, but I
only told them about our engagement—''

''Our *imaginary* engagement,'' she interrupted.

''I told them because people were starting to spread
nasty gossip about you.''

He was one step below her as she stood on the
porch, making their eyes level. ''You mean they were
spreading it about *you*, which, of course, wouldn't do.
Mr. Upstanding District Attorney must not be tainted
by a breath of scandal.''

"I don't care about that," he said, but he knew the words weren't entirely true.

"Of course you do. Which is why I'm saving you from yourself by not marrying you."

He took her hands. "Jennie, I'm not doing this to avoid a scandal. I *want* to marry you."

For just an instant, she believed him, which made her realize that part of her *wanted* to believe him. Part of her wanted to take a step down into his arms and say, yes, I'll be yours. But the sensible part of her knew it would be disastrous.

"Carter, there's no way I could be the kind of wife you need. I'd never be doing the right thing."

"I don't want a wife who'll do the right thing. I want a wife who's loving and generous and spirited and smart. I want *you,* Jennie."

Her heart had sped up and was doing its best to let her know that it wanted to be convinced. She backed a step away from him. "I can't marry you. The doctors say Kate will be weak when she comes home. And there'll be the baby to care for."

"So we'll live here. You can keep doing everything you have been doing, only you'll have my help."

She cocked her head. "You'd live here in this mixed-up household with a sister-in-law who has an illegitimate baby?"

"I'd live where you lived—wherever that had to be."

It was insane. She was never going to marry, and if she did, Carter Jones would be the least likely candidate on earth.

Carter felt his patience draining. "If you don't agree to marry me, I'll go to Kate, tell her that I seduced you and have to marry you to make an honest woman of you."

"You wouldn't!"

No, he wouldn't. But she didn't know that. He remained silent.

"We'd live here?" she asked, her voice weak.

Carter nodded. "As long as you need to. And as long as we can steal away to our own room and our own bed every night."

His words sent a rush through Jennie's midsection. Their own bed every night.

"So how about tomorrow?" Carter said, stepping up to her level and gripping her arms.

"What about tomorrow?" She felt dazed.

"For the wedding."

Jennie gasped, "Tomorrow?"

"Sweetheart, Kate's too ill to be here, so unless you want the lovely ladies from town making a big fuss over you, I don't see any reason to wait. And, as you know, after Virginia City, there may be reason *not* to wait."

There was that—the thing that had started this whole talk of marriage. What if she was carrying his child? She hugged her shawl around her. This was not the way to make this kind of a decision, but then, nothing about her dealings with Carter had made much sense. "I'd like to ask the Millards," she said, not believing her own words.

Carter gave something resembling a whoop. "Ask anyone you like, sweetheart. I'll stop by the church and tell the reverend to come by tomorrow night around seven.''

Jennie nodded.

Carter leaned over and gave her a kiss on the cheek, then turned and actually *leaped* down the entire flight of stairs to the walk below. Jennie gaped at him in the darkness.

"Go on into bed, now, sweetheart. I'll see you tomorrow night." She started to turn around obediently, then stopped as he called out one more time. "Jennie, do me a favor and don't think too much between now and then."

She gave a reluctant smile to which he responded by throwing her a kiss. Then he watched as she turned and went inside the house.

Jennie lay on her bed, fully dressed, too dazed to remove her clothes and find her nightgown. She'd just agreed to be married! It was beyond belief. But for some unknown reason she had not the least desire to run after Carter and tell him she'd changed her mind. She tried to tell herself that Carter had bullied her into it for his own purposes, as was the way with men. But she kept remembering instead the way his eyes had warmed when they'd looked at her just now in the moonlight. And how her heart had skipped when he'd talked about the two of them sharing a bed in her house.

It was time she admitted the truth. She loved him. It was impetuous, probably unwise and happening far too fast, but then, so had everything else in this past crazy year. It was as if, with the death of her parents last spring, she'd stepped onto a gigantic wave that was carrying her along to some unknown shore. And she was still riding.

Her room was dark, the house quiet. It must be past midnight. But suddenly she rolled to her feet. All right, if she was going to be married in less than twenty-four hours, there was work to do.

Resolutely she lit the lamp on her bedstead and pulled open her wardrobe. She'd never been much for female fussing, but she'd be darned if she was going to be married looking like a frump. And there was food to prepare, for the wedding, as well as for the miners at midday. Lordy, she still hadn't told Carter about that. Well, it would probably be only one of the many surprises they'd discover about each other after they became husband and wife.

She bit her lip as the words came to her head. Husband and wife—to love and care for each other until parted by death, just as her parents had been. Tears sprang to her eyes. Her parents wouldn't be at her wedding, but she knew they'd be with her in spirit. Be happy, Jennie, they'd say. Seize this love that has come so unexpectedly and suddenly into your life. Loving each other will make you both stronger, not weaker.

I'll try, she whispered, closing her eyes as the image of her parents' dear faces came into her mind. I'm going to try my very hardest to make this work.

Reverend Calder had grown absentminded in his old age, which suited their purposes just fine. It meant that he didn't question the suddenness of the wedding or why it should take place in the Sheridan parlor instead of over at the church with the whole town in attendance.

He read the vows in a shaky voice and omitted any homily that would have prolonged the time he had to remain standing holding the heavy Bible in his hands. In fact, he rushed the last three or four lines, and seemed relieved at the end.

He stayed for one of the custard cakes Jennie had hurriedly prepared that afternoon before Dorie had arrived to help her dress and arrange her hair.

Neither Carter nor Jennie minded the minister's perfunctory performance. They were too busy studying each other and letting the realization of what they'd just done sink in.

Carter was having trouble keeping his mind on the divine nature of the proceedings as he watched Jennie in a green taffeta dress with a tight bodice and scooped neck that had something soft and ruffly all along the top of her breasts. Several times he was at risk of being embarrassed by blatant signs of his arousal as he anticipated the moment when he could take her back to his hotel where they'd agreed to spend their wedding night.

Jennie had been up most of the night and had worked hard all day. She was exhausted, but at the same time exhilarated, as if she'd drunk a glass of champagne. Carter looked so handsome in a solid black suit and blue vest. And every time he glanced her way, his eyes held a special predatory, *proprietary* look that was so sensual it kept her cheeks constantly flushed.

The admission to herself last night that she was in love had opened the floodgate. By morning she'd been literally *singing* it. I'm in love. I love him. Jennie loves Carter. How long, she wondered, tapping her foot impatiently against the settee, would they have to sit here sipping cider and eating cakes and making inane conversation with Reverend Calder, the Millards and the silverheels? She wanted to be alone with him.

Dorie was their savior. "You men can sit here all night," she said, jumping to her feet with a clap of her hands. "But the wedding couple's leaving. They've got better things to do than watch you lugs gobbling pastries."

Jennie and Carter both stood immediately. Dennis Kelly popped the entire cake he was holding into his mouth and joined them on their feet. He winked at Jennie, then turned to Carter. "I guess you know you've got yourself a special little gal, Jones. You make her happy now, or you'll answer to us."

"You'll answer to a whole mine full of us," Smitty added. Unlike Dennis, he'd concentrated more on the hard cider than the cakes, and was not thinking sharply enough to remember that they didn't talk about Jennie's job at the mine. But no one seemed to notice his slip.

Carter was unconcerned about being accountable to Jennie's protectors. He slipped an arm around Jennie's waist and tried to concentrate on saying the proper goodbyes while his thoughts had already raced ahead to what he wanted to do to her when he got her alone.

Jennie moved away from him to shake hands with the reverend and give embraces to each of the miners, leaving all three blushing. Then she hugged Dorie and held a hand out to be squeezed by Dr. Millard. At the end of the line, almost hidden behind the doctor, was Barnaby. He was the only one in the room who wasn't smiling.

She put an arm on his shoulder and drew him against her. "Thank you for coming to my wedding," she said to him.

He looked at the floor and nodded without speaking.

"Are you going to be all right heading off to school by yourself tomorrow?"

Another nod.

Jennie lowered her voice and leaned close to him. "You're not sad about my marrying Carter, are you, Barneyboy?"

He looked at her then, his chestnut eyes wide and unsure. "I don't know," he answered, his voice on the edge of tears.

Jennie turned around and saw that the others were waiting in silence. She hesitated, then looked at Carter, her eyes asking for understanding. "I'm just going to tuck Barnaby into bed before we leave. I'll be right back."

She kept her arm around the boy's back and walked with him out of the parlor and to the tiny room in back of the kitchen where he slept. When they reached his small cot, she sat down next to him. "Now, tell me what's bothering you, honey. I thought you liked Carter."

"Will we still be a family, like you said?" he asked just above a whisper.

Jennie hugged him. "Of course we will. We *are* a family. You and me and Kate and now Carter, too."

"And the baby," Barnaby added shyly.

"Absolutely, and the baby."

"Carter's such an important man. I wasn't sure he'd want a family with bastards in it."

Jennie felt a tug on her heart and once again wished she could march over to school and stuff soap into the mouths of every one of those boys who had bullied Barnaby. "I told you to forget about that ugly name. Carter's happy to come live here and be part of our family."

"You asked him?"

Jennie nodded. "I wouldn't have married him if he hadn't wanted that."

Barnaby sat back on the cot with a look of relief. "He's not so…stiff anymore as he used to be when he first came around here."

Jennie smiled. "When he first came with those papers you wouldn't let him in the house."

"But he wasn't mad about it, was he?"

She gave him another hug of reassurance. Every now and then Jennie remembered the differences in their upbringing. She'd been raised by two strong parents who had never let her have a moment of doubt that she was loved. Barnaby had had no one, which meant that he was constantly worried about trying to please everyone else. Tonight she'd been too busy to pay much attention to him, but she noticed now that he'd donned his best suit and all by himself had found some kind of grease to slick back his unruly hair.

"Carter thinks the world of you, Barnaby, and I do, too. You were the only family I had tonight to see me properly wed, and I was so proud of you. You looked so handsome."

Barnaby beamed with pleasure, but he said, "Carter looked handsome, too, Jennie, and you look like a princess."

She laughed. "Why, thank you, Barneyboy. Now, I'm going to have to stop calling you that, because you practically aren't a boy anymore."

His eyes slid away from her. "I don't mind if you call me that, Jennie. I kinda like it. It reminds me of your ma."

She smiled and said, "Well, then I shall continue to call you Barneyboy until you're a grandpa. How about that?"

He giggled. "Maybe not that long."

She stood. "So are you feeling all right now?" At his nod, she leaned over to give him a kiss on the forehead, then stood. "I'll see you after school tomorrow."

"All right, Jennie."

His eyelids were already drooping and she had a feeling that without her prompting he would likely fall asleep in his good suit, but she didn't want to take any more time. It was her wedding night. And Carter was waiting.

Chapter Fifteen

They were oddly shy with each other as they mounted the hotel stairs to Carter's third-floor room. It would seem that since their relationship had run the gamut from a veritable shouting match to incredible passion, it should not be so disconcerting to face each other as man and wife. But both had been nearly silent since they'd left the house amid shouts of good wishes from their wedding guests.

"So Barnaby was all right after your talk?" Carter asked.

"He was half-asleep already when I left him. He just needed a little reassurance that he still would have a family left after all the changes."

"He reminds me of myself as a child."

Jennie couldn't imagine that the self-confident Carter had ever experienced the feeling of insecurity that Barnaby had; however, even as the thought came to her, she realized that she did not know a lot about his childhood. She'd told him about her parents and growing up first in the mountains and then in Vermillion, but he'd spoken little of his life before coming West. "He's had a tough life," she said. "And things still aren't all that easy for him. He's been upset lately by teasing from the boys at school. He says sometimes he wishes he could live alone in the mountains like we used to."

"Teasing is one of the hardest things for a child to deal with. But sometimes it can make you try harder because you want to show that you're better than your tormentors."

Jennie was surprised. He sounded as if he had experience with the subject. "Barnaby tries hard in everything."

Carter nodded. "I'm looking forward to spending more time with him."

Jennie felt a wave of happiness. Carter would be so good for Barnaby, and it was a relief for her to feel that she'd have help raising the boy. This was how it was supposed to be in a marriage—this feeling of no longer being alone to fight life's battles. She gave a squeeze with the hand Carter had tucked in his arm. He responded by looking down at her with a smile.

They'd reached the door and Carter released her hand as he fumbled in his pocket for the key. "Do I carry you over the threshold?" he joked, and Jennie realized that he was nervous, too. Perhaps for the first time in his life.

"Well, it's not as if..." She blushed. "We have been through this before, Carter."

He leaned over to give her a quick kiss, then managed to get the key in the door and open it. "Sweetheart, you're wrong. Neither of us has ever been through this before.''

He pushed open the door and stepped back for her to walk through. A lamp was already lit on the nightstand. The bed was tended with fresh linens with the feather comforter puffed high. A bouquet of wildflowers tied with a ribbon lay on one pillow. Jennie turned around with a pleased smile. ''You were expecting company tonight, I see.''

He reached to pull the shawl off her shoulders. ''I was expecting the company of my beautiful, desirable...*wife*.''

She felt his words all the way down to her toes. ''Wife,'' she murmured. ''I don't think I can quite believe it.''

He placed his hands on each side of her slender neck and tipped her head up toward him gently with his thumbs. ''I'll make you believe it, sweetheart,'' he said in a husky voice, and then he kissed her.

Her head tilted back and her eyes closed. His lips were soft and dry and so tender it almost brought tears to her eyes. Her arms fell limply to her side and she stood, swaying slightly, lost in the sensation of his kisses on her mouth, cheeks, eyes, forehead. He kissed every inch of her face without moving his hands from their place on her neck. Her knees threatened to buckle.

''That's so...so nice,'' she said. Then as he dropped his hands and pulled away she added, ''No, don't stop.''

She opened her eyes. He was watching her with

that teasing smile, his own eyes warm. "I'm not stopping, darlin'. Not until morning, maybe not then."

She smiled back at him and gave a sigh of happiness. The prospect of a long night with him was so enticing. Her stomach was already jumping as she remembered the feeling she'd had the last time they'd made love. He'd hardly touched her tonight, but the mere memory coupled with his restrained kisses had her passion already triggered. "Until morning?" she said archly.

He took her hand and led her over to the bed, where he picked up the bouquet of flowers and handed them to her. "I wanted roses, but these were the best I could find in Vermillion."

She sniffed their delicate fragrance. "These are lovely."

"Not as lovely as you," he said, then laughed softly. "I suppose the Harvard lawyer ought to be able to come up with a better line than that one."

"No, I thought it was just fine." She smiled at him, her heart swelling.

"Aw, sweetheart," he said, then he moved next to her and took her in his arms.

Jennie let herself melt against him, totally eager for the physical sensations that would match the emotions she'd been holding on to all day. She already knew that this time would be sweeter, more special than their night in Virginia City. This time she had finally allowed herself to admit that what she felt for Carter was nothing short of love—the real thing. Till death us do part.

He still hadn't said that he loved her, but she

sensed a new reverence in the way he held her. She could tell that he, too, realized that this night was something extraordinary. He kissed her again and again, sensual kisses that made her begin to ache with wanting. Then with murmured endearments, he undressed her, slowly, extending his kisses to each part of her body as he uncovered it. Halfway through the undressing, she glanced over at the lamp. He saw her hesitation, but he said in a husky voice. "Do you mind the light, sweetheart? I want to see you."

And looking at the intensity of his eyes, she realized that she wanted to see him, too. She shook her head, and he smiled and resumed his disrobing of her.

When she stood naked, he went down on his knees and pressed his cheek against her soft stomach, then turned his head to kiss her there. She held him to her for a long moment as the swells of passion moved over her body. Just when she'd reached the point that she was no longer sure if she could remain standing, he got to his feet and lifted her onto the bed. Then he quickly divested himself of his own clothing and lay beside her.

They needed few preliminaries. She was wet and aching for him, and he was hard and needy. He kissed her mouth again, then down to her neck and her breasts, and, as he tugged a taut nipple into his mouth, he arched and entered her. She cried out.

"I haven't hurt you, have I?" he whispered.

"No...no..." She sighed as she kissed him and moved in an age-old rhythm that started slow, then became more urgent. His mouth seized hers and suddenly their coupling became fast and frantic as they drove toward completion. It spiraled at her with such amazing force that she cried out again and softly bit the thick cord of his neck before giving herself up to the waves of feeling.

The sensation drained out of her slowly, leaving her body with a delicious lethargy. Carter lay heavily on her, still breathing fast. Neither spoke for several long moments. Finally he said, "That, my darling wife, was incredible."

She gave a happy laugh. It *had* been incredible, and what was more, she was liking the sound of that phrase that she'd never in her life expected to hear addressed to her. *My darling wife*. "I thought so, too," she said shyly.

He rolled off her and stretched out to turn off the lamp, leaving the room lit only by moonlight. Then he lay back down next to her, took her in his arms and pulled the sheets up around them. "Happy?" he asked her.

She nodded and nuzzled his shoulder. "So am I," he said, sounding almost surprised. "It's such a simple thing, really," he went on as if talking to himself, not to her. "All the scrambling, the struggling, the working to get ahead. When all along it's really just this simple."

She was a little confused at his rambling. "What is?" she asked.

He kissed her, thoroughly, before answering, "Happiness. This is what it's all about."

She wasn't sure precisely what he was referring to—the passion they'd just shared or the marriage or something else entirely. But she was too happy herself to question it. "Who would have predicted we'd end up together this way?" she asked.

He chuckled. "Not I. The first few times I met you, you kept wanting to throw me out on my ear."

"You deserved it."

"Mmm." He kissed her again.

She could feel his body stir against her leg.

"Somewhere along the line I must have decided it was easier to marry you than to close you down."

"I'm glad," she said, giving a little gasp as his kisses trailed down to her breast.

"I'll make a law-abiding citizen of you yet," he murmured, starting to focus attention once again on an erect nipple.

"I wouldn't count on it, Counselor," she said, but her voice was no longer steady.

He lifted his head and smiled at her. "Well, at least I'll have fun trying."

They hadn't quite fulfilled Carter's prediction of making love all night, but they'd come close. Somewhere a couple of hours before dawn, both had fallen into an exhausted sleep, so that when they awoke, well into midmorning, they'd had to scramble to get dressed and off to their respective duties. Carter had work piled up at his office, and Jennie had to get to the mine. She didn't have time to tell Carter the story behind her job there, so she decided not to mention it until they had a chance to talk that evening.

They'd given each other a long kiss before they left the room, then a shorter one in the hotel lobby, and had reluctantly parted for the day.

Jennie walked all the way to the mine by herself singing. Winter had definitely arrived—it was cold, but she thought it was a beautiful day. Today she thought the entire world was beautiful. By the time she arrived, her silverheels had told the other miners about her wedding. There were one or two long faces on the men who had developed an infatuation for their pretty cook, but most offered their congratulations.

Though she was busy, the day seemed to pass slowly as Jennie waited for evening when she would see Carter again. When she got back from the mine, she made a blackberry pie, his favorite, then raced through the rest of the supper preparations so she'd have time for a bath.

It felt so domestic and so *conventional* to be busy planning for her husband to come home from the office. She'd spent a long time rejecting such a life for herself, but now that it had happened, it felt simply grand.

The silverheels had offered to fix their own supper if she and Carter wanted another night alone at the hotel, but she turned them down. She was ready to begin her new life with Carter at Sheridan House, and she wanted to be sure that Barnaby didn't feel neglected. As Carter had said, as long as the two of them would be able to retire behind the door of her bedroom to privacy each night, they'd be fine.

She was bathed and combed and primped, the meal was ready, the silverheels had come down from the mine, and still he wasn't home. The anticipation of seeing him again was building up a tension that had her considering walking downtown to meet him. She wandered from the kitchen to the front hall and looked out the pane of glass next to the door. But it wasn't Carter she saw coming up the front walk. It was Lyle Wentworth.

She opened the door to let him in, trying to keep her temper even. After all, he'd helped Kate. He'd stayed with her when Jennie herself could not. And it wasn't Lyle's fault exactly that he'd been raised to be such a spoiled brat that Jennie had found him impossible to tolerate since before he'd graduated to long pants.

"Hello, Lyle," she said. "When did you come back to Vermillion? How was Kate when you left her?"

He removed his hat and gave her one of his supercilious smiles. How *could* Kate stand the man? she wondered. "I just came back today. Kate got your wire yesterday about the wedding. She was worried."

"I'm sorry to hear that. I thought about not telling her until the baby was born, but the way news seems to travel in this town…" The emphasis on the statement was obvious, but Lyle didn't have the grace to look embarrassed.

"I told her I thought it was a good thing, on the whole," he said briskly.

Jennie was surprised. "Well, thank you."

"For one thing, it will make this all easier to deal with. There's finally a man in the household I can talk to."

Behind Lyle, Jennie saw the man of the household coming up the walk. Some of the excitement over seeing Carter again this evening had dimmed with

Lyle's words. "What is it you want to talk about, Lyle?" she asked.

"About helping you girls get your lives straightened out." He seemed oblivious to Jennie's rising anger, but Carter was obviously aware that something was wrong the minute he walked in.

"What's going on?" he asked.

"Lyle's here to help us get our lives straightened out," Jennie said brightly.

"The girls' lives, not yours, Jones," Lyle clarified.

Carter gave him one of the smiles that he usually reserved for opposing attorneys. "That's big of you, Wentworth. But now that Jennie's my *wife*, I can't see as how you would have any business at all with her life or mine."

"Or Kate's," Jennie added.

Lyle's lips thinned. "It doesn't appear to me as if you're doing such a good job of handling things, Jones. You let your wife go traipsing off to spend all day up at the mine doing heaven knows what all alone with dozens of miners."

Carter hid his shock well, but shot Jennie a questioning glance. She gave an inward groan. "Lyle," she said wearily, "what business is this of yours? Why don't you just go away and leave us alone?"

"If Kate would agree to go away with me, I would," he said. "But she's determined to come back here to live. So until I can convince her otherwise, I'll just have to see to it that things go smoothly around here."

Jennie could tell that Carter was still puzzling over what Lyle had said about her job at the mine, but he put his own questions aside to say, "Listen, Went-worth, whatever your association may be with Kate, you have nothing to do with Jennie or with me."

"My association with Kate will be as her husband, once she sees reason about it," he said. "And once she realizes that the arrangements I've made for her baby are for the best."

"We've been through that, Lyle," Jennie said. "Kate's not giving up the baby, and she's not going to let your badgering change her mind."

"Women are too emotional about these things," Lyle replied. "Which is why I've come to talk to *your husband,* Jennie. He's the male head of the house-hold, now. I reckon he'll be making the decisions."

Jennie looked at Lyle in disbelief, then turned to Carter, expecting his immediate denial. He was watching her with an odd expression. "Well, tell him, Carter," she said with some exasperation. "Tell him that you don't intend to be making decisions for me or my sister."

Carter hesitated a long moment. "I don't intend to make decisions for you, Jennie, but, as I've told you, I think you should take a serious look at the idea of giving up the baby. Neither you nor Kate has any idea of what it means to raise a child without a father."

Lyle gave a smug smile. "Why is it that it takes a man to think things through clearly?" he asked.

Jennie felt as if the air had been knocked out of her chest. She stood staring at Carter, unable to be-lieve what she was hearing. Over the past two days she'd thought of nothing but how much she'd come to love this man. He'd made her heart fill and her body soar. And suddenly it was as if she were looking at a stranger.

Barnaby came racing into the hall from the kitchen, shouting "When do we eat?" He slowed to a stop as he saw the expressions on the faces of the three adults. "What's the matter?" he asked.

Jennie wondered if she could trust herself to speak. She reached to put a hand on Barnaby's head, then said, "Nothing's the matter, honey. I'll be back in the kitchen in a minute, just as soon as I see Mr. Wentworth out."

Barnaby looked warily at Lyle, his child's intuition telling him that his visit was causing some kind of negative response in Jennie. "Shall I call the silverheels for supper?" he asked.

She nodded. "Tell them we'll eat in five minutes."

He seemed to be satisfied by the definite nature of this statement, but Lyle was not.

As Barnaby turned to skip back toward the kitchen, Lyle said, "We can't put this off, Jennie. The doctors say Kate's almost ready. The baby could be born anytime. It's important to settle things about its disposition."

"Let's at least hear him out, Jennie," Carter suggested. "Let him tell you about this family he's found to raise the child."

Lyle gave him a look of approval. "It will have a good home with all the luxuries and, what's more important, a mother and father to raise it."

Jennie shook her head to see if it would clear out some of the anger and hurt. It had little effect. "Lyle, Kate left me with no doubt that she wants her baby.

If you persist in trying to persuade her otherwise or arranging to give it away behind her back, I'll get a court order prohibiting you from bothering her." She shot a scornful glance at Carter. "I should be able to find a lawyer *somewhere* who would help me."

"All I'm saying is that you could hear him out, Jennie." Carter sounded less positive. He was evidently finally realizing exactly how angry she was.

She ignored him and addressed Lyle. "I'm going to send a wire to Kate tomorrow. And I'll ask her to send me a wire every day letting me know that everything is going well toward the birth of the new Sheridan baby. If you interfere with that, Lyle, I swear you'll never see her again." She had to fold her arms in order to keep her hands from shaking, but her voice was deadly calm. Both men seemed to have no doubt that she was serious.

"We'll just see who Kate wants to listen to," he said stiffly. "We'll just have to see." Jennie watched with disgust as Lyle put on his hat and turned to leave. He had that petulant expression that made him look as he did back in grammar school when the other boys wouldn't let him have his way. She didn't bother to open the door for him or tell him goodbye as he left.

If Kate had had Jennie's support all along, she'd most likely never even have allowed Lyle to visit her. She certainly would never have listened to his talk of adoption for even an instant. It was just an unfortunate twist of fate that had made it necessary for the sisters to be separated at this important and emotional time in Kate's life. Once the baby was born and she could come home, Lyle Wentworth could be forgotten and everything would be back to normal, Jennie thought, trying to keep herself calm.

But as swiftly as the thought came, it was replaced by another. Things would *not* return to normal. Jennie now had a husband. She turned around to face him. His expression was unreadable. "How could you take Lyle's side?" she asked. For the first time since Lyle had arrived, her voice faltered.

"I'm not taking Wentworth's side," he answered carefully. "I'm thinking about the baby...*and* your sister."

Barnaby poked his head through the kitchen door. "The silverheels are ready." Once again he grew silent as he saw Jennie's face.

She forced herself to smile at him. "I'm coming. They can go ahead and sit down at the table."

Carter moved to try to put an arm around her, but she pulled away. "I have to get supper on," she said, her voice tight. Then she bolted into the kitchen.

All day Carter had been picturing the moment when he and Jennie would be able to slip away to her bedroom and start in again learning about the wonderful way their bodies interacted. They'd made love much of the previous night, but he didn't feel in the least bit sated. In fact, he could hardly wait to be with her again.

But instead of naked and happy in her bed, they sat across from each other in her tiny office, fully clothed, expressions stormy.

"If this *job* of yours is perfectly respectable, as you

claim, then why didn't you ever tell me about it?'' he asked.

''Because even though it was none of your business, you had conniptions that day when I was putting up my notice about maid service. I didn't know what kind of reaction to expect from you.''

He couldn't deny her assertion. He *had* acted badly that day. The thought of Jennie doing the same kind of drudge work that had worn down his mother had robbed him of his usual good reason. After he had overreacted that way, could he really blame her for keeping secret about the mine job? His voice softer, he said, ''Well, now that you're my wife, you don't have to worry about that anymore. I'll help you pay off the hospital bills with my savings, and my salary along with the miners' rents will cover the expenses here. You won't need the extra job.''

She shook her head. ''It would be silly for me to give up twenty dollars a week for a job that I *enjoy*. Sometimes being up there with the miners is the best part of my day.''

Carter straightened in his chair, trying to keep calm. ''I would think the best part of your day would be spent with your *husband,* not a group of strange men.''

''The silverheels are not strange. They compliment me and tell me jokes. They make me feel as if there had never been a cook like me in the history of the world. They're almost like another family,'' she concluded.

''Family. It's such an easy word with you. You think that everything can be a family—you and your miners, your sister and an illegitimate child, Barnaby. Putting together a bunch of people doesn't make them family."

She looked as if he had just slapped her across the face. "What is it you have against that word, Carter? I don't understand you. You yourself told me you wanted to marry me so that any child that might result from our union would have a family."

He stood up, too agitated to sit idly across from her. Pacing across the room, he answered her. "Precisely. So that our child could have a *legitimate* family. Not some kind of fabrication dreamed up by you to give people who don't belong the illusion that they do."

"Kate and I belong to each other. Her child will belong to both of us, just as Barnaby does. It doesn't matter what the law says. It doesn't matter what kind of last name you put on a person."

He reached the window, then turned to pace back to the desk. "You can't say that, Jennie. You *had* your father's last name. You had a legitimate family to grow up in—a mother and father to love you in this big, comfortable house. You don't know anything about growing up like Barnaby, never quite belonging, looking for love and acceptance and finding only loneliness. A child without a name has no chance for happiness in this heartless world we live in."

Jennie's head had been pounding since supper. She'd wished she could crawl into her bed all by herself and make the rest of the world go away, but Carter had specifically asked to discuss Lyle's visit, and she'd decided that her office would be easier ground to meet him on than the bedroom.

Of course, he was angry at finding out about her job through Lyle. He had a right to be, she supposed. She should have told him. But he'd been in the wrong, too, taking Lyle's side about Kate's baby.

Though now as his voice turned to a bitter tone Jennie had never heard before, she realized that Carter's view on this issue was something beyond a disinterested observer. All at once she understood that he wasn't talking about Barnaby. He was talking about himself. "You were illegitimate, too," she confirmed softly.

"Yes, Jennie. There was no Mr. Jones to love me and raise me to follow a father's example. I don't even know my father's name. Jones isn't even my mother's name, just a name she took when she couldn't live with the disgrace of bringing an unwanted child into the world."

"I'm sure she loved you," Jennie said, tears prickling her eyes.

"She didn't have time to love me. She was too busy cleaning other people's chamber pots in order to get enough money to feed us."

Jennie bit her lip. He had paced over to the window and back again, his arms folded, his hands gripping the sleeves of his coat as if trying to hold inside those years of hurting. She wanted to go to him and take him in her arms as he continued telling the story of his childhood, but he seemed to have almost forgotten that she was there.

Finally he sat down again, across from her. "Don't try to tell me about family, Jennie," he ended wearily.

She felt as if her heart had suddenly developed a crack. She could hear the pain from those early years in his voice, could see it in his face, but he was so wrong. Love was not dependent on legalities. Kate's child would never suffer as Carter had. She wished she could make him see that, but she didn't know how, especially not now as he sat across from her so stiff and distant.

"It's late," she said.

He looked at her sadly. "Yes. So are you planning to go up to the mine tomorrow?"

She nodded. "It's my job."

He shook his head. "If you want to write up that wire to Kate, I'll take it to the telegraph office in the morning."

She looked up in surprise. "Thank you. I'd appreciate the favor."

He looked irritated. "It's not a favor, Jennie. I'm your husband."

She nodded, her throat filling. She'd never felt farther away from him.

He watched her for a moment, then said, "I'm going for a walk." He looked exhausted.

"It's past midnight," Jennie protested.

"I know. You go on to bed."

With that, he was gone. The tears that had threatened all night fell, but she indulged them for only an instant. Then she sniffed, swiped her hand across her nose and stood up. In a way, this was easier. She'd been so confused over the past few days, trying to reconcile her resolution to be independent with her growing love for Carter. Tonight everything had become much clearer.

Carter had married her because he was afraid he would have a bastard child. It was as simple as that. He'd never said he loved her. With the childhood he'd had, it might be that he wasn't even capable of love. Jennie had supplied that part of it. She'd been the one to put the romantic interpretation on the events of the past couple days. She'd been the one foolish enough to imagine that their intense physical attraction meant equal intensity of emotion.

Well, this was easier. She was back to where she'd been in the first place—on her own to take care of her *family* herself with the love and care she'd learned from her own parents. She'd take her heart back from where she'd recklessly let it wander. She'd be her own woman again. And this time she'd stay that way.

Chapter Sixteen

Jennie had wanted to travel to Virginia City to bring Kate home, but Dr. Millard had insisted that it would be better if he had the whole carriage. Kate could ride comfortably with him in the front, and they could make a bed for little Caroline in the narrow rear seat. So Jennie had to be content with preparing a welcome-home party for mother and baby.

The news of the birth had brought badly needed cheer into the house. Since the night that Carter had told her the story of his childhood, they had hardly spoken. Lyle had not bothered them again, and Carter had not brought up the subject of adoption. But Jennie had stubbornly gone off to the mine each day to Carter's unspoken but obvious disapproval.

Their estrangement affected the entire household. The miners seemed confused by it, acting sympathetic but not quite knowing what help to offer. Barnaby was even more noticeably upset. Jennie had tried to keep things as normal as possible, but it seemed almost as if Barnaby had sensed everything that had occurred between her and Carter. He watched them both with grave, sad eyes, and had reverted to his habit of disappearing for long stretches.

It felt good to have a reason to celebrate. Everyone pitched in to get the house cleaned and Kate's room ready. Dennis and Brad had gone to the Millards' and brought home the wooden crib that had been Dorie's, which she'd insisted on giving to the new baby.

"At this rate, it's not likely I'll ever need one for a young'un of my own," she'd joked to Jennie. "Who'd have thought that you'd be married before me?"

But when Jennie had not seemed receptive to her teasing, she'd narrowed her eyes and fallen silent.

Now the crib was ready and tended with the baby blankets Jennie's mother had saved from her daughters' own infancies up in the mountains. The supper was prepared with a special chocolate cake for dessert, which Barnaby had decorated with real bottled cherries from the general store.

Dorie had arrived with an embroidered smock for the new baby and joined the group waiting impatiently in the parlor for her father's carriage to arrive with its precious cargo. Dennis suggested a game of whist, including the ladies, but Jennie said she was too nervous to concentrate on cards.

Carter had not come home from the office. During the past few days, he'd often stayed late, avoiding the uncomfortable silences that had grown up between them. But she'd expected that tonight at least he'd be home early. Perhaps he still resented her and Kate's decision to keep the baby. They hadn't discussed it again since that painful night, and Lyle had not made another appearance.

When he still hadn't arrived by six, she realized

she was angry. If that was the way he wanted it, fine. They'd have their celebration without him. She just hoped that she could keep Kate from finding out how disastrous her marriage had turned out to be. Dr. Millard had said that Kate would be weak for some time yet and shouldn't be upset.

"They're here!" Barnaby yelled from the post by the window he'd taken the minute he got home from school. With a flying leap he jumped off the stool and ran out the door. Jennie could see him tearing down the walk toward the carriage.

She followed at only a slightly more sedate pace, her heart thumping with excitement.

Kate looked absolutely fragile. The rounded stomach was gone, of course, but even her face looked much thinner than it had been in those carefree days before their parents' death. The year had taken its toll on both of them, Jennie reflected.

She pushed aside the gloomy thoughts as her eyes went to the tiny pink bundle in her sister's arms. Inside the blanket she could see minute arms flailing and a perfect little head with not one single hair, but with wide blue eyes that seemed to be taking in all the details of her new home.

Barnaby stood stock-still, looking at the baby in wonder.

"What do you think, Barnaby?" Kate asked him with a big smile. "Isn't she pretty?"

He nodded, too entranced to answer.

Jennie rushed to her sister and threw her arms around her and the baby together. "Welcome home!" she said, her voice quavery.

Kate gave her a kiss on the cheek, then held out

the baby. "Here's our little Caroline, Jennie. Didn't I tell you all along that she was a girl?"

Jennie nodded and took the bundle from her sister as if it were made of spun glass. It was love at first sight.

Kate leaned over and brushed her fingers lightly across the baby's bald head. "Caroline, this is your Aunt Jennie," she said. Her voice changed to a timbre Jennie had never heard before. It sounded, she realized in awe, like a mother's voice.

The miners stayed lined up on the porch, watching the scene a little self-consciously, but Dorie charged down the stairs after Jennie, gave Kate a hug and said, "I'm holding her next. Aunt Dorie. I get to be an aunt, too, don't I?" she demanded.

Kate laughed. "I'm sure Caroline will love to call you auntie. And she'll love sleeping in the crib you gave her." She put her arm around her friend's waist for another squeeze, then called up to the miners. "She doesn't bite yet, boys. You all can come closer than that if you want."

One by one they shuffled down the steps and came to view the new arrival, staying a safe step back. "She's so beautiful," Jennie said, getting used to the feeling of rocking her in her arms. "Thank you for bringing them, Dr. Millard," Jennie finally remembered to say to the old man who stood by the carriage watching the reunion with a fond smile.

Kate looked up at the house where the door stood open. "Where's Carter?"

Jennie slid her eyes away. "He's had a lot of work at the office lately. He'll be along directly. Come on. We'd better get our little gal inside, out of the cold."

Kate gave her a sharp glance, but didn't say anything as the whole household paraded back up the walk and into the house. Barnaby was the last to come inside, the look of amazement still on his face. Kate held her hand out to him.

"She's so little," he said, taking the offered hand.

"Yes, she is. But babies grow fast."

"What does she eat?"

"Right now she just drinks milk from a nursing bottle. In a while she'll start to eat oatmeal and mushy food."

"You were too sick to feed her yourself like some mamas do," he said. Jennie had patiently explained this to him along with all the other endless questions he'd had about his new little sister.

Kate nodded. "Yes, I was sorry about that. But she's happy with her bottle."

They walked up the steps and through the door. "Can I give it to her sometime?" he asked.

"Of course, I bet she'd like that."

"Can I tonight?"

"Well, yes. If she's not too fussy, you can feed her a bottle tonight."

He gave a nod of satisfaction and followed Kate into the house.

Carter knew he was acting churlishly by not being at home for Kate's arrival with the baby, but he simply hadn't been able to force himself out his office door and down the street. He had no desire to witness the homecoming celebration, knowing that it would simply reinforce the empty ache he'd had in his gut ever since the night he'd told Jennie about his past.

Telling his story and unleashing his feelings that night had been like opening a steam valve. He would never be able to change his past, to undo the slights he'd suffered or recover the love he'd missed out on. But it was the *past*. Now he had a chance to make his present into something entirely different. But it seemed that Jennie had turned away from him, as surely as all those other people who learned the truth about his origin. The difference was that those others had rejected him only because of his birth. But Jennie had rejected him because of his life.

There had been times during the past week as he'd watched her careful preparations for the arrival of Kate's baby that he'd wanted to pull her aside and tell her that he'd been wrong. Kate's baby would be loved—he could see that now. He would no longer talk about the idea of putting it up for adoption and would help her fight any move by Lyle to make Kate do so. But she'd been so stiff and cold, the words just wouldn't come.

He'd lain awake beside her for these past few nights, wanting desperately to take her in his arms. Sometimes he'd almost done it, but then he'd remember the way she'd looked at him with something akin to horror when he'd talked about giving up the baby. He'd remember that she'd said she never really wanted to depend on a man—how she'd gone to work rather than accept help from him when she'd needed money for the hospital. And how she'd been afraid to confide in him about her job at the mine.

They'd had the passion, but it appeared that Jennie no more accepted him as part of her life and her *family* than anyone else ever had. And no matter how he might wish things were different, he couldn't see how he could change that. He told himself that he'd been alone his whole life and done just fine. More than fine, he'd excelled. And he would again. He'd concentrate on his career, work hard, see where it took him. And he'd try not to think about the wedding night he'd spent with Jennie, that magical night when he'd been closer than ever before in his life to saying to another human being, "I love you." He wished he'd told her so that night. Now it appeared it was too late.

Supper was almost over by the time Carter came in, murmuring apologies for his tardiness. He leaned over Jennie's chair and gave her a perfunctory kiss on the cheek, his first in several days. Then he walked around to Kate and extended his hand. "Congratulations, Kate. I saw the baby sleeping across the hall. She's a pretty little thing."

"Thank you, Carter," Kate answered with a smile. "And congratulations to you. Though I don't know if I should forgive you for stealing my sister away from me when I was indisposed."

"Well, now I didn't exactly steal her away. She's right there, as you can see." He smiled and gestured toward Jennie, whose serious expression did not change.

Kate looked puzzled, but answered brightly, "For stealing away her *heart,* then. Don't worry, I'll forgive you eventually, as long as you continue to make her happy."

There was silence all around the table. Kate's expression grew more guarded.

"I'll do my best," Carter said after a minute. "Is there any supper left?" he asked, addressing the question to Barnaby.

The boy jumped up and turned toward the kitchen. "Jennie saved you a plate. I'll get it."

Carter's eyes went to Jennie. "Thank you," he said. She nodded back.

Kate watched the two of them with a sinking heart. From the very first time she'd heard that odd note in Jennie's voice when she'd talked about her meeting with the handsome prosecutor, Kate had held on to the hope that her sister would find the same kind of love Kate had thought she'd found with Sean—only for Jennie it would be the real thing.

But something was terribly wrong. Jennie and Carter hardly looked at each other. When they spoke directly, their voices changed, became more stilted. They hadn't sounded this way when they'd visited her together in Virginia City. What could have gone wrong?

A sudden thought struck her. Could their difficulties have something to do with Kate herself? She imagined that it wasn't easy for Carter to accept a sister-in-law like Kate when he held such an important public position. She sighed. She and Jennie had always confided in each other about everything, but she had a feeling that this was one confidence she'd have trouble wringing out of her sister.

Well, she was home for good now, and getting better every day. Caroline was happy and healthy. Lyle had stopped bothering her, at least for the moment. The world was looking pretty good to her right now. It was her turn to take over the balance for a while. She'd be the strong one. She'd help Jennie get out of whatever it was that was causing her such unhappiness. It might take some time, but she'd do it. It was her turn.

* * *

But after two weeks at home, Kate had still not been able to erase the unhappiness from Jennie's eyes or tease the stiffness from Carter's demeanor. The stubborn couple seemed determined to live side by side forever in endless misery. Kate was almost ready to wash her hands of the both of them.

Only the presence of little Caroline made them loosen their reserve. She'd seen them together playing with her little daughter and laughing over her increasingly human antics. It made Kate realize what fine parents they'd be to children of their own. But in a moment of despondency, Jennie had confided to her sister that she had that morning discovered that she definitely was not pregnant, and she'd implied that she had little hope of becoming so in the future.

Kate hadn't asked for more details. Jennie would let her know when it was time to discuss them.

But she decided to make an attempt to be more direct with her new brother-in-law. The miners had gone out for a night on the town. Carter had refused their invitation to join them. He didn't feel much like socializing these days. Jennie was helping Barnaby with his schoolwork back in her office, which left Kate and Carter alone in the parlor with Caroline.

"She sure is a cute little thing," he said, putting out a finger for the baby to grasp. She lay on a blanket in the center of the settee and Carter and Kate sat on either side of her.

"I'm very lucky," Kate answered.

Carter's voice held a bit of surprise. "Yes, I guess you really are."

Kate chuckled. "You can't quite believe that a

woman who's had an illegitimate child can call herself lucky, can you?''

· He looked a little embarrassed, but answered frankly, ''I've never thought so before, but then, being part of this household has changed my mind about a lot of things.''

Kate studied him across the settee. ''I'm glad to hear that, Carter, because I was afraid that it might be my baby that's been causing the trouble between you and Jennie.''

His head came up. ''Oh no, Kate. I'll admit we discussed it back when Lyle wanted…'' He paused.

''When Lyle wanted me to give her away,'' Kate supplied.

He nodded. ''Yes. But that's not the problem.'' His eyes went back down to the baby.

''What is the problem, then?'' Kate asked gently.

Carter shook his head, and his voice sounded thick when he answered. ''I don't know what to tell you, Kate. I don't think Jennie wants you to know that anything's wrong.''

''Jennie knows me well enough to realize that if she's not happy, I'm going to be aware of it. And she's *not* happy, Carter.''

''I know. I can't say that I've been having much fun lately, either.''

''So what exactly is the matter?''

Carter leaned forward to place his elbows on his knees and let his head drop into his hands. ''It was just a mistake. That's all. Jennie never wanted to marry me. She's happy here with you and the baby and her silverheels.''

''I don't see her inviting the miners to bed with her every night,'' Kate said dryly. ''Somewhere along the line you two must have decided that it was a good idea to get together.''

Carter looked embarrassed. ''We may have let ourselves get carried away by...you know...''

Kate laughed and patted her hand gently on Caroline's stomach. ''Yes, I *do* know, Carter. Believe me. But unlike my whirlwind lover, you're still here. Not only here, but married. So why aren't you two deliriously happy?''

He didn't look up at her. ''I don't know.''

Kate gave an exasperated sigh. ''Well, criminy, man. Have you asked her?''

He straightened up. ''She acts as if she doesn't want to talk to me.''

Caroline started to whimper and Kate picked her up and put her against her shoulder. ''Is this the dynamic young lawyer who came to make a name for himself in our humble town? Is this Carter Jones, future governor of the state? I thought talking was your business.''

Her outburst drew a reluctant smile. ''Most of the people I face in court aren't as prickly as Jennie,'' he said.

Kate glanced over him. ''You're a lot bigger than she is, Carter. I can't believe you're scared of her.''

His smile broadened. ''She's meaner than she looks.''

Kate made absentminded circles on the baby's back and rocked back and forth as she shook her head at him and said, ''My sister's not mean, Carter. And she's not scary. But she is stubborn.'' As he opened his mouth to agree, she held up one hand to stop him. ''So if you're in love with her, you're going to have to convince her of that. And it might take some convincing.''

She stood, shifting Caroline to the other shoulder and arranging the blanket with her other hand. Then she continued, ''I have faith in you. I think you really are going to get that governorship someday. And I believe you can work things out with my sister, that is…if you love her. Do you?''

''Yes.'' His answer was unequivocal.

Kate smiled. ''Good. Because Jennie loves you, too, and that's all that counts. The rest is details.''

Kate had taken the baby and gone up to her room for the night, but Carter still sat on the settee where she'd left him. Her words kept going through his head. *Jennie loves you, too,* she'd said. And suddenly he realized with blinding clarity that she was right.

In spite of her mistrust of men and her resolve to stay independent, Jennie had come to him willingly. She'd entrusted him with her body, and then with her heart. She'd married him, not out of fear that he'd tell her sister about them. They'd both known that that was an empty threat. There was only one reason she would have agreed to become his wife.

Neither one of them had spoken the words. That was part of their problem. After all their misunderstandings about her job at the mine and Kate's baby, he should have taken her in his arms and told her that he loved her. He should have taken her to bed and shown her how much she meant to him. Instead, he'd let the wall of silence grow so tall between them that it now seemed almost as if they were strangers.

But it was not too late. He heard her down the hall, saying good-night to Barnaby and then mounting the stairs. Soon she'd be slipping into her bed—*their* bed. And he'd join her there. It might take some convincing, Kate had said. Well, that was all right with him. He stood, turned off the lamp and made his way out of the parlor.

Hell, sometimes convincing could even be fun.

Jennie turned, startled, when he came into the room just behind her. "I thought you were down talking with Kate," she said.

"Kate's gone to bed. I heard you finish up with Barnaby and decided to join you."

She looked a little surprised, but she said simply, "Oh."

He walked across the room, took off his jacket and hung it on the clothes tree. Then he started to unbutton his shirt. Jennie watched him warily.

"Aren't you going to get undressed?" he asked her.

"Ah...yes." She looked over at the light burning brightly on her dresser.

Carter followed the direction of her gaze. "Do you want me to put it out?"

"I will," she said, walking over to do so. The room plunged into darkness.

He'd have preferred having this conversation while he could see her face, but the darkness might suit his purposes as well. "Little Caroline is blossoming," he said.

Jennie sounded relieved at his choice of topic. "Yes, she is. Kate's a good mother."

"You will be, too."

Jennie didn't answer.

Carter finished removing his clothes, then crossed

over to where she was fumbling in the dark with her own more complicated apparel.

"Do you need some help?" he asked, his voice low. In the dim light he could see her shake her head, but nevertheless he turned her around and began unfastening the hooks at the back of her dress. "Of course, there's one particular requirement to being a good mother," he continued.

"What's that?" she asked.

He finished with the hooks and slipped the dress off her shoulders, then turned her around to face him. "You have to have a baby."

His low tone vibrated somewhere deep in her midsection. His hands were running up and down her arms, raising a chill on her skin. Suddenly it was as if all the distance of the past few days had dissolved and they were back the way they had been together the night of their wedding.

But could she allow herself to go back there? What about all the hurt that had come since? She pulled away from him. "I'm just as happy being an aunt," she said.

"Well, I'm not." He pulled her back into his arms and brought her close to him, the silk of her shift slipping against his bare skin. "I want us to make our own baby, sweetheart."

His low-spoken words reverberated in her head as his lips claimed hers. She went up on her toes and pressed into him as his tongue began to weave magic inside her mouth.

She made a sound of acquiescence and desire and he pulled her up tighter. Their bodies pressed together below, his aroused manhood hard against the silk hollow of her abdomen. "Ah, Jennie," he whispered, bending to lift her in his arms.

Then he froze as someone knocked hard on their door.

"Jennie, Carter!" It was Kate, and she sounded frantic.

Carter put Jennie down and pulled a shawl off the bed to wrap around himself. Then he opened the door. Kate stood on the threshold, a baby bottle in one hand and one of Caroline's blankets in the other.

"She's gone!" she said, half sobbing.

Jennie ran to the door. "What are you saying, Katie?"

Kate took a deep, shuddering breath. "I went downstairs to warm the milk for Caroline's nighttime bottle. And when I came back up, her crib was empty."

Chapter Seventeen

Carter had an immediate suspicion as to the whereabouts of the baby, but he didn't say anything as he and Jennie helped Kate look through the upstairs rooms. They roused the miners, who then got dressed to aid in the search.

"I'll have to wake Barnaby," Jennie said as they finished the upstairs and started down. "He'll be so upset."

But Barnaby's room was empty, and Carter's fears were confirmed.

"They've taken them both," Jennie cried as Kate gave a wail.

Carter tucked his shirt inside his trousers and said grimly, "I don't think so." When both women looked at him questioningly, he explained, "Barnaby's taken Caroline. I don't think there's anyone else involved."

"Why in the world would you say such a thing?" Jennie asked, indignant.

Carter sighed. "Because he wants to protect her. I've seen him watching her. He doesn't want her to be subjected to the same kind of taunts he's had."

"But that's crazy," Kate gasped.

Carter raised an eyebrow. "Yes, but going through abuse like that can make you think strange things. With all due respect, Kate, you'll never really know exactly what it feels like. By the time you had to endure slurs of that type, you were an adult. It's a lot different when you're a child."

"We won't let Caroline be subjected to anything like that," Jennie said firmly.

Carter turned to her. "How are you going to guarantee that? Do you plan to keep her locked away in this house her entire life? No, Barnaby knows what little Caroline might have in store for her. He just isn't using his head too well as to what to do about it."

"Where could he have taken her?" Jennie asked, her voice shaken.

Kate had tears streaming down her face. "Are they outside somewhere? It's nighttime…and it's cold. She needs her bottle," she ended with a broken sob.

Jennie put her arm around her sister, then looked up hopefully as the front door opened. But it was only the three miners, who'd been looking around the outside of the house. "No sign of them," Dennis said, shaking his head.

Carter's mind was whirring. If Barnaby had decided to escape with Caroline he hoped the boy would be smart enough to know that he'd need to find shelter, at least at night. The most logical place to find refuge would be one of the mines dotting the surrounding canyons.

"Has Barnaby been up to the Longley mine with you fellows?" he asked the miners.

"He's been there with me," Jennie answered. "Just last week."

"Well, it's a place to start looking," Carter said.

He turned to Kate. "Do you want to trust us to find him, Kate, or would you like me to go into town and get the sheriff?"

Kate shuddered. "There's already been far too much talk about us in town. Let's try to find them on our own first."

Carter nodded his approval. "You stay here in case he comes back or you get some news. Dennis, Brad, Smitty and I will head up into the hills and check all the nearby mines."

"I'm going, too," Jennie said quickly.

Carter walked over to her and planted a kiss on her mouth. "I won't *tell* you no," he said with a small smile. "But I'll *ask* you to stay here with Kate. She's not in any shape to be left alone."

It was obvious from one look at Kate's trembling form that Carter was right. Jennie put an arm around her and said, "Come on, Katie. We're going to go make some coffee. We'll all be needing it."

The women headed back toward the kitchen. Carter sent Smitty to fetch Dr. Millard and Dorie, then briefly sketched out a strategy with Brad and Dennis on how best to cover the nearby territory. Carter himself would go up to Longley. He didn't know if it was the affinity he'd always felt with Barnaby or just a wild hunch, but somehow he was almost certain that that was where he would find the misguided young fugitive.

He didn't have to walk all the way to the mine. He'd been on the trail only about twenty minutes when he heard the sound of something around the bend. At first he thought it might be an animal, but then he heard a tiny mewing that was unmistakably a small and unhappy baby.

He closed his eyes in relief and waited for the boy to walk toward him.

"She's too little," Barnaby said with a hiccup in his voice. He'd evidently been crying.

"She certainly is," Carter said, reaching to take the baby from his arms.

"I think she's missing her ma. I fed her a whole bottle but she kept crying."

Carter tried not to show all the anger he felt for the worry Barnaby had put them all through. There would be time enough to deal with it all rationally. The important thing was that they both were safe. "Babies need their mothers all the time when they're this tiny. It was very wrong of you to take her off like that."

Barnaby hung his head and said in a low voice, "It was because of what you said."

Carter jerked back in surprise. "What I said?"

"The other night. I couldn't sleep and I was going down to the office to see Jennie, but you and she were arguing and you told her that a baby without a name has no chance for happiness."

Carter's chest constricted. "Oh, Barnaby…"

"So I was going to take her to live in the mountains like Mr. and Mrs. Sheridan did before they came to Vermillion. Then it wouldn't matter if she didn't have a name."

Carter couldn't believe that his heedless words had been the cause of all this. "How were you planning to feed her and take care of her?" he asked, wondering just how many hours Barnaby had spent since that night planning this.

"I found my own food for years before I came to

the Sheridans. I'd hunt for us. She can have mushy food now. I asked Dr. Millard.''

Carter winced as he remembered how attentive Barnaby had been to every detail of the baby's care. Perhaps he should have suspected that the boy was thinking about something like this.

Caroline had fallen asleep in his arms. He rocked her gently and found the sensation comforting. ''Children need more than food to be happy, Barnaby. They need love. You and I know that better than most people,'' he concluded gently. All the anger had drained out of him.

''I love her, Carter,'' Barnaby whispered, his head hanging. ''I love her something fierce.''

Carter hesitated, then shifted the baby to one arm so that he could put the other around Barnaby's small shoulders. ''I know you do, lad. But you'll have to promise me that you'll never do anything this crazy again. The way you can best help Caroline grow into a happy young lady is to do your best to be a responsible member of our family.''

''You mean Jennie and Kate and you and me and the baby?''

''Yup, that's what I mean. We're a family. We have to support each other and love each other and stay together.''

''And can we keep the boys from calling Caroline bad names?''

Carter turned to walk down the path, keeping one arm around the baby and the other around Barnaby. ''We'll do our best. But if a bad name or two slips through, she'll have her big brother to cheer her up.''

It had turned quite cold and Barnaby was dressed in only a shirt. It made Carter sick to think about what might have happened if they hadn't been able to find him. There'd be snow in the mountains any day.

"Carter?"

"Yes, son?" Barnaby's steps were flagging and Carter knew the boy must be exhausted, but he didn't want to slow down.

"Maybe you could give Caroline your last name."

Carter was touched by the boy's suggestion, but he said, "Caroline has a perfectly good last name, Barnaby. It's Sheridan. It's a better one than mine, to tell you the truth."

"I like Jones. It's a nice name."

Carter smiled a little sadly. "Yes, it is. I like it, too."

They were silent for several minutes, then Barnaby said, "Could I have it?"

"Have what?"

"Could I be a Jones? I'm not saying I'd be your kid or anything like that…"

The prickling behind Carter's eyes felt suspiciously like tears. He blinked rapidly. "I'd be honored for you to have my name, Barnaby, if that's what you want."

"Would it really be my name? I mean legal-like?"

Carter ruffled the boy's hair. The lights of town had come into view below them. "Say now, aren't I a lawyer? We'll make it more legal than if you'd been born that way."

"Barnaby Jones. I like the sound of that," he said happily.

"I do, too," Carter replied. In fact, his name had never sounded so sweet.

Jennie stayed with Kate and Caroline all night. The baby had awakened as soon as Carter and Barnaby got down from the mountain and they'd been unable to calm her down. Kate was still shaky and exhausted and Jennie was afraid to leave her alone, she explained to Carter with a little sigh of regret. Now that the excitement was over, both had hoped to be able to continue where they had left off when Kate interrupted them.

"We'll talk in the morning," Carter had whispered to her. "I don't intend on going into the office tomorrow until I've said some things I need to get off my chest." Then he'd given her a brief kiss goodnight and let her go on down the hall to Kate's room.

Jennie wished they could talk tonight, but Kate's grateful look when she walked into her bedroom was worth the delay. Still, as she sat watching over Kate and her niece she couldn't help wondering what the new day would bring. She had a feeling that she was going to like what Carter had to say. In fact, since he'd joined her earlier that night and they'd kissed, much of the tension of these past few days had miraculously dissipated.

I want us to make a baby, he'd said. Jennie might be still naive, but she was smart enough to know that a couple didn't do that by sleeping at opposite ends of the bed the way she and Carter had been doing. The mere thought stirred her and made her want to creep down the hall and crawl into bed next to him. But she had Kate and the baby to think about first.

Tomorrow, she thought sleepily. She had some things to say to him, as well.

Barnaby had apologized to Kate and asked everyone to forgive him for all the trouble he'd caused. He was so obviously contrite that no one had the heart to suggest further punishment. In fact, when he asked if he could stay home from school for a day, Jennie had agreed.

She and Carter were both waiting for the opportunity for their private talk, but things weren't working out in their favor. First, Dr. Millard had come by to check over Caroline and be sure she'd suffered no ill effects from her exposure to the night air. Dorie had come along with him with news from town for Kate and Jennie.

They all sat around the dining room table waiting for her father. "The Wentworths, father and son, had a shouting match yesterday in the middle of the street right in front of the bank," Dorie reported with glee. "I don't know who won, but Lucinda swooned in the middle of it and didn't revive until they carried her over to Papa's office."

Carter had smiled at the gossip, then had pulled his watch from his pocket and looked ruefully at Jennie.

Unfortunately, when Dr. Millard came downstairs after checking the baby, he accepted Jennie's half-hearted offer of a cup of coffee, and Dorie declared that she wouldn't mind another of Jennie's cinnamon buns.

Jennie returned Carter's look with a helpless shrug. Before long it would be time for her to head up to the mine.

Then, just as the Millards finally got up to leave, there was a knock on the front door, and Barnaby appeared in the dining room entryway to announce, "There's a bunch of people from town here to see you, Jennie." He sounded scared. "You didn't tell them about last night, did you?"

She assured him that no one knew about their adventure of the previous evening, then said, "You might as well tell them to come in here. There's more room than out in the hall."

He disappeared for a minute, then returned followed by Mrs. Billingsley, Miss Potter, Mrs. Wentworth and at the tail end, Lyle. Jennie forced herself not to groan, and managed to say calmly, "Good morning."

As usual, Mrs. Billingsley led the charge. "It's just as well you're here, Mr. Jones, because perhaps we'll be able to get this straight once and for all. We had an agreement to allow this establishment to operate if certain undesirable elements were not to be present." She looked pointedly over at Kate, then gestured to Margaret Potter, who pulled a folded paper from her reticule.

"Undesirable elements such as my sister?" Jennie asked, steaming.

"Fornication is against the law in this town, Jennie," Miss Potter said.

Carter stood and gave the ladies one of his lawyer smiles. "Well, then, it's a wonder the Vermillion jail's not full to overflowing, isn't it? Perhaps I can clear this problem up. Some time ago I obtained a license for Sheridan House as a multiple residence. It doesn't require business zoning. Its presence here is perfectly legal."

Jennie looked at Carter in surprise. He'd never told her about the license. But then, they hadn't been communicating too well recently.

Mrs. Billingsley looked as if she wanted to spit as she turned on him and said, "Are you aware, Mr. Jones, that while you're working hard at your office every day, your *wife* is spending time unchaperoned at Longley mine surrounded by dozens of those coarse miners?''

Jennie's mouth fell open as Carter dropped all pretense of a smile, pulled himself up to his full height and answered, ''My wife has a job at the Longley mine. I'm incredibly proud of her for being able to work there and also be completely responsible for the running of Sheridan House all these months. She's a remarkable woman, ladies. If you all worked as hard as she did, you wouldn't have so much time for your vicious gossip and petty meddling.''

Mrs. Wentworth gasped. Henrietta Billingsley pointed a finger at her and shouted, ''Don't you dare swoon, Lucinda.''

Lyle stepped up to put an arm around his mother. ''I told you ladies to let me handle things.''

Mrs. Billingsley made a harrumphing sound at the back of her throat. ''A big help you've been, Lyle. You said the child would never be brought back here. The truth is you've always been so besotted with Kate that you can't see these girls for what they are.''

Lyle sent Kate an apologetic glance. ''As I told my father yesterday, the Sheridans have as much right as anyone to be a part of this town. As for the child, Kate and I will be discussing more about its disposition when she's fully recovered her health.''

Kate stood up from the table, her eyes shooting blue fire. ''Don't bet on it, Lyle Wentworth,'' she said. ''In fact, if you ever even again mention to me the possibility of giving up my child, it will be the last time you're welcome in this house.''

In spite of her vehemence, Lyle didn't look convinced. His mother reached up to pat him at the side of his tightened jaw. "You see, dear. This is what your father was trying to tell you."

He pulled away from her touch.

"I'm going to suggest that we all get on with our daily business," Carter said loudly. "I hear Caroline crying for her mother upstairs. And neither my wife nor I have time to waste listening to pointless whining."

Mrs. Billingsley and Miss Potter looked as if they wanted to continue the confrontation, but both Lyle and his mother were ready to leave and turned to do so. Kate also got up and left the room to go upstairs to her baby. Jennie stood and said, "Good day, ladies," then walked into the kitchen.

Carter smiled. "Did you need someone to show you the way out?" he asked them.

Finally the two women turned to leave, their faces glowering. Carter watched them go, took a look at his pocket watch once more, then moved toward the kitchen.

"I couldn't believe you said those things," Jennie said without turning around when he came in through the swinging kitchen door.

"To the battle-axes? I should have said them a long time ago."

"But what about…couldn't they hurt you if you stand for election?"

Carter shrugged and walked across the kitchen to take her shoulders and turn her around to face him. "I don't care. I'm more concerned with them hurting Kate and her sister, who happens to also be the woman I love."

Jennie looked up at him, her brown eyes wide. "The woman you love?" she repeated softly.

He nodded. "The woman I've probably loved from the time she first stood on that stoop out there and ordered me off her property."

Jennie smiled and shook her head. "You couldn't have loved me then."

"You may be right. It might have still been lust at that point."

She burst out laughing. "Lust, eh? I've been warned about men like you, Mr. Jones."

He had backed her up against the kitchen counter so that the lower portions of their bodies were pressed together. "I would hope so, Mrs. Jones."

"I've been warned against lustful, ambitious men who use people for their own purposes, then discard them like old newspapers." She was having trouble finishing her speech because Carter had started nuzzling her neck and his hands were making small circles on her breasts.

"Discard them sometimes that very same day," he agreed in grave tones between gentle nips along her jaw.

"So how would I ever learn to trust a man like that?" The question became breathless toward the end.

"I've heard that once in a great while it's possible to tame such a scoundrel."

Jennie drew in a sharp breath as his fingers pulled at her nipples. "How...ahh...how would one go about doing that?"

Carter whispered low in her ear. "You make him fall in love with you."

She smiled against his cheek. "I didn't think that kind of man fell in love."

"Yes, they do. If they're smart enough. And then they find that all those ambitions aren't quite as important as they once thought they were."

He pulled away from her to let her see that he was serious. But she moved him back against her. "And what about the lust? Do they give that up, too?" she asked archly.

"No. I think that's the one vice that never gets tamed." Then he kissed her, thoroughly and taking his time about it.

When she could speak again she made a little sound of contentment at the back of her throat and then murmured, "Oh, sweetheart, I'm so glad to hear that."

His eyebrow raised and he gave her a wicked grin. "What would your silverheels do if their lunch was late today?"

She smiled back. "There'd be a riot most likely."

Carter lifted her in his arms. "Hmm. A public disturbance, eh? Too bad. I hope they won't call on the town prosecutor for help. He won't be in his office."

Jennie tucked her face into his shoulder as he started to carry her across the kitchen. "Where will he be?"

Carter paused a moment at the door and kissed her hard. "He'll be busy making love to the cook."

"In the middle of the day?" she asked, blushing.

"Uh-huh." He nuzzled her neck as he pushed open the kitchen door and headed toward the stairs. "Do you think we may cause another scandal for Vermillion's busybody matrons?"

Jennie returned her husband's kiss, then gave a satisfied sigh. "I certainly hope so," she said.

Award-winning author

Gayle Wilson

writes timeless historical novels and
cutting-edge contemporary stories.

Watch for her latest releases:

HONOR'S BRIDE—September 1998
(Harlequin Historical, ISBN 29032-2)

*A Regency tale of a viscount who falls for the courageous wife
of a treacherous fellow officer.*

and

NEVER LET HER GO—October 1998
(Harlequin Intrigue, ISBN 22490-7)

*A thriller about a blinded FBI agent and the woman assigned
to protect him who secretly carries his child.*

Available at your favorite retail outlet.

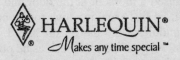

HARLEQUIN®
Makes any time special™

Look us up on-line at: http://www.romance.net   HHGWHB

Mysterious, sexy, sizzling...

THE AUSTRALIANS

Stories of romance Australian-style, guaranteed to
fulfill that sense of adventure!

This November look for

Borrowed—One Bride
by **Trisha David**

Beth Lister is surprised when Kell Hallam kidnaps her on her
wedding day and takes her to his dusty ranch, Coolbuma. Just
who is Kell, and what is his mysterious plan? But Beth is even
more surprised when passion begins to rise between her and
her captor!

*The Wonder from Down Under: where spirited women win
the hearts of Australia's most independent men!*

Available November 1998
where books are sold.

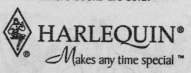

HARLEQUIN®
Makes any time special ™

Look us up on-line at: http://www.romance.net

PHAUS5

AWARD-WINNING
AUTHOR
TORI PHILLIPS
INTRODUCES...

An illegitimate noblewoman
and a shy earl to a most delicious
marriage of convenience in

THREE DOG
KNIGHT

Available in October 1998
wherever Harlequin Historicals are sold.

**Harlequin®
Historical**

Look us up on-line at: http://www.romance.net

HHCC